Davidia and SENORA COLLEGE

Ken Spargo

Published in Australia by Sid Harta Publishers Pty Ltd,
ABN: 46 119 415 842
23 Stirling Crescent, Glen Waverley, Victoria 3150 Australia
Telephone: +61 3 9560 9920, Facsimile: +61 3 9545 1742
E-mail: author@sidharta.com.au

First published in Australia 2020
This edition published 2020
Copyright © Ken Spargo 2020
Cover design, typesetting: WorkingType (www.workingtype.com.au)

Spargo, Ken
Davidia and Senora College
ISBN: 978-1-925707-13-7
pp276

ABOUT THE AUTHOR

Ken lives in Melbourne, Australia.

His first venture into writing began on a sewerage farm whilst engaged in an aquaculture project in 2002. On a boring Friday afternoon, his imagination got the better of him and he decided to fill in his time by writing a nonsense short story called *The Frog who Hopped on One Leg*.

Within a year he had written a series of short stories and a year later began his first novel *Stumped*.

Imagination supplies an endless source of ideas used to create and craft his crime and fantasy fiction novels, his preferred genres.

He loves to travel; with many places he has visited providing inspiration for his novels. He has travelled extensively throughout Europe, Asia and other parts of the world and lived and worked in Austria, Europe, New Zealand and Papua New Guinea. Caravanning locally is also of great interest.

Ken's primary occupation is as an accountant and runs his own business.

Sport has been a major influence in Ken's life. His two crime fiction novels have both been influenced by his involvement with sport (cricket and golf).

Ken's inspiration for writing the Davidia series of novels has been his daughter, Sophie. He has assisted in raising two children.

All novels have been written with a sense of humour, which is a refreshing feeling and allows the seriousness of life to relax. We all need escapism at times.

Other titles in the Davidia series:
Davidia and the Prince of Triplock
Davidia and the Six Sisters
Davidia and Grandma's Memories
Davidia and the Knowledge Tree
Davidia and the Foreboding Dinner
Davidia and Aunty's Curse

CONTENTS

PROLOGUE

'They will comply with our wishes, otherwise it will be a termination that will have to be invoked. They are so stubborn and rude. They ignore the respect of elders and most of all they answer back in forceful terms which is unheard of in our college.'

Two senior education controllers were discussing the visit of exchange students, Davidia and Slirander, to Senora College, where the only real addition to their education was chaos. A strict regime of educational control was enforced with an iron fist. Students were kept in cages, or were they stand-alone student accommodation, educational centres fully fitted with total digital management?

'We offer the best there is in a new approach to education and they don't like it,' said Miss Alpine.

'They do derive from an inferior education unit than what we provide, so there's bound to be resistance for a new approach. It will take time to adapt, but adapt they will,' replied Mr. Avalanche.

'Monitor their every move and don't let them near another student. Their constant escorts will ensure compliance to our rules and ways.'

In another dimension, education was taught with strict controls about being the "new" way to learn. Davidia and Slirander were now students not appreciating the efforts of control that stifled the freedom of learning. They were to be trained "puppies" in future education and upon return to their own college will instigate the odd new way of learning. The girls were konnockered, which was an electrically controlled device knee implant, which controlled all students.

'We must escape from here,' said Davidia, feeling trapped in her student accommodation. It was a rectangular shape of suffocation. She had contact with Slirander via thought processes. She was also isolated and alone.

'There must be an exit that we haven't located yet,' replied Slirander.

'It's miserable being alone. Where are the other students? We must locate them.'

'That will invoke serious disharmony and risk.'

'I'm prepared for it. It is better to try and succeed than not try and fail.'

A plan was set in motion, as to whose detriment was yet to be determined.

Suffice to say, chaos was introduced without a class lesson.

The girls had taken that step forward, which cannot be reversed.

And so, it began.

1 CHALLENGE

It wasn't a particularly pleasant day at school. Tension amongst the older-age students was a simmering pot full of mixed feelings and emotions, none which anyone dared mention in case a rude and offensive retaliatory remark was foisted upon them. It wasn't a pleasant or natural experience for some, nor was a visit from the school psychologist to trim the school's intelligence quota to keep the high achievement standards of the school intact.

It was nearing year-end exam expectations and students were filled with anxiety about their ability to achieve that fabled mark, whatever that was in their personal in-tray that translated as individual success. The corridors ebbed and flowed with endless foot traffic. Was it used as an in-between class session, a stress relief exercise, or a time-filler? Some students displayed confident smiles, but is that because they spotted a person of interest in the opposite sex, or was it flashed around as a front to hide the stress they may want kept hidden? Frowning only damaged the porcelain-perfect skin many possessed, and that structure had to remain intact for the future of remaining eternally young. Magazines emphasised for both genders the importance of the permanent smile and the perfect shape. Ageing didn't exist in the magazines because that snapshot in time was a forever photograph, reality wasn't as kind.

'How do you think you will perform in the exams?' Davidia asked one of the stressed students.

In a few years' time she would be in the exact same position.

She didn't know her background so she was unaware if such a simple question would create an affront.

The student sized up Davidia as a pugilist does when prepared to snot an opponent and switch off their lights with a right or left cross. It didn't matter which. It was the result that was important. Davidia sensed the change in her body. Fists began to form. An unpleasant facial skin exercise appeared instantly like a lightning bolt and the larger frame turned toward her with non-existent dialogue. A huge, pinkish tongue often used in the discourse of the English language, was u-shaped and full of a slimy liquid agitating for an escape. No wonder she couldn't express herself with a gob full of spit.

Slirander was nearby, observing her friend. She too felt danger with a large D was looming. She quickly sprinted the three steps required and accidentally bumped the to-be offender to trouble by dropping a book on the floor and scurrying to retrieve it. That quick-thinking technique saved a saliva wash and the offender expended her gift for Davidia over a few nearby lockers instead, one of which was hers. The liquid dribbled to the floor leaving slime trails behind that any slug would be proud to claim. Before any ramifications were dealt out, Slirander and Davidia had retreated along the corridor to safety.

'I could have handled that without your interference,' said an incensed Davidia.

She felt she could always fight her own battles; however, a friend is still a great ally.

'I could see that. She's an older and larger student than you. Your mum wouldn't be pleased with the dental bill,' replied Slirander. 'What was it about?'

'I asked her how she might perform in the upcoming exams. That's all.'

'I suppose that's innocent enough; however, there is a lot of tension at this time of the year and stress does weird things to people. Everyone gets a little on edge. Remember, that might be us in a few years.'

Davidia nodded and thought, *Yeah, could be.*

They both moved on to their next class.

*

The winds in the corridor of school power were circulating ominously in the staff meeting room. It was also filled with tension, but of a different dimension than that for the students. Members were agitated and experiencing anxiety about whether their individual skills had been sufficient to maintain the school's premier position as the top academic school in the state. They wouldn't know the truth of that until after the exams. As the dialogue flowed like free wine, a surprise had been presented to the school principal that he thought they had to meet. He had pondered for days wondering what the purpose of the proposal was. It worried him.

The school principal, a Mr. Jack Jim Jones, was a tallish man tipping the height scales as a Collingwood six-footer. Dress sense was not a classroom topic when it came to him. A tie was a foreign animal. An ironed shirt was a mystery and by not tucking it in, it allowed free flowing material to comfort an enlarging bubble. Long pants met the ground with floor drag fraying the cuffs into a modern-edged dish rag. His feet were imprisoned with shoe leather and laces that had no meaning of teamwork or togetherness. They were a tripping hazard often let loose to flay helplessly as they were dragged along the floor. His hair was on top of his head, but, with incessant scratching, no one knew what lived there. It gave the impression of falling snowflakes that sat on his shoulders, hence the nickname

"Snowflake". A suit was in a deck of cards, not in his wardrobe. There was a jumbled collection of garments cobbled together, which gave the impression of a uniform appearance, jacket with pants and shoes leaving his colour coordination on the paint charts in any hardware store. It was an imponderable puzzle. He had a very high IQ, great manners, empathy in his school world; and with both staff and students he was a valuable listener. He occasionally asserted his strict side when necessary. Now he had a problem that he needed to share with the staff. Such a weighty decision stooped his posture in thoughtful pose as he stroked his chin, feeling the rough of the stubble from an ineffective early morning shaving exercise with a blunt razor. His breathing was heightened. There was no need for the school defibrillator. His mid-forty age range still gave him good health.

'Thank you for your attendance,' he began. 'I have a worrying message from another school.' He waved the letter as a gesture that it was the real thing. No one was shown its header or postmark from whence sent. 'The school has been challenged to an unusual debate or contest. I'm not sure of the truth of it; however, we have been given an ultimatum to achieve the highest academic results in the state. If not, we are threatened with financial cuts to all our programs.'

'Like who has like given us the challenge like?' said Miss Onna Meg Green, known simply as "OMG". She possessed student school-speak and by just listening without seeing her, one assumed that it was a student that you were hearing. She was late twenties, single, full of potential and a great advocate for all things positive. The glasses she wore framed a piercing set of eyes. Once they bored into a student, an imaginary burn was felt. Lesson learnt.

"Tomorrow, two representatives from Senora College will be

in attendance to answer any questions. We must confront the challenge if we are being put at great risk. The students' welfare is our main priority.'

'I have never like heard of this like college. Where like is it?' said Miss Green.

'Apparently it has had a name change and used to be better-known as Sycamore College.'

The staff nodded, as if they had all heard of Sycamore College. The name wasn't questioned and passed through to the all knowledge group as a given.

'It should be an interesting experience being challenged for the premier academic title,' said another teacher, proud of their abilities. Her class won't fail, they were taught to impress.

That night, a few thoughts were spread like treacle jam amongst the teachers wondering about tomorrow.

Principal Jones had more to ponder about than school success.

*

'Have you heard the rumours?' said Davidia.

'What rumours?' said Slirander.

The two girls were walking between classes, enjoying a free moment from learning stress. The word in the corridor had it that an argument with another school was about to erupt over who had the brightest group of senior students. Had it been the Year 10s, then there was no dispute, according to the girls.

'Two academics are arriving tomorrow to sort out the school principal. Apparently, he received an important invitation today to arrange a school function with another school. I wonder if it's to dump, or should it be reclassify, the not-so-academic elsewhere at that school.'

'Is that school policy to transfer students for selfish ideals?

Shouldn't we all be able to complete our studies at our school of choice?'

Slirander was incensed, if the rumour had any merit, that such a practice would exist. She gave her odd ear a tug, which was a customary habit, but for some unknown reason, this time it required more attention. It wasn't quite up to an incessant itching standard, or had an infestation of bugs, but it was warning her of an uncertain feeling. It was in her unexplainable basket. Even her friend, Davidia, who usually understood most things about her odd friend, would have to wait until this one blossomed into an understandable reason.

'They wouldn't do that, not at this school, surely.'

'Money is an insidious force. If they replaced the students and the school achieved better grades, more fee-paying students would want to come here and study. It is a logical consequence. I think it's called, business management. My parents are university lecturers. They may have heard of this other school.'

Slirander had her thinking cap on. It wasn't part of any supplied school uniform. It was a personal choice as to who wore one. Imagination had to invent a physical appearance to wonder what one looked like. Did they really exist?

'I'll ask mum if she has heard of this other school too.'

The school bell rang. All rumoured thoughts evaporated as the message to go home had been delivered. No rumour could compete effectively with leaving school for the day.

Davidia wondered if any of the other students were aware of the rumours. Earlier in the day, she had been passing the staff room when she saw Principal Jones wave a piece of paper over his head, appearing as if he was brushing away an annoying insect. Her curiosity rose like a self-raising pudding – and poof, product everywhere. The rectangular glass in the doorway, plain not frosty, allowed her clear sight; however, she was particularly keen to remain undetected, so only one of her eyes peered in from the edge of the frame. She noticed the theatrical performance: paper waving, stilted walking, and facial contortions accompanying a set of expressive words, and the principal did dress indifferently. Her lip-reading skills were imperfect, so it was understandable that what was said wasn't exactly absorbed, nor could it be accurately understood and repeated correctly. Hence, some misunderstanding arises when a rumour is born. Its parent or parents can sometimes be born out of ignorance and/or misinterpretation. Today had a great start. Davidia was at first base to begin the gossip.

That night at home, she asked her mother if she had ever heard of Senora College. Her response was a definitive, 'No'.

Slirander also asked her parents the same question with the same result. She thought it strange that her parents didn't know; and they were in the education system.

The telephone rang. The ring tone was mildly humourous. She thought, *grunting pigs aren't that popular, are they?*

'Slirander. It's Davidia.'

'Hi.'

'That rumour today. I asked my mum and she hasn't heard of Senora College.'

'My parents gave me the same answer. It's odd that no one has heard of the name.'

'Why not look up Dr. Google? He sorts out every other complaint.'

'What a great idea. Stay on the line.'

Slirander found her laptop, turned it on and after the screen-saver pleasantries, thought that she might update it. That last scene was a past memory filed under "F" for forgotten. What was his name again? Who cares? Back to Dr. Google. The screen acted as a window into the world. Press a few buttons, keystrokes and press enter, and a whole information dimension is accessed. *No, I'm not looking for a relationship. No, I'm not sending buff coloured pictures to you. I'm not subscribing to that porn site, which had been cleverly misspelt, conning subscribers into believing it's a chess club, another misspelt word for club type.* Danger doesn't only lurk in a school corridor, outside parks or streets in the general community; it can accompany you anywhere an electronic gadget is located. It's back to Dr. Google again. Finally, the tool bar reappeared and Slirander typed in "Senora College". An instant collection of names appeared, as if they all required to be immediately opened. She scrolled down all the variations and, yes, there was a Senora College listed, but strangely, it was in the United States of America; San Francisco as a matter of fact. There were no other names listed under education either. She thought that must be it.

'Davidia, the only school I can find and Dr. Google isn't ill either, is near San Francisco, in America. They don't list their personnel. I suppose it's legitimate.'

'Why would you think that it isn't?'

'My ear acted strangely today when you mentioned rumours. I can't explain it.'

'It is unusual that we are being visited by representatives of an American school. Maybe they have an offshoot here, but under another name. It's a pity we can't be at the meeting to hear what's going on. They are meeting the principal tomorrow and we aren't on any guest list. We'll just have to wait until the truth comes out. It is delicious to think foreigners are visiting our school. They might be offering American scholarships to the school. I'd love to win one.'

Davidia's penchant for mental exaggeration was being buffed by a bout of positive thinking. Did she also have a personal thinking cap? What colour was hers?

'Let's think on it and see what tomorrow brings.'

'Another set of fresh memories. Goodnight, Slirander.'

'Goodnight, Davidia.'

The two friends had fields of thought as their heads hit the pillow, wallowing in rumours.

What about the one …?

*

The doorbell rang. It had no offensive ring tone. It was 7.00am. Davidia's mum opened it. There was no one there. She was about to close it when the wire door section wouldn't shut. She looked down and there was a small, patterned box neatly tied with a striking red bow. A small card dangled loosely attached by a thin red ribbon. The card twisted as it was picked up. The card read, *To Davidia, from a secret admirer.* Her mother was shocked. She immediately panicked. She hoped that she wasn't dating behind her back. If she was, she was upset at not being included in the emotional loop. She smelt the pungent perfume reeling in its intensity. It must have been spilt in transit. She wondered who would deliver a weird-smelling package so early by no one. It was a poser. She called out to Davidia to check if she was awake.

'Yes, mum?' drawled a response from within the bowels of the house.

'There's a parcel for you. It was left at the front door.'

Davidia hadn't recently entered any love-struck competition for free perfume, or any competition at all. Boyfriends were listed on the absent calendar full of blank pages, so it wasn't one of them. She hadn't subscribed to any magazines either, so she was at a loss as to who might have sent it. After a refreshing shower and clean clothes, she bounded down the stairs as light as a fairy, landing feet upright at the bottom of the stairs. It was perfect placement every time.

'Hi, mum. Is Slirander here yet? We are walking to school together today.'

'She hasn't turned up. There's only this small box for you. You would tell me, wouldn't you, if you were dating anyone?'

'Of course, mum. My studies come first,' she said tongue-in-cheek.

Boys have their interesting side, but none had presented theirs to Davidia yet.

She read the card. The handwriting was familiar. She wondered what Slirander was up to. It was from her friend, wasn't it? She twirled the small package around a few times, not intentionally trying to dislodge any part of it. It began to feel heavy and heavier. A muffled sound struggled to escape from it.

'What the …?' said Davidia.

She dropped it onto the floor. Another louder muffled sound could be heard. She thought, *No animal lives in such a confined space.* She stood back a few paces and watched the small package writhe like a wriggling worm. Suddenly, one side burst open and out fell a lipstick tube with attitude.

'Why did you have to drop me? It's a long way down to the floor. Next time be careful. My container could dint and then my use would be short-lived. I take pride in my appearance.'

Davidia watched the cameo performance with interest.

'Who and what are you?' questioned Davidia.

She was aware that lipsticks are inanimate objects, yet this one was feisty, spoke, and, for its size, was a serious opponent.

'Open your eyes. It's me,' said Slirander. 'Pick me up and see for yourself.'

Davidia cautiously picked it up. She didn't want an unwanted surprise. Her fingers slid up and down the slink gold casing, flipping in and out two subtly-placed levers.

'Stop playing with my arms.'

With the top cap removed, a brilliant red lipstick with magnificent shading like a full-gloss, matt finish was revealed

'I must try it on,' said Davidia out loud.

'No, you don't. Keep your succulent lips off me. I'm not a lip moisturiser either.'

Davidia placed the uncooperative little case on her bathroom wash basin and watched it.

'Haven't you woken up yet that it's me,' said an incensed Slirander. 'Come closer.'

Davidia crept carefully and could see very small movements occurring. Were they agitated actions?

'You can speak. How is that possible? I can hear you better now that I'm nearer. Why can I hear a talking lipstick? You aren't a circus trick or alien, are you? I'm not being wire-tapped, am I?'

'It's me, Slirander. It's me, you hear, albeit rather feint.'

'Why imitate a lipstick? Surely, there's something larger you can be.'

'We have to get into the school staff room today and listen in on the proposal those two Senora College representatives are going to make. What better way than to be small and unnoticeable. You have to somehow smuggle me in.'

'Won't it be dangerous? You are so small. You could easily be misplaced or stolen and that very attractive colour will ensure a female won't leave you alone for long. Even I almost tried it.'

'The lipstick section is real enough. I'm in the compartment below it. Safely secure from prying banana lips.'

'I won't ask how you did it.'

'Better not. I'm still your friend, large or small. At least I'm still going with you to school today, just like you told your mum. There's one last thing to do. Pick me up for safekeeping.'

As Davidia did so, she felt a sharp and nasty pain on her right digit finger. It began to pulsate in agony. What had happened? There were no self-harm scissors in sight, no broken shower screen glass to blame, nor was her shaver lying around as a loose object. She wrung her hand for a second or two.

'You big wimp,' said Slirander. 'It was only a pin-prick anyway.'

'You did this to me. I ought to toss you in the bin, you nasty bitch.'

'Before you overdose on stupidity, place your finger in your ear and see what happens.'

Davidia was wary of following orders. She detested having fingers in her ears at the best of times. She thought, *it is such a ridiculous place to put a hurt finger.* What would she know? It was her head. She hadn't any reason to disagree and did as suggested. She was amazed at the instantaneous relief.

'Can you hear me better?' said Slirander. 'I bit you. I'm glad I'm not a cannibal. You might be tasty to the boys, but you don't taste all that good. I almost puked. I doubt a good dose of salt would improve the taste; however, your finger acts as a receiver when put in your ear. It's a communication tool, so you don't need to be near me to converse.'

'You're saying my finger in my ear is a communication antenna plugged into an ear receiver? Yes? I'll look stupid with my hand up there.'

'It is the only safe way to relay what is going on. This time, our disguises will last one full day. By this time tomorrow I'll be me again. No more lippy and no more radio station.'

Davidia was reeling from what she was experiencing. There was nothing more to do at home.

'Mum, I'm off to school now.'

'Aren't you waiting for Slirander? By the way, what was in that package?'

'Just some lipstick one of my friends recently bought on *eBay* and thought I'd like it. I'll take it to school to show the other girls. I'll catch Slirander at school. She's obviously not coming with me today.'

What would the challenge be for the two young schoolgirls?

2   STAFF ROOM

Students were normally banned from the teacher's staff room and access was usually by invitation only. The invitation was not always based on a good feeling.

Today would be a pot-pourri of ideas, questions and answers about that special letter received by the school principal, which he seemed to be full of angst over. No one knew for sure what had piqued his anxiety. He was the only individual to have read its contents. His troubled, stubbled chin was worn bare by rubbing. He had no need to shave this morning. A mottled rash had developed in its place and appeared as if he had a dose of youthful acne.

The teaching staff was in full gossip mode prior to the arrival of the principal and his guests. It wasn't only the students the staff discussed in a variety of descriptive words and phrases. They had an array of commentary based on being awake and filling their minds with thought trash. Fiction can quickly become fact, gossip that is camouflaged as truthful dialogue can cause damage to the innocent and perception doubles as reality. The spoken word based on these discussions usually ended up in the outbox in the mind's tray of forgotten thoughts.

The meeting was to be held after morning recess at 11.00am. By that time the school day would be in its normal routine. A few members visiting the school would hardly be noticed. The staff began to assemble. The atmosphere was abuzz with expectation of an interesting morning. The air felt fresh like a new beginning was dawning but, of course, it wasn't. It was already late morning.

Principal Jones sat at the front table observing the jostling groups of who sat with whom. Various cliques had developed amongst the school employees.

How does a rumour grow? How is it planted? Is it purchased in a shop? How is such a growth product acquired? Davidia had already made her summation by peering through the door window frame. She didn't know if it would match what the staff room could produce, or whether they had any of their own. She wasn't about to divulge hers. Was she correct in her observations, or had she taken literary licence with her interpretative knowledge? Why is everyone happy to share it within earshot of each other? There's no definitive answer for such a popular pastime. The fact that everybody can participate is probably its most attractive feature.

A few staffers began to chat amongst themselves.

'That new secretary to Principal Jones was at the chemist last week. Have you noticed how her body is rounding up and her clothes are tightening? I reckon she could be you-know-what.'

The suggestion could be weight gain, pregnancy, or she couldn't read the label size when she had purchased her new clothes and was too proud to return them. The maxim, one size fits all, isn't quite true; however, that's not a rumour, that's a fact.

The staff room was in full swing with literary discourse permeating the thoughts of all those present about the impending guests. The wait was deafening. Before any further misleading comments emerged, the staff had been seated near each other to avoid any whispering conversations.

The staff room door opened.

*

Davidia had arrived at school with her new brand of complaining lipstick. Her hair was neatly tied into a ponytail with a plain white ribbon. Its two long loose ends dangled, freely swaying as if a breeze existed as she walked. She had carefully placed the lipstick inside her jacket pocket for easy retrieval. The problem of access to the staff room seemed insurmountable. There wasn't any misdemeanour she could instigate to give her access and plant her partner in crime. Her thought basket was quite light-on at present. Normally, that's an unusual situation for such a bright-ideas girl.

'Davidia, have you thought about how we gain access to the staff room without being noticed?' said Slirander, who was tiring of being stuffed in a pocket. She craved fresher air.

'I'm still thinking. It's so obvious if I walk past, I'll easily be seen. I need a disguise.'

As soon as Davidia had turned into the corridor that led to the staff room, there were two other adults in front of her around her height heading in the same direction. They were no taller than she. One appeared from behind to be male, the other female. Their gait had a slowness of sway which attracted her attention as well as the longer than normal hands dangling by their sides. One carried a thin briefcase. She quickly took Slirander out of her pocket and pointed her in their direction.

'Do you notice anything peculiar about them?' asked Davidia.

There was no response. Then she begrudgingly remembered that to communicate with Slirander she had to place her finger in her ear in full view of anyone who may be around. She wanted confirmation of her first thoughts. Her receiver was firmly placed in her ear.

'Ugh!' She repeated her first question. 'Do you notice anything peculiar about them?'

Slirander took a moment or two.

'Rather short, aren't they?'

'Anything else?'

'They have long, thin hands and are extremely well-groomed. They seem quite ordinary.'

Suddenly, one turned toward the other and conversed with their counterpart. They both looked directly at one another and in doing so, produced an interesting profile an artist would crave to have as a human study to place on canvas. Slirander suddenly felt slimy to Davidia's touch and almost slipped from her grasp.

'Don't drop me, I'm delicate,' Slirander yelled.

'I look stupid with my finger stuck in my ear.'

'Pay attention then and be more careful with me. Those visitors may have more in their briefcase than an exercise in paperwork. I've seen those profiles before and if my memory serves me correctly, it wasn't a pleasant outcome. I can't figure out from where they seem familiar.'

'Are they dangerous?'

'Wait and see. We have yet to find out about the rumour of the school contest. We are nearing the staff room. Withdraw your finger, it looks ridiculous.'

'You're telling me.'

Davidia withdrew her finger, much to her relief and pending embarrassment. A cold wind rushed into the previously warm, finger-filled space. Her head spun with the impact.

The two visitors neared the staff room with Davidia in tow. She hadn't yet discovered her brilliant access thought into the staff room; however, she had it in her hand all the time, but hadn't recognised it. She waited at a distance to avoid being labelled a stalker. The visitors were about to turn right and push against the door aptly labelled "staff room". Davidia's thought bubble burst with her usual ingenuity. It was a minor explosion this time. She had to get ahead of the visitors and beat them into the staff room she wasn't invited into.

'Excuse me, excuse me,' she called out, as she quickened her pace toward them.

The two startled visitors turned around and took up defensive stances to bat whatever it was that was fast approaching. It was an automatic response. Danger took various forms and in the modern world it was preferable to be ready than not. Their faces tinged with yellow anger. They quickly realised that it was an inoffensive schoolgirl who had attracted their attention. Davidia was almost upon them.

'What can we do for you and why have you called to us? We have never met,' said the female, with the manners of royalty.

'I'm sorry. I got lost looking for the principal's office. It's such a big school. Do you know where it is?' Her pleading, blue eyes would melt the stiffest of defences.

'We are new here and have no idea where it might be. Why don't you ask one of the teachers in the staff room we are about to enter?'

Davidia didn't want to be trapped by appearing seemingly stupid to ask a question she already knew the answer to. The teachers would all be aware that she knew where it was. She had visited many times before under various guises of achieving better behaviour. By this time, she had edged herself close enough to be one step away from the door and in-between the visitors and the door. The staff had all seen the commotion outside in the corridor and curiosity was born this time and it wasn't a rumour. A few had left their seats for a proper inspection. Davidia was desperate. She had to improvise and get Slirander into the staff room to spy on the upcoming event. What to do? Before the staff had made it to the door, Davidia displayed the lipstick in so obvious a manner by holding it in her hand high above her head. She knew it would be immediately confiscated. Even the visiting teachers were aware of the "no lipstick" policy in school, or at least the "garish lipstick" policy. In an unprecedented move, the male politely swiped it from Davidia's hand, and she feigned complete surprise. Her ruse had worked.

'I'll pass this on to the principal. He'll know how to deal with the issue.'

'But, that's my favourite lipstick. Please, may I have it back?'

'No, and may a lesson be learnt.'

Davidia had done her thespian stint, albeit short, and quickly retreated along the corridor and out into the schoolyard before any staff member could approach her. The visitors now had her listening post which they would kindly hand to the principal. It would be placed on the front desk in full view of the innocent. It wasn't technically legal, but snooping had a certain amount of adventure. The staff waited after the corridor noise had subsided.

The staff room door opened.

*

Principal Jones stepped forward, hand held in front for the normal five-fingered handshake embrace. The visitors also replicated the action, but only one finger was presented as a greeting. The clasping had a certain futility about it when holding one finger wasn't quite a welcoming feeling. Principal Jones did his best to perform the greeting grasp, but felt he was cheated. Where's the real handshake gone? Maybe the educational do-gooders had purloined common sense and introduced this new behaviour without advising the general school community? It was a mystery. The thin, bony finger felt like grasping a naked knuckle that a complete skeleton kept in a museum would be proud of. Facial exercises immediately followed with welcoming features. The visitors were less emotional. They were all business. Their eyes were inert. They looked like the missing centres of a doughnut.

'I'm Principal Jones. Welcome to Vlad College. These are my colleagues.'

He waved his arm in an arc, encompassing his educational flock. They all stood up as an act of respect.

'This is Miss Alpine and I'm Mr. Avalanche. We are pleased to be visiting your school for the further education of all students.' Polite applause greeted the opening comments. 'We have been researching a new educational form of learning and are pleased to give your school the first opportunity to participate. Principal Jones has received a proposal of our ideas and their implementation. It is a different approach but, nevertheless, educational. Improvement in mental skills is a common goal for all. We almost forgot. We confiscated this lipstick from one of your students. This type of product shouldn't be used by them.' The male handed the offending lipstick to Principal Jones.

It all sounded plausible, reasonable and balanced, but it was only a few basic sentences. The substance and structure would follow.

Principal Jones gratefully received the small offering. He placed it on his desk at the front of the room. He ushered the two visitors to nearby chairs and the meeting was ready to commence.

Slirander was placed upright and had good vision of the whole room and, more importantly, the desktop. It held the proposal that everyone was eager to hear about. The sea of expectant faces littered around the room could also have been seen in the audience of any rock concert. The two visitors sat motionless, gazing at their prey. Once in History class, that might have been appropriate, but today it was only an expression. A hush came over the room as Principal Jones stood tall to commence his presentation. He stood tall like the Pope in front of a passionate audience.

Slirander wanted to read the letter of proposals before Principal Jones had stood up. She quietly flapped her two arms unseen and was able to roll over onto the letter unnoticed. She quickly read the letter by rolling back and forth across the page. Time was fleeting. She relayed everything read to Davidia, who she hoped was prepared for receivership.

Davidia had hidden herself in a section of the school gardens where she could listen undisturbed and unseen. It happened to be directly outside the staff room. It was dirty and uncomfortable sitting on the bark mulch. Those bulgy little woodchips weren't at all comfortable. She didn't care about later excuses for soiled clothing. She was now an undercover operative on a secret assignment. The dread of placing her finger in her ear for reception duties was still uncomfortable. A spy must do what is required without complaint.

'Testing, ready,' she said, as her finger tingled with an incoming message. It was Slirander.

'Finally. I was worried you weren't in position.'

'Have you found anything interesting? Go ahead. I'm safe. No one can see me. Are you safe?'

'I'm fine. Listen carefully.'

Slirander had almost read the letter word for word when Principal Jones picked it up just as she was about to read the conclusions. There was static on the line as Slirander was placed to one side. No one had paid any attention to a fallen lipstick. They often overbalanced at the slightest touch. No one was any the wiser about the listening post. It was time to listen to a speech, impressive or otherwise. Davidia had momentarily lost contact.

'Slirander, what's happening?'

'I couldn't read the conclusions; however, Principal Jones might read them out. He's about to present to the crowd. It's a rather weird set of points made. I also noticed that the letterhead had no address and I felt seasick as each sentence seemed to undulate. It felt like they were trying to escape. I didn't read one happy sentence. Listen to the speech and see what sense you can make of it.'

'I hope it's not too long. My ear is beginning to hurt.'

The speech that was to change her school's educational advantage began.

'Fellow staff members and invited guests, I have in front of me a set of innovative proposals that may increase the gain in the school's academic results whereby we can become the premier educational institution in the State. Senora College have kindly lent us their two most senior educationalists to assist in achievement of that goal by agreeing to implement a range of approaches and experiences not previously taught. They certainly haven't been made available under normal educational guidelines. This would be a first. We can lead by example.'

Principal Jones paused for a freshening mouthful of water. Not the ordinary pure tap water that ran through the school's watering system, but a $5 special bottle of overseas introduced, exquisite mountain-dew, bubbly-imbued, triple-filtered and extra-trickly, bottled water discovered by the ancient monks in a European mountain village and walked out of the hills on the back of yaks. The school budget was in perennial pain from the thirsty staff. Ordinary tap water did the same job cheaper and was normally healthier and more natural.

'What are these ideas?' asked a staffer.

'As a trial they have invited the school to provide two students from each of Years 10, 11 and 12 to their school to undergo these new teaching techniques.'

'What are these new techniques and why have they remained hidden to date?' asked another staffer.

'They will be slowly introduced to the amazement of all. The selected students will attend Senora College daily and once these new techniques have been applied, they can relay them to the school. It is also suggested that the school takes six selected students from their school to be taught at our school and they may gain from us also.'

'So, it's an exchange program then?'

'It's an enlightenment of ideas not thought of before. They will be taught with special procedures.'

'Can you explain any one of those special procedures?'

'They can only be revealed within the relevant school system and are so secret, their integrity needs to be maintained to prevent stealing by other institutions.'

'Will we be given access to these new and innovative teaching ideas?'

'In the planning stage we need to take the first steps very carefully.'

The speech ended up with a tumultuous applause from the mesmerised staff. Not one of them had understood the thirty-minute speech's contents, nor did they have any idea of what was said. It appeared to be a winner no matter how it was presented. The two visitors gazed over the crowd, pleased with the nothing presentation. No one was running for political office today.

'I invite questions to be directed at our two visitors, who can explain in detail these revolutionary ideas.'

'Where is your school located? None of us here have ever heard of it.'

'It's in the development stage on the outskirts of the city being built on the site of a swampy tip near Hilbridgeburg. Classroom classes commence next week. We are mainly interested in the Year 12 exams to be held in the next few weeks as we have a few off-campus students being home-tutored who need to flex their knowledge. They are our priority.'

'Where's Hilbridgeburg again? I seem to have misplaced my SatNav.'

'It is where it has been explained,' said the yellow-tinged Mr. Avalanche.

His body posture stiffened like a surfboard. That was one wave to miss.

Principal Jones stepped forward in a general-like manner and promptly ended proceedings. He already had his dose of applause and now he sensed it would be withdrawn with too many intrusive and inquisitive questions his guests weren't particularly keen to answer. He'd had his success and that was that. School policy would involve these new innovations in quality teaching. His decision was made. He didn't need any union interference. He was the boss. No one was really any the wiser whether the comments would be instituted or were real; however, a salesman had sold them an unknown innovation without any explanation. Wow! Knowledge and ignorance in the same sentence would give rise to questionable benefits. Time would tell.

'No more questions then?' he said, as he dismissed the adult assembly.

*

'Slirander, is the agony over?' whispered Davidia, afraid she'd be overheard by another student. Hiding in the garden bed is a questionable activity at the best of times.

'Yes. The speech wasn't the same as that written on that letter. Somehow it all changed when spoken out loud. There's something amiss in the translation from written to oral. Did you remember what I read out from the letter?'

'Some of it and it wasn't very pleasant. Principal Jones may have been misled. He fortunately didn't read that written advice.'

'His water could have been tampered with a dose of rambling nonsense. It was the only thing he consumed. I hear it's the new trend in education hailed by the academic set. Those two visitors with the mountainous names were the only ones nearby. There's a mystery about them. Have you noticed the yellow tinge around their faces and those thin fingers?'

'They might have a vitamin deficiency or yellow jaundice. Either that, or it could be a body halo? Often religious groups like to stand out with an oddity, perhaps that's theirs? What's happening now?'

'The staff room is almost empty. Only the two visitors and Principal Jones are left. I can hear them discussing selection, isolation and therapeutic treatment. I'm not sure if they are offering the use of a private spa. It's indistinct. I don't know what educational quality would be produced by being nude in a spa. How would it improve male diction and who should be in there in the name of education? Definitely not a student.'

'Are you sure that's what they are discussing? It doesn't sound like the school curriculum to me.'

'Shush, they are coming nearby. I might get to read the conclusions of that letter.'

'Thank you, Principal Jones, for allowing us to meet your staff and present our ideas. The letter of proposal is a lead document for the future of education. We are glad that you have an open mind to the proposals, and we will jointly implement them during the next week. Is this the letter we sent to you? As it is a private missive, we must retain its possession. We don't want any snoopers to get hold of it, do we? Secrecy is paramount.'

'Certainly not! Let's work together on the joint venture of future education.'

The three adults shook hands again with renewed enthusiasm. Principal Jones didn't even mind the hugging of a bony finger this time. They parted, but before they did, there was "Lipstickgate" to deal with.

Slirander just had time to read the ending conclusion of that interesting letter before it was snatched off the desktop. She did wonder about the purpose of retrieval. It had sinister written in capital letters all over it.

'What about the lipstick? It has a magnificent hue. Miss Alpine would love to decorate her lips with it. I could then see more clearly where all her words come from. Besides, it's expressly banned for our students,' said Mr. Avalanche.

'It's a gift,' said Principal Jones, as he departed the staff room.

The space seemed empty even though the two visitors filled a small floor area. Even with a crowd of those visitors, the space would still feel like a vacuum.

'No, no! Davidia, I've been bagnapped. You must come and save me, if you can. I have no idea where I'm going. I won't be home tonight. My parents will worry. You can tell them I am having a study sleepover at your house. This is a nightmare.'

Before Davidia had expressed the emotion, 'Shit,' she wanted to know what the conclusions were on the proposal letter.

'Did you read the conclusions?'

'I tried to, but I didn't get them all. The words group (candidate selection), cage (personal learning space) and therapeutic (connived result) were all I could glean. The words satisfaction and failure were mentioned, but not in what consequence. They were written in capital letters and emphasised in red ink. That's it. Now I'm in a handbag or personal carry-all. It's rough, stinks and bounces like a trampoline. You must come and get me. No one else knows I exist as a lipstick.'

'I can't go home either. I need to follow you. I'll tell your parents that you are staying with me and my parents that I am staying with you. I don't like white lies, but what else can we do? Wait a minute. That means that I must have my finger stuck in my ear all night without any sleep. I could get arrested for stupid behaviour.'

'I'm afraid so.'

Davidia needed relief from her finger incarceration. She emerged from her hiding place looking like a landscape gardener's assistant. Her finger was still trapped. It didn't enjoy the probe, but it had to be borne. Sacrifices to become a heroine had to be made. A few fellow students noticed her strange behaviour. A few snide comments were made.

'Are you looking for your brains?'

'You should be reported for being a blonde.'

'It won't come out the other side, will it?'

'What an air hole!'

'They should be pristine clear by now.'

'You don't eat it, do you?'

A few sniggers and the band of merriment passed by. Davidia extracted her finger much to her relief and set off looking for the two visitors who had her friend without knowing it. She didn't have any plan on how to retrieve the lipstick. It was almost too late. Within twenty-four hours Slirander will materialise as herself again. The two visitors were seen leaving the schoolyard heading toward the tram station.

Davidia whipped out her telephone, rang both their parents with the plausible sleepover excuse and sprinted to her locker. She retrieved her older age make-up kit, available for girl emergencies when trying to impress the males, and a small backpack. She was last seen creating dust particles out of the schoolyard.

Would she and Slirander be missed in class?

3   LIPSTICKGATE

'Honey, Davidia just rang to say she's having a sleepover at Slirander's tonight. I didn't know she had that planned. She must have taken her nightwear and toiletries to school. Slirander didn't go with her this morning either, which I thought was a tad unusual. I'll check her room.'

Davidia's mum normally didn't venture into the realm of the mysterious, in case she was surprised by what she found and had to accept with greater certainty that her girl was growing up. The independence streak of youth seemed to emerge far earlier than when she was a young girl. The bathroom was neat and tidy. Nothing was disturbed in there. The bed was made as if the coverings had been ironed stiff. The wardrobe offered nothing except a large range of brand-name clothing. None of them were ordinary day wear. She concluded that nothing was removed from the room at all, except Davidia's school wear. Doubt circled her mind threatening to cloud her impeccable judgement. For a moment, disaster exploded in her thoughts. The pain was unimaginable, when just as suddenly reason came floating through on a cloud, calming her nerves. She thought now that Davidia's developing into a serious teenager, responsibility goes with that; therefore, she could look after herself. She hoped that the life lessons that she had been taught to date would overcome any situation her daughter was mixed up in. She was a very capable young girl. Mum relaxed, closed the door and headed to the kitchen for a soothing beverage. The type wasn't mentioned.

Slirander's parents were more relaxed. They were more

accepting of their daughter's behaviour, dress and general activity. They thanked Davidia for alerting them to her non-appearance that night and wished them both a pleasant evening. How simple was that? Not all parents are that accepting. Once again, young developing girls, or early women, have a capacity about them that allows some leeway, whilst having faith in them at all times? Mmm.

The pleasantness of the evening for the girls was an unknown. Would it remain so?

*

The tram stop near the school was bustling with an array of individual activity. Small children tested a parent's patience. Many youth and older aged persons had long, thin, black strands growing from their ears colloquially known as "black spaghetti", which ended up plugged into a small hand-held object. Very few took notice of anyone else as they searched their telephones for the endless messages of being involved in the digital world. It appeared that their souls were tapped into a magical source. Waste food wrappings clung to the ground as an edifice to good eating and poor rubbish recycling manners. Seating was at a premium. Many were occupied by youthful firm backsides which could have been offered to those that were much older and obviously less firm. The selfie and selfish worlds collide.

Davidia made it to the tram stop unnoticed by anyone. Who was interested in a teenage schoolgirl when their world was normally more important? She was a part of the crowd swill. This allowed her time to readjust her school uniform by overlaying it with a fine top, hiding her student identity from view. She loosened her white hair ribbons. Her long tresses cascaded around her face in a hugging embrace. Her new disguise as an ordinary youth would allow her to place her finger in her ear in a more private manner and hide her face from view. Being incognito on a spy mission was of the utmost importance. Her backpack of goodies was a godsend to altering her appearance. She was now ready to track, except for the important placement of her finger. Would that cause her any embarrassment? She couldn't afford any. She thought it better to wait until she entered the tram and took one of the seats with her firm backside. The tram arrived. A mad scramble ensued. The two adults she was chasing sat down at the far end of the tram facing away from her, whilst she sat in the first section inside the door where she could observe unnoticed. A corner seat was available, which meant that she could lean one arm along the back of a seat and pretend to support her head whilst placing that all important finger in the correct hearing orifice, hidden by all that hair.

Slirander felt lonely and discarded. She hadn't been in contact with her Davidia lifeline for some time. It was impossible to know what she was up to. Then it happened. Miss Alpine extracted her new lipstick from her carry-all. The hapless Slirander was about to be smeared onto the thinnest set of lips which presented as stretched elastic. The shock almost sent Slirander into meltdown. If she "ran", the rubbish bin would be her new home.

'I should have picked a better disguise,' she wailed to herself.

The real her wasn't affected because she was in the bottom half, but her red top was about to be decimated. A residual feeling would be felt throughout.

'I've got to bear this,' she said. She shut her eyes tight.

Miss Alpine toyed with the gold object for a moment or two. She was probably unsure how to open the damn thing. Both arms were flicked sharply causing Slirander some pain.

'I hope the bitch isn't going to break my arms off,' she said, quite annoyed.

'Slirander, where are you? I'm on the tram following you.'

Davidia was back online. Slirander couldn't answer for two reasons: discovery and use.

Miss Alpine brought out one of her unattractive mirrors and proceeded to redden her thin lips. Slirander winced as she felt a scratching across her red top. The sight she couldn't see wasn't worth reporting. She was sure an offence had occurred. After the smearing and a few top and bottom lip sucks, Miss Alpine managed to apply it correctly and could now identify her mouth more easily. The same crap still came out of the same place, but it sounded better when said. Even Mr. Avalanche nodded complimentarily. Words would have given him away. Slirander held her breath in case she was of any further use. In the next instant she had been thrown into the carry-all. It was relief all around.

'Slirander, can you hear me?' said Davidia.

'Yes. I've had the most dreadful experience. I've been used as a real lipstick. I never realised how unpleasant it could be. Where have you been? Are you nearby?'

'I'm on the tram following your bag nappers. Is most of you okay?'

'I have one more use and that's it. Whatever I do, which isn't much in this format, I can only be used once more. I'm then at personal risk after my cover is removed. I risk being a discarded lipstick forever. My parents would lose their daughter and you, my best friend.'

'That's not going to happen. Can your top be replaced?'

'Yes, but you would have to tell my father. He doesn't know my current predicament. It's not always the case that daddy knows best. We have to solve this situation ourselves.'

'Are they talking to each other?'

'Not a word. They haven't discussed anything at all. They act like mutes. I can't risk implementing any discussions. I can only listen. Where are we so far?'

'I'm not sure. I have been so busy worrying and listening to you I haven't paid any attention.'

Davidia peered out of the windows and was astonished to find that they were in a country area travelling through a swamp. All passengers on board were still there and she realised that the tram hadn't made one stop. How peculiar? Where was she? Her arm suddenly slipped off the back of the seat and bumped a fellow seater. Her face was filtered from view with all that hair; however, the seated passenger was enraged, with a face taking on a yellow tinge for being unceremoniously and accidentally bumped. Was that a facial halo? Who's the make-up artist? It didn't look healthy. What's with the sickness colour? She then glanced along the tram and noted that everyone was seated and had a variation of the same facial colour. Were manners in vogue on this journey? They all paid no attention to each other. It was deathly quiet, like holidaying in a graveyard with all your friends on the funeral tram. Davidia began to fear for her safety. An ill chill sent shudders through her petite frame, when she noticed a light frost creep up her leg to knee height. It stopped. She had frosted leggings. They would make a suitable addition to her mounting wardrobe. Everyone else in the train wore the same items. Her eyes almost jumped out of her eye sockets as she observed the emergence of a protruding kneecap on each leg that she could see. Did it occur to her? She leant over to view the floor and checked. Her knees were normal. A fellow passenger spoke to her because she had made a substantial personal movement, which was a rarity when any of the group travelled.

'Is your konnocker properly formed?'

'My what? Oh, yes, my konnocker is rather small, but beautifully formed. Would you like to see it?'

'That isn't allowed if it is covered. You look pale. Your colouring is too light.'

Silence followed.

Davidia had noticed that all the other fellow passengers possessed a slight yellow facial tinge, which brightened when angered. She opened her backpack and found a yellow *Texta* exactly the right colour. She needed both hands for Operation T. She was in spy mode and it sounded apt. Her hands disappeared behind her hair mass and she carefully drew around her face a yellow *Texta* fringe to blend in with all the others. It was oil-based and not water-based, so it would last a while. This would keep her cover intact if she didn't act too stupidly and give herself away.

'Next stop, Hilbridgeburg.'

Slirander felt the jolt. She couldn't see a damn thing inside the carry-all. Super vision would be wonderful had it been bestowed upon her. Davidia sat bolt upright, prepared for the next segment of her journey. She replaced her finger in her ear to update Slirander.

'This place is weird. It's not one of our suburbs. We are in a place called Hilbridgeburg. The tram has stopped. Your carrier and companion got off first. Oops, I must follow them. Talk later. Finger removed.'

What awaits Davidia in this foreign educational environment?

*

Principal Jones sat behind his huge desk contemplating the speech that he had delivered earlier in the day. His head sat heavily in his hands. It wasn't that his brain capacity had grown at all. It was more to do with what he had said to the staff. The missing letter that he had based his speech upon was no longer in his possession and its existence as evidence upon which it was based was missing. He wondered whether he was sane with his commentary. Another deep breath stretched his shirt and gave him more carbon dioxide to exhale as stress relief. A knock on his door refocused him. It was Miss Green.

'Like that was an incredible like speech, sir. What did it like mean? Can you like explain it like to me, so I like don't appear incapable like of like accepting new ideas?'

'When I read the original letter of proposal, it seemed an excellent basis for future educational discussions. When I presented those details, I felt like a puppet being controlled by a puppeteer and appearing perfectly natural in presenting it. How did it appear to you? I feel miserable.'

'Well, sir, it sounded like this to me. Are you able to like tolerate criticism? I like my job and would rather like say nothing like than to risk ongoing unemployment.'

'Feel free to express your opinion. I'm sure everyone else has. Unfortunately, I don't have the original letter to refer to, nor do I remember all its contents. How embarrassing for a school principal is that?'

'Like I don't want to like swear, sir, but it went like the crapper. That's it. No one understood like what any of these new like ideas are. It's Blanksville. How did these visitors from like Senora College contact you?'

'By mail.'

'Did you like check them out?'

'Not really, but their letterhead and content appeared authentic.'

'So, it's like this. You didn't like find anything about them.'

'Not really. How gullible am I?'

'I'm not like prepared to like answer that question, sir, except that you are like a male. I reckon it's an educational scam. That's it! Scamgate! You did like say we are introducing like new programs like what? It's like a real mystery, sir. Are they like contacting you again? If they do, like would you like me to be there, sir? Another set of eyes might like see something new. Remember, sir, we're a team.'

'Thank you, Miss Green. I understand that in the next few days a proper program will be forwarded. We'll wait until then. Did I appear hypnotised to you, because my memory bells keep ringing to tell me that I said absolutely nothing about what the letter suggested?'

'Sir, it's like a memory loss. I would never like call you a like Zombie, but you have a headful of good like information, but you like left it at home. A few like sanity rumours have started, but I like stopped spreading them. Sorry, sir. It was a day like for the like weird. The other teachers like don't spread like rumours, but who has control like of the English language? You might like need a sedative, sir, and not one like found in a packet. That special adult medical like bottle with a foreign name like after a northern Englishman like Scot that you have like hidden in those like shelves is worth a like visit. Is that his like name, Scotch? I have like met him on many an occasion like. He hasn't like asked me out yet like, but I'm sure he will. You do know like I'm single.'

'Yes, Miss Green. I'm fully aware of your marital status as you are mine. I'm also single but married to the job.'

'What's your wife like?'

'Controlling and occasionally suffocating.'

'You know like, sir, you can like sniff the flowers like now and then.'

'And what flower style should that be?'

'Any that may grow in the ground. Well, sir, it's time for my like next class. Remember, sir, teamwork.'

Miss Green was sometimes provocative but made good sense. Could he, after his embarrassing speech? The future of his comments and the contact with Senora College will have to be carefully managed.

What will that relationship be?

*

Davidia approached a fellow passenger and asked what time the tram leaves to go back to where they had previously caught it. The passenger's eyes disappeared into an abyss. It was like looking at a set of micro dots.

'Are you new here? Have you been recruited?'

Davidia had to think quickly.

'Yes, this is my first tram journey here.'

'It won't be your last.'

'When I take my next trip from here, does the tram leave from this station?'

'You really are new. The station has gone. See, it doesn't exist anymore. Tram journeys are ever only made once from any station.'

'But where is the next station? I can't see any and where did the tram tracks go?'

'They will appear again elsewhere, when the next drive is on.'

Davidia couldn't believe a place with disappearing tram lines, tram and station existed. She angrily placed her finger in her ear to see if that was a myth also. Slirander answered, none too happy. Words full of rhyming with itch commencing with the letters b and w, crackled over the finger waves. It was really alright. Slirander had reacted appropriately.

'What is this town? It's not on my dad's SatNav, which I recently misplaced.'

'It's Hilbridgeburg. Discovery is your journey. Don't do that here. It's offensive and a dirty habit.'

Cheeky bloody stranger.

'I can place my finger anywhere I want on my body,' she said, incensed at the impertinence of her having any dirty bad habits. If she did, she wasn't aware of them.

The passenger departed and left her alone standing like a foreign sentinel in a strange land.

It was supposedly still broad daylight when she noticed a dark shadow cover the sky like a thin sheet drawn over a bed. Her quarry was fast disappearing into the distance. Fortunately, her youth and speed were enough to make up ground quite easily. Miss Alpine and Mr. Avalanche never looked behind them, so she was still undiscovered. They walked past a few monocoloured buildings alternately painted in either miserable grey or depressing black. Each structure was square, not rectangular or triangular, just plain boring square. The imaginative architect who had designed this rudimentary collection of what was supposed to be housing, must have done it whilst asleep, at death's door or on an insanity trip. Ugly couldn't adequately give it the description it deserved. Davidia felt oppressed by the monotony of it all.

She felt her finger tingle. It was an incoming call. She hadn't handed her finger out to anyone. Oops! She realised that it was Slirander, her only unit caller.

'This isn't a holiday in here. What's happening out there? Are you nearby?'

It must be a miserable existence for any lipstick to be bounced in the dark and still be expected to perform at optimum capacity when the lips of the perpetrator need to be embraced with a covering that enhances their appearance and kissability. Slirander wasn't in a mood to be that nice.

Davidia peered around her in case another offensive local comment was made. It was all clear. She placed the antennae into the receiver. By the time that ear was no longer required for surveillance, it would be free of any wax impurities.

'Slirander, I'm not far behind. This place is weirdo land. Remind me never to do drugs if the mind ends up in a permanently regurgitated existence like this. It's so depressing. They should call this joint Boxland. Nothing is different. Even the inhabitants melt into buildings without opening any doors. It's the stuff of ghosts.'

'Shut up with the rambling. Have you discovered anything about the two visitors?'

'I'm only following them at this stage. I'll wear my Wonder Woman costume a little later, shall I? Just a moment, they are entering a huge bulbous building with the name Senora College emblazoned across it on a flashing screen. It certainly stands out from the others. I don't believe it. They didn't enter through any door. The whole damn bulb lifted off the ground and they walked in underneath it. That's incredible. I hope we aren't in Galaxy 72 or wherever *Star Trek* travels. I must get inside.

Somehow you must get out of that carry-all so you can see what I see. I don't want to be the only insane one. We could be in serious trouble here. Gotta go; my stalking technique needs activating. Talk later.'

Davidia crept up to the bulbous building, which was made of a special one-way glass. You could see out but not in. It was constructed to withstand any natural devastation or assault that Nature, in a moment of a natural hissy-fit, could throw at it.

The staff monitoring the access and exit points noted that the "trainee" or "recruit" was quite incapable of gaining access on her own. It was like watching an animal at the Zoo chasing its surrounds searching for its prey. This time it was Davidia. She walked along its circumference, which wasn't all that far, probing any defect in its walls to allow entrance. The staff finally had enough amusement and raised the dome to allow Davidia in. The surprise had her mouth agape and standing in a schoolgirl pose, pretending shyness: you know, look at the ground, feign a stupid grin, eyes down, cross legs over one another with hands held firmly at the front of the skirt, and perform a silly wiggle. Where's Oscar when you have the perfect performance?

'Come, come, child,' said a matronly staff member. 'No need to be coy with us. We knew that entrance was impossible for you because you don't have the code and you don't exist on our records. How you arrived here undetected is amazing. It has never happened before.'

'Where exactly am I?'

'In Hilbridgeburg, obviously. You are our first free visitor. How did you get here?'

'I caught a tram. I must have got on the wrong one. It was at my regular stop.'

'We've heard of inoperative activity where all members weren't properly scanned before getting on board. Have you got a konnocker?'

Davidia knew that she didn't have a real one, but one of her knees had a slight deformity from a childhood injury. Would that suffice in a superficial examination?

Had it been the reason she went undetected? She had seen one grow on the knee of a fellow passenger and pretended hers was in the process of forming properly.

'I'm not sure. Is it a requirement?'

'Everyone must have a konnocker to allow exit and entrance to the town and any of the buildings. Anything less is an intruder with consequences not discussed. We have all been processed, coded and given the immortal lump. Show me what you have masquerading under your skirt. Knee exposure is mandatory.'

Davidia felt vulnerable at this point. With mistaken access, no konnocker, no explainable reason to be here, and non-coded, her visit to Hilbridgeburg might be a disaster, and what about Slirander? No, she must clever her way through it. Her friend needs her. Besides, what is it about this town? Education hadn't yet appeared except in the name of the college.

Davidia fumbled with her clothing. She wasn't particularly keen to show other women her perfect set of pins in case closer examination, other than vision, was sought. She needn't have worried. She raised her dress to the appropriate height. The two staff members walked out from behind their desk and approached. Two sets of beady eyes focused on the reveal.

'That's a very small konnocker,' said the matronly lady. 'It looks like it has an inhibitive growth pattern. You can see by that innocuous lump it has tried to grow but failed miserably. You have the start of a good konnocker albeit embarrassing to show anyone else. Look here.'

The matronly staffer raised her skirt and proudly showed Davidia, her lumpy growth.

'Now that is a konnocker. Knock your socks off.'

It was a huge knobbly growth bulging out from her kneecap. Each inhabitant possessed one in some form. Davidia's deformity saved her. She now had to be coded to allow unfettered access to all buildings. Once the ladies had settled, Davidia suggested that she be coded and become part of the society. Another young, intelligent, female youth would certainly liven up the town.

'I'm impressed by the size of your growth. Does it continue to grow whilst you are alive?'

'Each konnocker is coded with a definitive growth date and when that is reached, we are replaced by another. The population here to date is stable; however, there is a rumour that amongst us there is a plan to expand elsewhere. Where to, no one yet knows? Trials are being carried out.'

'Are you able to code me? Perhaps I could be part of that development. I come from a different place and have arrived very recently.'

'It is normally approved by Miss Alpine or Mr. Avalanche.'

'It would be a complete surprise for them. I'm only sixteen. I have lots of time for development. Aren't they your educationalists?'

Davidia had almost said too much. She retracted her statement by saying she had seen them at her school earlier in the day and had assumed that they were their educationalists.

Phew! Problem resolved.

'Place your knee here,' said the matronly lady.

Davidia lifted her leg onto a flat table at leg height. An automatic strap fastened her leg. Her kneecap was surrounded by a vibrant light. She felt a burning sensation. It was over in seconds. She placed her leg on the floor. It felt okay. She lifted her skirt to find she had an ugly konnocker protruding from her left knee. The code was hidden inside.

'You realise that it's for life.'

Davidia almost choked. What about her dating capacity? She couldn't be seen again in a swimsuit, play sport or show what was one of her best features ever again. There must be an antidote. Any real explanation would sound ludicrous. What a damn mess. Where's Slirander?

'Is there any cure for this unseemly bulge?'

'No one knows if there is. You now have free access everywhere. Welcome to the group.'

'Can you tell me where Miss Alpine might live? I'm a new trainee for educational future.'

'That's a plan we know she is working on. Follow that corridor. At the end of it is her office. We can't disclose where she lives, because we don't know.'

Davidia was pissed off with being permanently branded and had gone to all this trouble because of a damn lipstick, albeit her closest friend. She was owed one.

Would Slirander be smeared again?

4 RECRUITS

Davidia felt no side effects of her konnocker attachment. It didn't inhibit her ability to walk correctly. She'd love Slirander to have one too because of all the effort she had gone through to follow and perhaps save her. It was time to impersonate what was a work in progress. A spy continually evaluates their situation to adapt to any procedure for survival. Davidia was still mentally digesting her predicament as she carefully walked along the stranger corridor to Miss Alpine's office. She could see the office door easily within eyesight; however, she didn't seem to be any closer, yet when she looked behind her, the two staffers were dust specks in the distance. The floor was stationary, or it appeared so. Was there a hidden walkway that she couldn't feel? She wasn't floating. On either side of the walkway she visioned, or thought she did, glimpses of movement in large cages. It was impossible to tell what sort of animals they were. The walls were frosted. Could it be a zoo or a rescue facility for endangered animals? The building lacked warmth even though it had an operational heating system.

Her konnocker suddenly felt itchy. A mini vibration had tickled her skin. She scratched it as a matter-of-fact and, before any thought could fill her mind's in-tray, she was standing outside the door of Miss Alpine's office. What the …? It was so surprising. The bad language effect that accompanied such a surprise was sadly absent. Reaction time had instantly disappeared. Davidia composed herself. She wondered what was in there. She raised a hand as an offensive tool to pound the door, when an open space appeared. Another, what the …? In the distance standing in a confrontational position was Miss Alpine. She had felt an unhealthy tremor in Davidia's konnocker and wasn't quite sure what it meant. Now she could see the individual she had summoned with the vibrating knee technique and realised she was a young schoolgirl. Educationalists know these things. Her manner of nastiness subsided. She even practised a smile, which was, at best, a good attempt. No yellow-tinged colour change in anger framed her face. Her doughnut eyes bored into Davidia's. She was staring at a stranger. This had her strategically on the back foot, so she took a step forward to be on her front foot. She always had to have the pre-eminent position in her world. No youth would best her. Davidia scanned the office and noticed the carry-all thrown loosely, like a forgotten rag, across the back of a chair. It hung limply by one strap, lacking any care in placement. She thought of Slirander as a prisoner in that saggy space. Her friend needed her more than ever as they were in the territory of the "enemy".

'Hello there,' said Miss Alpine. 'Who might you be and how did you get here?'

Davidia's explanation had to be acceptable, otherwise there was no telling what the ramifications might be.

'My name is Davidia. I was going home for lunch from school yesterday from Vlad College, hopped on the tram at the stop and ended up here, wherever I am?' replied Davidia. She had no intention of disclosing the real reason that she was there.

'What year are you in?'

'I'm in Year 10.'

Miss Alpine thought that was perfect. It was another exchange student to educate. It was unfortunate that Davidia was by herself. Her aim was two Year 10s from Vlad College once Principal Jones had agreed to the student exchange program in the name of better education. One student in advance might work.

'I see you already have a konnocker. That's very impressive

and you have obtained it without proper permission, which isn't allowed. If there is an impurity in it, it means a leg amputation. We can only have original invitees here. Any stragglers or stranger arrivals might jeopardise our educational program. Bring your leg here.'

Davidia followed orders whilst she formulated any plan that sprung to mind. Miss Alpine placed her hand on her konnocker and felt its bulginess.

'It is on the correct knee, isn't it?' said Davidia.

No female had ever placed a hand on her knee, and she was primed to kick Miss Alpine in the groin when she withdrew her hand.

'Perfect job. You will make an appropriate candidate.'

'That's a lovely shade of lipstick you are wearing. Can I buy that shade here somewhere? I didn't see any shopping mall.'

Davidia had recognised Slirander's red top bumping gums on a pair of banana boat-shaped lips; however, she already knew that.

'It's not allowed amongst students here to wear any false items. Educationalists, because of the age difference, have that ability. Your time will come.'

'Is it possible to see where such beauty comes from?'

Miss Alpine hesitated. No student, and I mean no student, had ever asked a question like that before. Their training didn't allow disobedient questions. Adults often performed rational thoughts to process a measured response. Was there any danger associated with the question? It had been a long while since Miss Alpine had felt the emotion of doubt. One meeting with this new "student" had re-ignited that absent feeling. She hoped that Davidia wasn't going to be trouble. We all hope that, don't we?

'You are rather curious for a student. Why do you want to know?'

'When I become an older-age teenager, I will probably visit

shopping malls and cosmetic shops. If they had that colour in a lipstick, then I could select that exact same colour and credit the selection of my purchase to you.' Someone's ego, regardless of size, was being gently massaged.

Davidia felt a movement in Miss Alpine, yet she was ramrod still. Then, the unexpected happened. She walked over to her carry-all and extracted that lipstick under discussion. Davidia's eyes lit up. Miss Alpine noticed. Why? Was Miss Alpine teasing her? Davidia had to hold in any excitement. She was still a "spy", and control; it was all about control. She waited until it was offered to her. Slirander was almost within her grasp. The few seconds seemed like an endless spacewalk. Was it really going to happen? Her palms moistened. Her heart rate tried to push her chest out of her school shirt. It was doing an excellent job until Miss Alpine requested Davidia to sit down whilst still holding her friend. She thought that the bitch wouldn't give it to her. Breathe, breathe to calm her nerves. She sat down with her whole being tingling with alertness.

'Is this the item of interest that you desire?'

'Is that it? I thought a lipstick case would be more impressive than that dented gold insignificant item. It's hard to believe that such a small thing created such radiance.'

Davidia wasn't that uncharitable to suggest that it was misused on Miss Alpine. Rubbish! It would look better had it been scrawled as graffiti over a disused factory wall. Davidia's smile might have been smeared across her face, but it was a façade. Her eyes; it was in the eyes. Drill, drill, bore, bore. Two strong-minded women of different ages spanning the decades sat opposite each other. Miss Alpine wasn't normally a sharing person.

'Kindly return this item to me. Look at it only. It is not to be used. I'm not normally this charitable. I enforce the education in this town. Soon you will be part of it too.'

Miss Alpine passed the lipstick to Davidia. Slirander finally felt the familiar feeling of her friend. She hadn't been abandoned after all. As Davidia twirled the lipstick in her hand, Slirander bit her finger again, this time in anger, not as a reception centre, wondering why she hadn't been saved earlier. Davidia winced with the pin-prick pain. Slirander could see once again and scanned the room. Her appraisal had been instant. Davidia couldn't place her finger in her ear as a communication tool because she would be discovered talking with what or whom? Her deviousness had to be exemplary. She pretended to sneeze. Her backpack held a pack of tissues which doubled as a handkerchief. Often, when people travel, they carry the all-purpose toilet roll which has a multitude of practical uses. No need to list them all. You would recognise your particular use amongst them, if they were. Her act was so convincing. A translucent, white substance began to pool at the end of her nose. Where did that come from? She made a dive for the backpack. Miss Alpine was quick as a flash and stood before her and her saviour. Davidia had created a quirkiness of behaviour that she wasn't used to. It bothered her.

'I have a tissue which needs me,' she said. 'Otherwise, do you want to wipe it?'

The situation was worsening. Miss Alpine stood aside, stunned. If a mishap occurred, the cleaning staff would need to be called. Davidia hurriedly sorted through her "goodies".

Once, when she was at a school dance, one of the other girls had a new scarf that Davidia fancied to wear just for the sake of putting it on. She wore her own scarf of a lesser brand. On the dance floor the other girl was wildly gyrating to impress one of the boys with the big intelligence, the school footballer of the year. Davidia wasn't interested in her date, nice lad though he was. He was the conduit to get closer to her goal of temporary thievery. Girls can be so deceptive. A smile, a wink, a wave and a male talking gibberish often followed. Fashion had a high price to pay for envy eyes when their budget didn't extend to a prize they wanted. It will soon be mine. Davidia wound up her lithe torso and flung it loose like a spinning top onto the dance floor. If no one had paid any attention to her to date, they did now. There was no need to turn the heating up. The lighting was dim, the crowd moved like a restless kelp bed and the obvious happened. Davidia already had her scarf in hand. She deliberately bumped her arrival, pretended to fall, flung her arms around the other for support, not for an emotional embrace, whipped off her scarf, replaced it and then landed in the arms of the footballer of the year. Wow! No goals scored tonight. The look of jealousy from her "opponent" would mean a prison term for someone. The crowd resettled. After ten minutes with her prize, she realised it wasn't worth the effort. She sought out the real owner, walked past her, flung it across her knees in an act of modesty as the footballer of the year was almost on the playing field again. The scarf covered the centre bounce area. Even though girls can be protagonists, they can also be great modesty friends. Davidia didn't want her scarf back either. No one was any the wiser that the deception of scarf swapping had occurred.

Davidia rummaged for the necessary tissue box. It took only a second or two; however, it wasn't only the tissues she was seeking. A girl must always have an appropriate range of essentials when wanting to look older than their years without the parents knowing, especially at an after-school talking session to attract an expectant boyfriend. She had a lipstick, similar in colour to Slirander, who she let slip into her backpack and replaced her with the "imposter". Davidia withdrew both the tissues and lipstick. A quick wipe did "job one" and she handed back the lipstick to Miss Alpine, who gratefully received its return. There was no indication that she was aware that she had been given a replacement. Davidia now had Slirander safely in her keeping.

'Ouch. I'll be having a few words with Davidia when I next speak to her,' said Slirander, being tossed around like wind-blown seeds rolling around the bottom of the backpack.

She still had no clear vision or communication with Davidia. Slirander wondered why Davidia didn't stick her finger in her ear and relieve her of the tension of not knowing. She was feeling a surge of anger and perhaps helplessness. All she could really do was to be applied as a dress-up item. That's not very worthy of the talents of this young girl; however, the situation called for patience.

'Davidia, you have trespassed your presence into my school. Accommodation for your stay is available. You will be a special guest of Senora College. I will contact Principal Jones and advise that you will be one of the exchange students from Year 10 for the new era of education. I hope he will provide another Year 10 student as part of the program.'

'Can't I go home? I only got lost. My parents might worry. I don't have a complete change of clothing. I can't wear the same clothes over and over again. What about my extensive cosmetic range, fluffy pillows, slippers, night dresses, the special lingerie I take selfies in and my soaps? They'll all miss me.'

'Everything to make you comfortable has been done. This is an educational institution, not a seedy parlour. It awaits you.'

Miss Alpine raised an arm. She wore a short-sleeved dress. Her armpit was clean-shaven without any offending hairy growth, which normally hung down like thin spaghetti vines. Davidia was transfixed. She normally didn't stare, but had noticed a rounded tattoo with a dark centre covering the whole area. It would be impossible to tell whether it was a clean skin or a patch. She averted her eyes to elsewhere in the room. Miss Alpine lowered her arm. A door opened and two escorts, both the proportion of medium sized dogs, which they were, appeared on either side of her. Davidia picked up her backpack and wondered what next? She glanced at her escorts. Maybe they were trained circus dogs?

'My name is Randy,' said one.

'My name is randy with a small "r" not a capital letter "R",' said the other. 'Together, when we bark, we make the sound RRRrrr like any normal pooch. So, effectively, we have been named after a sound. You'll like learning here during your internship. There are so many things to discover. We are to be your buddies. If you need anything, just call RRRrrr and we'll be there. Please follow us.'

'Davidia, please follow the two Rr's. Until tomorrow then, when the induction into Senora College occurs.'

It was still only today that she had arrived. The twenty-four hours of Slirander's lipstick incarceration would soon be over. Maybe time in this place was different to her normal time? Davidia was fascinated. She didn't feel any fear factor as she moved. She wasn't sure if she was walking, but it appeared to be so. Her two new companions walked upright on their two hind legs. One had an air of a professor and the other an astute educationalist. It was a female intuition thing. It was too early for any explanations about a what, where or why? The day had already been confusing enough. Maybe a rest and discussion with Slirander would make sense of it all. This wasn't a normal school day.

'Where are we going?' asked Davidia. 'I like to know things in advance.'

'To your accommodation,' said randy. The small "r" randy was the chatty dog.

'Will there be any others besides me?'

'All educating students will be there? Your special room will be enjoyable. Almost there.'

Davidia didn't see any other students anywhere. They walked through walls as if they were a mist. Senora College disappeared behind her, yet they were still indoors. A tunnel corridor opened in front of her. There were a long series of doors as far as the eye could see. There was no sound. It was mute land. Even the escorts said nothing. Signals were used instead, with paw pointing, head twists and leg movements. Davidia tried to speak, but there was no sound. Had someone stolen her voice-box? A young girl losing the ability to speak was not as big a disaster as confiscation of her *iPhone*; however, it could be a traumatic experience just the same. Davidia was made of sterner stuff. Little randy pointed to a wall space and beckoned Davidia's entrance. Her konnocker was the key used to enter anywhere within the town of Hilbridgeburg, yet there were some secret places that it couldn't allow access.

Was there a hidden secret?

Davidia stood in her room alone.

*

'The exchange students are prepped and ready to go?' said Mr. Avalanche, who was responsible for selection and training of the "infiltrators".

He inspected the fortunate six: a boy and a girl each from Years 10, 11 and 12, who were to experience education outside of their normal schooling in what was perceived to be a hostile environment. That was the initial strategy to enable different learning techniques to be adopted and imported into Senora College; however, over the years it had become more difficult to absorb those teaching techniques. The college had, instead, developed their own encapsulated learning program and sent their students out to compete with other colleges and schools to prove the success of their educational system. No one knew the existence of the world of Senora College because all exchange students, once having returned to their normal environment related it to a dream. No adults were ever invited or allowed entrance to Hilbridgeburg. The population was home-grown. Unfortunately, side-effects, not drugs related, have a way of uprising from within normality. There was no way known when this untaught and unknown behaviour would occur and the ramifications that would erupt.

Mr. Avalanche thought that he had the best and most intelligent six to learn other ways. He had no idea a rogue element was within them all. Could it be a disaster and what damage would it wreak at Davidia and Slirander's school? Before departure, each student underwent the process of temporary konnocker removal in case too many questions were asked about a knee bulge that looked like a tree burr. Communication to their home would still be through the konnocker remnants, which would remain intact. It was their antennae and receiver. The student would place their palm on their knee and listen. Thoughts were transmitted both ways to maintain any secrecy from being overheard. All was in readiness. Where was the tram that would transport them to their new school? Mr. Avalanche suddenly raised his arm and placed his other hand, as if he was preparing an armpit fart, under his armpit and seemed to tug at something. It was the signal to the tram to materialise, pick up the passengers and send them on their way. He had a tattoo identical to that of Miss Alpine in the same spot. They were the tram spotters, which was very privileged positions to hold. It was the only possible way to exit Hilbridgeburg. Davidia had seen it, but didn't know what it meant.

*

A single, young, youthful girl, full of vitality, much like a vitamin pill, stood alone in a large room with four plain walls. It was prison cell square. That there was enough room for at least one full-size tennis court, for singles or doubles, was irrelevant. She did a three-sixty and found the view the same no matter where she looked. Her bewildered eyes registered sameness. She thought that there had to be more here than the dull colour scheme. Was she under surveillance? Were there hidden cameras undetectable to her eyesight? Was she really a prisoner or a trainee student? Whilst she was contemplating her situation, she remembered Slirander who would be at the base of the backpack under all sorts of weights. Davidia dug her out.

'*There you are,*' she said in mime, because she hadn't yet placed her finger in her ear.

She could see Slirander's two little arms waving furiously at the side of the lipstick. It was difficult to understand what that fluttering was all about. It wasn't peaceful. Davidia reluctantly placed her finger in her ear. A little static but hearing was clear.

'At last! Have you ignored me? What is going on in this place?' said Slirander.

'I am apparently enrolled as a trainee exchange student to be taught a new educational way of learning. It's weird: mist doors, disappearing floors, floating, strange konnocker knee bulges, dog escorts, no other students, and two quite strange leaders. Look at this room. It's my accommodation of four plain walls. There must be an electronic basis to operate what we can't see.'

Davidia held up Slirander so that she could see and enable her assessment of the situation.

'It's odd, isn't it? Walk over toward that far corner.'

Davidia slowly walked forward, it was preferable to going backwards and, before she knew it, a bed had appeared out of the wall. The fluffy doona wasn't the same as hers at home.

She turned toward the next corner and a desk, complete with computer screens, laptop, desktop and an electrical equipment console, materialised. She could have been flying an aircraft, there was so much of it. She continued the walk of square and, as she did so, a kitchen, bathroom, small lounge room area and toilet all came into existence. Once she was a certain distance from each area, it recoiled into the wall, so only one item at a time, depending on the function, was in the room. The kitchen was fully stocked with a variety of foods, most of which were familiar. On the refrigerator door, there was a computerised menu for 24-7 service. She only had to touch to order. There was no room service charge. It was fabulous to have all these items, but it felt lonely. She had never been inside a mausoleum but imagined it felt something like this. An unwelcome chill ran up her body from floor to ceiling. Her petite frame shook for a moment.

'It's not actually paradise, is it?' Davidia checked with Slirander.

'It's more like an underground cage. Something obviously automatic must operate all of this.'

'My konnocker is the key to its operation. If you were here as I am, you would have one too. After today, you won't have a choice.'

Davidia kept scanning the room with Slirander held aloft in front of her leading the way as a torchlight. She walked around about four times and everything operated in the same manner.

'There's no doubt about it. It is all computer controlled. Nothing left to be imaginative about, but it is impressive.'

Davidia must have looked odd walking around with a finger in one ear speaking out aloud. It triggered management curiosity. A voice from the ceiling split the silence. It boomed in an unfriendly manner.

'It is not allowed to talk inside the Crates. Cease that incessant activity immediately. Why are you speaking?'

Davidia suddenly realised that she was under surveillance. It was expected with such a lavish set-up; however, was it by sight and full-time? Where was her privacy? Had it been hidden in a cupboard? Had she agreed to a vow of silence though she wasn't a monk?

'I speak to myself when I'm nervous or in a new place.' She paused for a moment for a response. 'Am I under surveillance?'

'Yes, but only by sound and not by sight. You can relax here. Your treatment, I mean education, commences tomorrow. You will be advised of your timetable by ring sounds. There is a chart on your desk which you must learn to recognise. Twenty-four hours of each of your days are controlled and monitored. Enjoy your stay.' The computer voice faded.

It was deathly silent. There was no conceivable sound heard anywhere. She thought that her room must also be sound-proofed. Davidia unplugged her ear. Now, she could speak to no one. Even Slirander had free sound time. Both girls had time to contemplate their predicament. Guinea pigs are pets that people look after, feed, love and clean their cage; however, a human one usually has a different usage and outcome.

What would the girls be fed?

Slirander would materialise overnight.

How would that be explained?

5 EXCHANGE

rincipal Jones received a second letter from Senora College with explicit conditions to apply to their exchange students. If it was to take place, then an approved signature needed to be applied and returned to the address on the letterhead. So far, it had only been Principal Jones and the staff who had discussed the offer in any detail. The idea of being top college in the State was certainly an attractive biscuit to bite; however, the real decision had to be approved by the school council. Often it was a committee sitting around a table comprised of some parents with self-interest at the forefront; well, in this case it was. It was akin to a group of vultures tearing at a hapless carcass called education. They could be so self-opinionated that it was difficult to focus on the reason they were there; for the kids and education, or for self.

Prestige was often sought within the position. Who would the local mayor invite for a high tea reception? Who would open a building in their honour? Who would sit front and centre at the local sports day? Seat reshuffles around the table were as regular as the amenities used as factions sided together. Principal Jones had convened a special meeting and had sent each school councillor a copy of the letter and agenda. He had hoped they would have been prepared to make a decision after a short discussion at council. The meeting was held at the local municipal offices in the Whitten Room. It was used for special occasions. The large boardroom table sat twelve, similar to the Last Supper group in Leonardo da Vinci's famous painting in Milan. The high-backed chairs prevented both their anatomy and excess brains to fall over backwards. Apparently if that occurred, only the backs would be damaged. Spring water without the spring sat motionless in pewter urns with a hint of condensation sliding down their sides. A prepared glass was already waiting to be sipped, if water was the beverage of choice. A cuppa and a coffee were available afterwards with some delicious club sandwiches for supper. Leftovers weren't taken home. The council budget didn't extend to excess because that was the incorrect style for the councillors. All seated. The meeting began.

'I hope you have all read the agenda and letter forwarded to each of you,' began Principal Jones. 'The letter has requested that our school be used as part of an exchange program with Senora College. They wish to exchange six of our students, two from each of Years 10, 11 and 12 to learn new ways of being educated with six of theirs from the same years. We would need to accommodate each of them in the home of the student who is exchanged. They haven't stated the length of time of the exchange, but I assume it's for one term only.'

'Isn't it too close to year-end exams to be entertaining this idea?' said a parent.

Heads nodded. Everyone was still awake.

'I agree it is rather poor timing, but the offer is a once-only deal. Do we take these opportunities as they arise or stagnate as an educational institution? We should learn from others, as they from us. It should be minimal interruption as most students sitting the exams should already be up-to-date with their studies, if they have planned correctly. Remember, we are a top educational institution and proud of our name.'

Principal Jones was rooting for a "yes" vote. He had forgotten the old adage, pride before a fall. He didn't know how high up the ladder he could climb before the scream of gravity ran him back to the ground.

'It has the hallmarks of a sensible decision; however, how will the six students exchanged pass their exams? They won't be here and, besides, who is to select them?' said another parent.

'We can credit their results by their participation. When they return with their individual reports, we can assess that information. It is a most unusual request; however, sometimes special solutions require special decisions. Another school may not make this style of call on education. Being a leader is not to ignore progress. On the matter of selection of who might best represent us, it should, I believe, be left to the teaching staff with an intimate knowledge of which students to select and we should trust their judgement. In new times, new ideas need to be embraced.'

Once again, the group nodded in agreement. The anticipated argumentative approach and the lengthy disagreement schedule with the, "I am first" principle, were all put aside to the amazement of Principal Jones. The school council finally agreed in a positive manner without any dissent on all points suggested. It was recorded in the minutes for posterity. Apparently, Principal Jones was to later frame it as a memoir item as a first for his school. The supper preparation was almost caught short with an early finish. The letter of acceptance was signed.

Had a deal with the Devil, or an equally nasty mythical character, been done?

What did this action really mean?

Would education suffer or excel?

Davidia and Slirander weren't considered in the process to date as they were already there.

No one knew that they were missing.

*

Senora College had received the letter of acceptance of the exchange program. Miss Alpine was rather pleased. She contacted Mr. Avalanche immediately.

'Vlad College have agreed to our terms. Our education can now move forward. That new student, Davidia, needs to have a close eye kept on her. She checks out for suitability, but is very proactive in thought. She might be too unusual for our standards.'

'The special treatment room is always available at a moment's notice for rectification. It has been a long time since we've thought of mentioning it, when the student involved hasn't even commenced with her education.'

Both the A's felt danger associated with Davidia. Who'd have thought, eh!

'Are the students ready for departure?'

'They are keen to perform.'

'Send the tram.'

'I need to check on the students one last time to ensure that they have all they need.'

Mr. Avalanche arrived at the departure point and admired his half dozen representatives. Each wore a stiff, starched, ironed uniform. He checked each of their konnockers in case any of them hadn't been expertly removed. Each knee was as normal as a knee could be. The only possible give-away that they were different would be that the knee would enlarge slightly when anger provoked. The excuse to satisfy any curiosity was that it was fluid from a sporting injury. That did it. They also possessed a real oddity, rarely used. It was a lengthening finger. If they were about to lie, state a mistruth or misrepresent reality, the middle finger on the right hand would enlarge, somewhat like the nose in the story of Pinocchio. It was known simply as the "sossurge" (soss-urge). It replicated giving someone the bird in modern day rudeness. It subsided with a retraction of the lie. The students were taught to meddle with the truth, but not sufficiently to sossurge someone, especially staff. No one would understand this odd affliction anyway. There was no need to test this skill as he was quite confident that he knew their capabilities. He should have looked into their eyes; something wasn't quite round. Maybe the education for the new class of knowledge had been overcooked. A visit would soon tell.

'All aboard,' he said, as he performed the armpit fart.

They were on their way.

*

Davidia needed a night's rest. The day had been long and full of differences. Her room was still a huge square. There wasn't a softening toy, ornament or huggable item available. Her stomach rumbled. She didn't have an uninvited intruder, did she? Anything seemed possible in her strange surrounds. It was dinner time. She approached the refrigerator. A menu appeared. A button said "press me". She did. A menu materialised. Please select. She did. A few minutes later a wall opened and on a trolley tray was her meal. She sniffed, prodded, cut and finger-licked the offering and was finally satisfied that it wasn't poisoned. It was real food. Each mouthful was given the maximum jaw presses before swallowing. It was a visual meal only. Taste was absent, though filling. It suited her surrounds. Once the meal had been dispensed with, she located the shower. The water was clean but grey in colour. The shampoo lathered into a sudsy mess. It was also grey. The colour scheme had a similarity about it. The word happy couldn't describe it adequately. The bed was the next leg in the night-time process. When it emerged, the non-fluffy doona was patterned with words crossing all over it. Grey was still the predominant colour. She slipped in between the sheets as easily as Cinderella's foot did into the glass slipper. How did she change into her night attire? The bed was warm. A special underfloor heater kept the room at an ambient temperature. There was no further advice. She placed Slirander on the bedside table and whispered goodnight. Slirander couldn't react. She fumed at her loneliness and being a visitor in a small space.

During the night, strange movements flittered around her room. It appeared that there were fingers of intrusion searching the room that everything was in order. They looked like a series of eyes on the end of fibre sticks. Slirander felt the airwaves undulate. Were they now under visual as well as sound surveillance? She kept vigil all night. Who to trust was an issue? In the early hours of the morning another strange event occurred. The lipstick case began to enlarge and the metamorphosis of a lipstick into a human occurred. Had a new scientific discovery been created in Senora College without any approved experimentation? How would Miss Alpine react when another uninvited student turns up and in Davidia's room? The dented gold case was left behind as evidence of Slirander's last incarceration. She stood tall, once again stretching all her extremities as herself. Another intelligent Year 10 had emerged as an uninvited exchange student. It was almost a plague. Senora College now had a fistful of attitudes to deal with; two Year 10 exchange student representatives from Vlad College. Slirander couldn't be sent back. She had to be incorporated into the educational program, like it or not. It was noted that Davidia didn't snore. Her breathing undulations reminded one of a gentle, restless sea with two consistent waves heaving in rhythm.

A gong sounded at 8.00am. Davidia bounced out of bed in pogo stick fashion, eyes alert; on a high and alone. She hadn't seen Slirander yet.

'Is it breakfast for two?' said Slirander.

The surprise startled Davidia. Her friend was back. She turned around and hugged her closely in affirmation of their friendship. Team D and S were together again, watch out.

'How do you do that?' said Davidia.

She had never really fully understood Slirander's extraordinary ability to change into anything. Acceptance of it was the easier option. Before any further activity ensued, a voice tinged with frustration split the air.

'Intruder, intruder,' it whined. 'Keep still. Don't move. The intruder is to be eradicated. Davidia, stay safe.'

A gap in the wall expelled two large-sized robotic machines. Was that a head of someone peeping over the dashboard? They circled Slirander and sprayed her with a disabling agent.

'Stop that!' yelled a furious Davidia. 'She's my friend and no one spits at her.'

She bravely went over to one machine and swiped the peeping head with such force that it fell off. The other machine stopped dead in its tracks. Nothing had ever tampered or resisted their mechanisation before. It was a stunning performance. Senora College had certainly imported attitude. The second machine sent a plea for help. It didn't want to be beheaded. The technology in the repair shop would be too awful to confront. It had never been repaired before. Slirander didn't succumb to the spray. Maybe it was thought that she was a dangerous weed. The room was a stand-off. Only the girls weren't damaged.

Another gap in a wall opened and in walked Miss Alpine. Her face was a vivid yellow like a very happy sunflower plant, but she wasn't happy. She was spitting something, but it wasn't knives. Had her saliva glands been in a greater rush than her words? She had a face that probably matched the rear of her anatomy. It was an assumption because no one had seen it. Fury was certainly another regurgitated emotion that she hadn't experienced for a while. What is it with this Davidia, the wrecking student? She stared out of her doughnut rings.

'Who is this student?' she demanded. 'What is she doing here?'

Davidia didn't know that she was to be an exchange student forced on Senora College by her unexpected visit. First there was one, now two. Are there any more?

'This is my friend, Slirander. She's a student in Year 10 like me. It looks like she got on the wrong tram too. What an unbelievable coincidence.'

Miss Alpine wasn't amused.

Davidia was becoming used to confrontation. She was a developing sixteen-year-old forging her way in the real world. Backward steps were only found at the rear of her house in her world. Sitting indoors dabbing on a computer keyboard wasn't for her. It was an element in the learning process, but she had gained confidence and knowledge by fronting her demons. Once at school, an older girl had threatened and bullied her online with the most unflattering comments about her body shape, lack of boyfriends and her looks. She didn't take to it too kindly, especially when she sent the message in text accompanied by atrocious spelling. She located the perpetrator at school the next day and in the schoolyard, in front of an agitating crowd, they met. Was it fists at one metre, kicks at two or verbal insults at three? Davidia was a girl with smarts. She chose the third option. The pain of words lasts far longer than an instant pain, no matter where inflicted. The unpleasantness began. After two minutes, it was obvious the older girl was faltering – you can fill in your own nasty dialogue of what might have been said. A series of witty, scything remarks sliced her veneer of boldness and soon she retreated with a handkerchief covering her face. Later that day, Davidia confronted her again, not for the purpose of revenge or further hurt, but to pass an olive branch of friendship, so it never occurred again. Maybe Miss Alpine needed that olive branch full of juicy olives right now?

Miss Alpine studied Slirander closely. She thought girlfriend, student, same college, relevant study year, present without searching for another exchange student and how did she really get here? Davidia had told the truth. She did catch the wrong tram, albeit in a different form. Was she as feisty as Davidia? Her school was being invaded with emotionally-charged young girls. She looked directly at Slirander.

'My name is Miss Alpine. You have trespassed without permission; however, as you are from the same college and year as Davidia, you will be accepted into the college as an exchange student. We expect the arrival of four others from your school very shortly to join our education program. You may know them. In the meantime, Slirander must be coded, konnockered and settled into her own accommodation. All students have their own space. Slirander, please go with the two escorts provided.'

Two small animals the size of a regular watermelon emerged. They didn't have any legs, eyes or any discernible features. They were just a moving shape consisting of a series of bursting bubbles making inoffensive plop, plop sounds. Slirander took a double-take. What were those things? They just floated like a hovercraft.

'Hello, there! Please come with us,' said one of them.

'And if I refuse?' replied Slirander.

She thought that her height gave her the advantage of refusal.

Miss Alpine thought, *Not another one.*

'Please come with us,' said one of them.

It was evident that after the refusal, a few extra bubbles were shed. It was like simmering soup on a hot stove.

'Who are you?'

'A direct question deserves a direct answer. My name is "Bubb" with a capital "B" and my twin is called "les" with a lower-case

"1". Together, we are named Bubbles. We aren't identical. I pass less wind. It's hard to tell the difference. Don't upset us or we can explode. And you are?'

'My name is Slirander. Davidia is my friend. We are schoolgirl visitors.'

'That is precisely our task. We are to escort you to your accommodation.'

'Why can't I stay here with Davidia? We're friends.'

'The protocol is one person per cage.'

'Don't you mean room?'

'The accommodation has a variety of names. Some are named after pets. Please come.'

Slirander was about to act stubbornly when she thought better of it. How could she communicate with Davidia, if it was disallowed electronically? There wasn't much time. She walked over to Davidia and, surprisingly, pretended to kick her. She didn't actually. It was a ruse. Davidia fell backwards in surprise and Slirander caught her. As she did so, she sunk her teeth into her arm, quite painfully. Davidia screamed.

'You bloody bitch! What did I do to you? You're no friend. I've done nothing to deserve being bitten. Are you some form of bloody vampire? Gee, that hurts.'

Slirander whispered in her ear.

'A scab will form in twenty minutes. If you touch it, it will signal me. We can't speak, but it will transmit thought waves between the two of us. You must hold your complete hand over it when we "speak". Release it and there's no contact. We are under constant surveillance. There is an unpleasant smell about this place. It may not be what it seems. Be careful. Scream at me again.'

'You rotten, bloody bitch. Piss off and find another friend.'

Davidia sobbed and wiped a few made-up tears from her face. It seemed real enough.

'Bubbles, let's go.'

Slirander was whisked away by the balloon ball twins to another location nearby.

*

Principal Jones had requested his staff to select the six exchange students to be sent to Senora College; however, before a final decision was made, Slirander's dad turned up at school. He had made an appointment with Principal Jones. He was also a fellow professor. Principal Jones thought the meeting would be a discussion about Slirander's schooling ability, which was very impressive. His office was cluttered with so many family photographs that each struggled for a surface upon which to hang or sit. The cleaners often had nightmares after dusting the collection, there were so many. The leather settee was so old it was a history lesson in itself.

'Good morning, Principal Jones,' said Slirander's dad.

'Good morning, Rotan,' said Principal Jones.

No one knew their family surname. How is that possible if Slirander is enrolled in school? The explanation is yet to be explained.

'How can I be of assistance?'

'My daughter isn't at school today, nor is her friend, Davidia. Do you know of their whereabouts? They should be here.'

Principal Jones' face mimicked a puzzle.

'Really, they haven't run away from home, have they? Young girls are prone to do silly things.'

'Not these two. They are amongst your best students. Can you check, please?'

'I'll ask Miss Green to pop in. She'll know.'

Principal Jones asked Miss Green to his office. She checked

her reflection in a corridor window, wondering if her facial redness was rouge or emotion? She knocked on the door.

'Come in, Miss Green. This is Slirander's dad, Rotan. Has his daughter and her friend, Davidia, been in attendance at school today?'

Miss Green realised that they hadn't. She hoped that she wouldn't be up on a charge of attendance inattention.

'No, sir. Strangely enough, they weren't there like yesterday afternoon either. Has something like happened to them?' she said.

'I understand that you have an exchange program with Senora College and are contemplating sending six students from your college to theirs and vice versa,' said Rotan.

'That's privileged information you shouldn't know. There must be a leak in my systems. I'll sack the perpetrator for lack of loyalty.' Principal Jones was tensing like a high wire across a valley.

'I want my daughter and Davidia to be your Year 10 exchange students as they are already there and, furthermore, please ensure that an exchange student is sent to my home and Davidia's home.'

'That's not possible. We don't know where Senora College exactly is at present.'

'I do. Take your students to the local tram stop as advised by Senora College and they will all safely arrive at their destination.'

'You couldn't possibly know that. Why should I believe you?'

'Because, I'm Slirander's dad. I am fully aware of your exchange student plans and can assist at any time. I'm in contact with my daughter.'

'She isn't allowed a mobile telephone and her school *iPad* remains on the premises. How is it possible to contact her?'

He jokingly expressed the opinion that she didn't have extra sensory perception (ESP). Slirander's dad sighed.

'Please include them in the exchange program. It's not important to know how I communicate, just to know I can.'

Principal Jones was perplexed. It was impossible to know the information Slirander's dad had displayed. He always thought that Slirander was a strange girl and her dad's performance strengthened that opinion. Or was it a leak that bothered him? He decided to agree with that suggestion and arranged for the two Years 11 and 12 students to be sent.

*

The six exchange students arrived at Vlad College for distribution and billeting out to the various exchange families. Each student was well dressed, well groomed and well mannered. Already they had outdone the Vlad College students. They each carried a small suitcase full of the necessary items for a short home stay. No one could access these cases unless they were the individual owners and it was only by using their konnocker to knee, that its outer casing could be opened. It was a special security coded system. Odd perhaps, but it worked for them. Personal effects were the property of the owner and why should anyone snoop amongst them. They didn't hide a secret, did they?

Principal Jones and staff greeted the new breed of students in the staff room and were suitably impressed by their appearance at least. The parents of the exchange students were in attendance to meet their substitute children. The thin, bony, one-fingered handshake given startled the parents. It felt like a stick had been placed in their hands. Once the formalities were dispensed with and the parents and students had been matched, it was the end of the school day.

'That went smoothly,' said Principal Jones, pleased that there were no embarrassments.

'That was like easy, sir,' said Miss Green, 'you certainly have the like ability to manage like students and parents. You can like manage staff too like, sir.'

Miss Green was giving off some sort of mating signal, but receiving them flew past a set of perfectly good hearing ears.

'I wonder how that student with Slirander's dad will fare. I have a sneaking suspicion we'll be hearing more from him. This whole experiment has me concerned. Am I doing the right thing or has this exchange been cleverly foisted upon me? I'm not sure.'

'There is no need for like doubt, sir,' said a comforting Miss Green. 'See you like tomorrow.'

Principal Jones relaxed. It was after school hours and as nobody was watching, he fumbled for his alcoholic friend and took a nip of a soothing beverage as a stress reliever for the day. It was only one. It was also time to go home.

*

Slirander's dad eyed the exchange student as a replacement for his daughter as they travelled home. He sensed something about her. She was a pleasantly attractive young lady who said absolutely nothing whilst in the car. It was motion muteness. She had been trained never to converse in a moving vehicle. It was a safety issue. Nothing said, no information given and secrets remain thus because they aren't spoken about. The car stopped. Slirander's dad walked around and opened the passenger side door and was greeted with a bright, disarming smile. It was all normal and pleasant. It was almost a perfect day; well almost.

At the front door stood Slirander's mum. She proudly waited for the student to greet her and to welcome her into her new, if temporary, home. The student walked straight past her ignoring any pleasantries with her luggage case firmly grasped by her side.

Both parents looked stunned. They thought, *The rude, arrogant, little bitch*. She had the manners of defiance and not compliance. It was fortunate that not all thoughts are spoken. The door shut and they turned to engage with their guest.

'I'm Rolet, your host mum during your stay,' said Slirander's mum.

'I'm Rotan, your host dad during your stay,' said Slirander's dad. 'Welcome to our home. We hope that you enjoy your stay with us. What is your name?'

'My label is Casesix. I am a student with a high IQ and pleased to be meeting you. Where is my space and free food?'

'Oh! You mean your room and dinner. Follow me, it's upstairs.'

'Up what? I don't up anything. I need flat space. Feet flat, floor flat, I walk flat so flat space is needed.'

Fortunately, there was a spare bedroom on the ground floor, which was usually for guests; however, the thought of providing a nicer upstairs bedroom seemed an inadequate choice for Casesix. Rolet showed her the bedroom. A cursory glance was met with a frown. She walked around the walls and was surprised to find that they didn't move at all. There was nothing happening.

'I hope you like it,' said Rolet. 'I chose the colours myself.'

'Where is the grey? This is too bright.'

'You'll get used to it. Dinner will be in fifteen minutes. You must be famished, travelling all that way. How far did you travel today?'

It was a simple question. The reaction wasn't.

'I cannot say. I don't carry an odometer and the tram isn't equipped with a kilometre recorder. Speaking isn't allowed when travelling, nor is paying any attention to the surrounds. We sit in a semi state of disinterest until we are advised to alight the tram. Now, I'm here.'

Casesix was reacting to a program-learning technique called

Responses, which so far was supplying answers that could possibly offend. Emotional balance and niceties were obviously missing ingredients. Perhaps the program could be tweaked somewhat.

'You must be tired. Freshen up and dinner will be served shortly,' said Rolet, wondering what the rude-mannered girl was really like and were they in for a tough ride?

Raising Slirander was difficult enough without having to case-manage someone else's firebrand.

'I will attend when ready,' replied Casesix, as she slammed the door shut.

The door lock tumbled tight. In her world, she was locked in her space every night. This was no different.

'I suppose it will take time to get used to her,' said Rolet.

'I wonder what Slirander is up to in a strange place,' said Rotan. 'I'm in contact with her via my tooth transmitter, so we know that she and Davidia are safe.'

With the exchange students safely housed, the night could close without further misunderstandings, or could it? Suddenly, Casesix opened the door dressed in her night attire of grey.

'Where's my food?' she demanded.

She sat at the kitchen table with arms crossed and a face full of selfishness; ugly puss, sour puss or even unpleasant puss etched across her features. The pouting lips suggested a "not happy" disposition. It was the "Why am I here" look. Ugh! This could be a fun stay for the family.

'In our house we don't demand, we ask politely,' said Rolet, trying to be nice and caring.

'You are to serve me whilst I'm here. That's how it is at home. Now, where's my food?'

Rotan sat next to her and spoke to her with kind eyes. She stared blankly back.

'We will teach you our ways so that you can cope with your new environment more easily.' He had a way of reaching the hearts of young people. Casesix sighed.

The evening meal was quickly consumed and Casesix returned to her room to study whatever her program was for the next day at school.

That evening a set of parents pondered over their "new child".

Apparently, all sets of parents with the exchange students, had "day one" difficulties. Maybe, the two school cultures were too different. Time would reveal that truth.

Rotan pressed a molar and it tingled. Slirander received the message.

6 NEW SCHOOLS

'We can't have any weaknesses here,' said Miss Alpine, once Slirander had been removed from the room after that nasty between-girl interaction. 'Does your wound need dressing?'

'It's only a nip, really. That friend of mine can be quite cannibalistic at times. Look, it's almost healed already.'

Sure enough, a healthy scab had appeared for a cameo performance. It would remain whilst she stayed in Hilbridgeburg. Slirander had her tingly molar to pass thoughts with. She used her tongue, sight unseen, by putting upward pressure on the molar to trigger its response. Then her mind would thought-activate through the tooth. It only worked obviously if the receiving parties – her dad and his molar and Davidia and her arm scab – had made the relevant contact on their bodies. At least information flow couldn't be impeded. No one was going to amputate Davidia's arm, or give Slirander a set of falsies to chew with. This was an educational institution, not a torture chamber.

'It's almost time for your induction into the school system. When the next gong sounds, Randy and randy will escort you to another section of the school where you will be officially greeted.'

Miss Alpine didn't say by whom. It was assumed to be by fellow student introductions. Davidia was quite excited to make new friends. Miss Alpine left. Davidia sensed she should try her arm scab communicator. She placed her full hand over it and waited. It soon tingled. Her thoughts were being interfered with because Slirander was trying to fill her head space with her thoughts whilst Davidia's lot were trying to escape at the same time. It took thirty seconds before a logical sequence kicked in.

'This place is unusual,' said Slirander. 'My space is exactly like yours. They seem to be cloned. I'm up for a konnocker shortly, then to the induction. See you there.'

Their communication ceased.

'Rather typical to get all the words in. She didn't even let me say one lousy thought,' moaned Davidia.

She wondered if her friend was nearby. A gong sounded.

'RRRrrr,' said the Randy and randy escorts. 'It's time to be infused into college life. Please come with us.'

There was no protest.

'What type of induction is it? Do I get bathed? Do I have holy water poured over me and receive a diploma of introduction? Am I trussed up in leg manacles and chains? I've never been inducted before, not even when I was born. Can't you tell me something about it? It won't hurt, will it, please?'

'No. Please walk in silence,' replied randy. He pointed a paw toward the exit. 'Please walk.'

Davidia paced toward what seemingly was a flat wall; however, when she neared it, it magically opened and resealed once she had passed through. It acted somewhat like beach sand does when you remove a handful, the sides cave in and swallow the space that you had previously created. The corridor was identical no matter which way she walked; or was she floating? It was difficult to tell. There were no signature points to create any bearings from. A grey mist with no end could best describe it.

The two escorts kept closely by her side in case she "strayed" from her path and discovered something she wasn't meant to. Davidia absorbed what she could from her surrounds, which wasn't much. Suddenly, a huge light space opened up in front of her. In comparison to what she had experienced to date, it felt like the sun was invited into her room as a special guest. This time the room was also square, but at least it was lit with a good-feel light. Her escorts didn't intrude into the light space. They just pawed her to move forward. She was alone, surrounded by her thoughts and that incessant bright light. A few moments passed. It was deathly quiet.

As a child she had often played in the local cemetery and she remembered it gave her the same creepy feeling. It never improved after any visit. She wondered about the school induction process and what form it would take. She didn't have to wait long. The sides of the room began to shrink until she stood in a small cubicle as wide and as tall as a coffin found in that foreboding cemetery she once played in as a child.

To her surprise, another coffin cubicle was placed beside her. It was Slirander. She looked as equally as happy as she did. Slirander turned toward her friend and displayed her new konnocker. It was as equally as impressive as hers, but there was no point in bragging about an unsightly knee bulge. Other anatomical parts might better qualify for complimentary dialogue instead. They both blinked and smiled at each other. That was their last visual joint moment. The bright light disappeared and a green glow followed. Both girls were in the rectification rooms, to be introduced into the school structure. The girls felt that they were being tampered with in a strange manner, but were unaware what it immediately meant. Wispy green, spaghetti-like fingers moved through the air. They couldn't access the cubicles; however, when the greenness was outside the cubicle, if you looked closely enough, long bony fingers seemed to be pointing at them like scolding a recalcitrant child. Had they been sossurged? This could mean that they were being warned about bad behaviour and not displaying it in the school. The process lasted a few minutes. Behind the walls a conversation took place.

'Are these girls suitable to be adopted into our plans?' said Miss Alpine, who was on top of every aspect in the whole school process.

'They both possess an obstinate streak far greater than we expected.'

'Is it a challenge that we can overcome? You know what failure means.'

Both teachers watched carefully for any non-compliant behaviour. Fortunately for the girls, they waited patiently as obedient lambs ready for their next milk bottle. The green tinges circulating around the room were a "truth" light that permeated the girls' mental state and the surprises in there were as scary an encounter as ever made. It was felt; however, that they were worth the challenge. That old saying about "biting off more than you can chew" applied to the girls, with the qualifier of how much had to be spat out, because the task was far greater than the solution. Miss Alpine pressed a button, the air cleared and Davidia was once again in the well-lit room alone. Where had Slirander gone? What had happened to her?

'Thank you Davidia, your induction is over. Please return to your room,' said the disguised voice of Miss Alpine. 'I am the manager of Senora College and you have been accepted into our teaching standards.'

Did the voice appear as a threat? Davidia had heard similar sounds listening into her earphones whilst she went jogging. She took as much notice of what was played and the dialogue as she did of this voice, which was very little.

'Where are the other students? I expected to meet them here. I can't make new friends if there's no one to talk to.'

'Precisely. Idle chatter is banned. You are here to learn. That is all.'

'What about my exams in a few weeks' time?'

'Priorities, it's all about priorities and you now have new ones.'

Davidia began to realise that Senora College was one strange place. Her senses told her to be alert, careful and observe. That propensity to open her mouth and blither out any witty or offensive dialogue before thinking would need to be reined in. Her words would have to be chosen as carefully as the extensive shopping time for the latest brand named "bargains". Davidia felt that the sound of the voice held a certain feint fear factor. Should she warn Slirander? In full view, she placed her hand over her arm scab in an embrace as if she was comforting pain. No one took any notice. Slirander's tooth tingled. She pressed her tongue against her molar and thought transmission began.

'This induction nonsense is pathetic. There have been no questions and no other students to meet. There is no one here except a voice and that odd green mist. How did your induction go?' said Davidia.

'It was the same. Boredom with a capital B. I wondered what it was all about,' replied Slirander. She also felt a sense of danger. It was time to be on guard. 'I don't know what the purpose was. I didn't learn anything really; however, to me this is not a trusting place.'

'Perhaps it's a form of interrogation. That green mist could have been a "truth" wind of some sort.' Davidia's imagination joined in. 'I get the impression it is an isolated existence here, even though there are many other students. I haven't seen any others. How could they be the premier academic school if students learn alone? What about family life? It's a mystery of some sort.'

'I think Principal Jones has been misled. There is something not quite right in the world of education, especially with our predicament. It's time to go. I've been asked to return to my space.'

Slirander returned her tongue to its normal resting spot in

her mouth. It was indented with a small hole where she had pressed it against her molar. She could now speak properly, if required, without mumbled diction caused by an incorrect tongue placement.

'Slirander, please return to your space,' said the same voice.

Bubbles appeared as her escort as soon as she exited the square light room. Once again, during her return to her space, it was a silent journey. The only sound was the light popping of wind bubbles.

Communication ceased with Davidia. She removed her arm from the scab and noticed, as she did so, that it glowed a dull red, then disappeared to be a normal scrubby colour. Maybe that's what it does when Slirander and I contact each other? It's a signal.

What does the future hold for the girls if they believed that they were in an education prison and, worse still, how do they extricate themselves?

It will be an interesting puzzle.

'Davidia, please return to your space,' repeated the voice.

'Certainly, and thank you for the induction. I feel like I'm actually a proper Senora College student now,' she said, through fake humility, just to earn acceptance and be perceived as no threat to the school for whatever reason.

Camouflage was important, both physical and mental, to achieve results without being noticed. It was terribly hard to ignore either Davidia or Slirander. They were two young, strong women going somewhere in life and it wasn't home.

The two Rrandys woofed their reappearance as she also exited the square light room. Her return journey to her space was also in silence. She wasn't taking any vows of silence for the ministry of God's work; however, it felt like she was. She was once again pawed to her room and left alone in that dull space to begin her "new" education.

A gong sounded. It was 9.00am.

*

Vlad College had a slightly different induction process. The six new students from Senora College were to be presented to the whole school as a group at morning assembly and be welcomed. This was the prime opportunity for Principal Jones to say something favourable in a once-off public forum to them about their new environment. It was meant to be a feel-good speech for all concerned and it was hoped that the new students would blend in seamlessly.

*

'Casesix, it's almost time to leave for school,' said Rolet, having prepared a hands-on breakfast for her guest student.

Of course, in her previous environment it was all touch buttons without company. Having another person also to invade her breakfast space generated some hostility.

'What is it? I didn't order it. Where's the menu? I select my own food from the list.'

Casesix had never experienced any personal attention as was being displayed towards her. Aggression was her form of emotional-handle to manage any new changes that she was unfamiliar with. For the moment, that was the excuse of justification. There's possibly an undercurrent of another emotional-level program in there somewhere which, like a self-rising cake, is yet to rise.

'It's bacon and eggs. It's our daily breakfast and I decide each morning what to eat,' replied Rolet with an intense look of prying trying to discover the cause of such anger.

'I prefer to order. I suggest that you prepare a proper menu,' replied Casesix, angrily.

'Then I assume you don't want it,' said Rolet, who had thoughts of throwing it straight into the bin.

The look of determination on her face said, "challenge me".

It did smell delicious – fresh bacon rashers teased to cooking perfection where a knife didn't have to be an antagonist but a best friend, as it sliced through the soft, edible product. The edges were tinged with a thin layer of crispiness, which crackled to the mouthful. The aromas that swirled in the kitchen could be directly from the best chef's kitchen in the country.

Casesix was in a new, controlled environment, but without her having control. A learning curve for her had just begun.

'No, I'll eat it.'

'When completed, kindly collect all your school belongings for the journey to school.'

'I expect you to do that. At home I had servants, albeit electronic, to attend to those requirements. Leave me to finish my breakfast.'

Casesix was heading for a brick wall without knowing it. After breakfast, she stood out the front of the house waiting to be picked up. Rolet and Rotan were both going to accompany her to school. She saw Rolet come outside with nothing but the house and car keys.

'Where's my schoolbag, books and tablet?' she asked.

'They're still sitting in your room. They apparently don't move by themselves. We'll wait for you.'

Casesix's face flared into a vivid yellow. At home she was feted. Here, she felt ignored. Rolet saw the sun flash and wondered whether she was well. Casesix stormed inside as a petulant, angry and disagreeable youth does at times, collected all her things and returned shortly, still pulsating in sun yellow.

'Kindly sit in the rear.'

The door was slammed shut. Her mouth was shut tight and her body was as tense as a supporter with their team in front by a point in the Grand Final and the opposition were having a shot at goal after the siren. There was no telling if she sweated or where that moisture went. The trip to school was in silence, which was similar in tone as to when Davidia travelled her new school highways. Rolet and Rotan glanced at each other with both sets of eyebrows raised in an arch. Youth, a perennial part of growing up, is a different experience for all. They arrived at school. The car disgorged its cargo of three. They became a part of the assembly with Casesix being directed to the front of the hall to join her fellow exchange students. They huddled together like a rugby scrum, patting each other but not inappropriately.

'This is a weird place. They have different rules to us. Have any of our konnockers been activated?'

No one had been contacted from their home college.

'What about the sossurge?'

Once again it was a unanimous "no". So far, no one had experienced too traumatic a change, but it was change nevertheless. Principal Jones strode to the front of the assembly and addressed all attendees. He thanked the new students for becoming part of their education process, the billeting parents for their care of the relevant student and the school community in anticipation of adopting the new students as their own. It was a rah-rah moment all around. The exchange students began their new education experience; however, what was it that they were actually after? It hadn't been clearly explained.

'Casesix, we will collect you after school. Be at the meeting point at 3.00pm. Enjoy your day.'

Rolet and Rotan waved goodbye. They wondered whether she would be as much trouble as Slirander.

Time will reveal all.

*

A droning sound filled Davidia's space. It sounded like a woeful, failed, single-track record played purposely to the annoyance of any listener. The language sounded like English but wasn't. Perhaps a few musicians had been out on the tiles the night before and cleverly decided at 4.00am in the morning to team up their instruments in a tangled ensemble of recognisable notes; however, harmonising was left at the starting post in race six and didn't finish. The constant droning ensured the student tried to block it out and when they put on the headphones, a more subtle message was delivered. It was "drone washing" – ignore that lot but accept the more palatable notes with an insidious message, not obvious at the beginning. Davidia was directed by a voice to sit at the desk, read the screen and put on the headphones. Her school day had commenced.

'Good morning, Davidia. Welcome to Senora College. Your first lesson of the day is prepared on the screen in front of you. Your morning task is to memorise the given text. Any break will be signalled to you. Under no circumstances are you able to leave the desk without express permission. Please be seated,' said the voice.

'I'll be there in a moment. I have to visit the bathroom first.'

Before she had taken one step toward her intended visit, a series of clouded figures surrounded her and she felt a shove, or was it a nudge or a push toward the desk. It was as if she was magnetized and drawn forward to the seat. She resisted by flaying her arms and forcing her feet into the floor as resistance. It was useless. She knew when she was beaten and acknowledged acceptance. Her visit was put on hold.

'Thank you for your cooperation. Please commence your lesson.'

As she sat down, once again she felt someone tampering with her legs. Maybe someone wanted to inspect her konnocker? A clamp was attached to both ankles. She was immobilised from leaving the desk. She thought, *This isn't proper schooling.* Slirander had warned her and now, with her imaginative ideas, she had to play smarter than her tutors and learn all she could to understand what it was they wanted. She doubted if it was premier education excellence. She wondered how her replacement was faring. After leaving this strict environment, Vlad College and her parents, in comparison, would be a breath of fresh air. Here, it was all recirculated.

Her small screen filled with the text that she had to memorise. It was a series of sentences, each consisting of fourteen words per line and ten sentences long, with the last word rhyming with another sentence-ending word.

'This is repetitious. What nonsense, learning like a trained parrot. There's nothing of interest in the content either,' she said to herself.

Davidia was furious. She thought that it was a waste of her time learning how to repeat verse like a poet. It lacked humour, depth and any large words. She wondered what sort of "new" education this was purported to be. There had to be a good reason for her to learn the text. She complied and knew it word perfect when the screen lit up with the word "break". The manacles magically disappeared and she dashed headlong to her seated rest area. She placed her palm on her scab and Slirander's tooth tingled. What's a girl to do in the privacy of the small room, except gossip with her girlfriend?

'Slirander, what have they got you learning? I'm reading text. It's useless and boring.'

'I'm doing the same thing. I haven't seen the curriculum yet, but do exactly as they ask. They haven't got us repeating words as time-wasting. They'll have another reason. It could be a compliance test to determine how willing we are to learn and obey the rules.'

'You mean an assessment of some sort. I'm on a short break.'

'Me too.'

'They certainly have us regimented. Maybe we could escape our rooms and find out more about this Senora College?'

'Not on our first day. Earn some trust first.'

'You mean suck up to them.'

Before her emotions grew into angry words, the gong sounded, communication ceased and Davidia returned to her desk on time. She was normally headstrong and had her own definite views on issues. This was perhaps a time to wait, look and learn and not create confrontation. Patience was required. Would Davidia make use of hers? The screen said, "Welcome back", but not where from. It was exercising its digital manners. Davidia gently touched the screen for text reactivation and more boringness to learn. The manacles reattached themselves.

Ten minutes after being seated, the screen flashed at her as if in malfunction mode. Was she being hacked? It was impossible to know. She wasn't allowed to interfere with the screen except turn it on and off. She waited for the correction. None occurred. Dare she touch the screen? Curiosity often leads to temptation, or is it the other way around? Davidia couldn't resist. When something is constantly flashing at you, the feeling is to do something about it and wait for any consequence. It's only a digital screen. Electrocution was a possibility but was highly improbable. She took a deep breath. Her fine fingers darted like a lizard's tongue lightly brushing the screen. Suddenly, the screen faltered. The word *"Help"* flashed across it in italic font like it had been pushed over before it was sent. It disappeared and the screen returned with its boring repetitive content. Davidia wondered what it was about. She was sure that the security measures would be too strict for anyone to bypass, yet there was a plea from somewhere. Once again, she pressed her palm onto her scab and waited.

'Slirander, please reply,' she said.

There was no immediate answer. This made Davidia think that Slirander had been to the dentist and had her molar removed. Panic almost made an unnecessary visit.

'Sorry, Davidia. I was concentrating hard on learning the text and I almost ignored the tingling. What's up?'

'I had the strangest message sent across my screen. The word "*Help*" flashed past. Someone might need our assistance. I mean, manacles, isolation and rote learning don't give me that feeling of freedom. Maybe someone else feels that way too or they are being tortured.'

'As I said earlier, learn and observe. It's all sameness here. Who knows if we can conjure up a meeting with an excuse later on? Gotta go. Spellcheck needs correcting.'

Silence again. Davidia now had another focus to ponder. Learn first, investigate later. Suddenly, the screen text had another meaning. The balance of the day was rather bland but that call for help flashed often in and out of Davidia's mind. It wouldn't leave her alone, much like a persistent admirer who you would never date.

At the end of the first day's lessons, Davidia touch-screened her computer. The security check flashed across her screen and then it switched off. The evening had arrived. At least there was food for thought for a hungry mind within that one word, "*Help*".

*

'How was your first day at your new school?' asked Rotan, when Casesix was picked up after school. 'Did you make any new friends?'

'I don't have any friends, only acquaintances. It's not allowed to be engulfed by someone else's emotions. I'm here to learn, not fraternise.'

The anger lines of undulating frown furrows on an innocent face seemed totally out of place. A lip pout also suggested a not-happy moment.

'Is the teaching here similar to your school?'

'Why all the nosey questions? I'm a student, that's it. Education is education.'

Casesix had never experienced such mental or physical freedom before and coping to understand it was difficult to deal with.

'Will your parents visit you whilst here? We'd love to meet them.'

'No. I expected relief from an inquisition when I arrived here. It's just the same.'

'Have you any homework?'

'No.'

'We ask our daughter the same questions when she comes home. I wonder how she is enjoying being an exchange student. What's your school like?'

Casesix was struggling with the pleasantries. There was no way she would reveal how she had been educated, nor what their daughter would experience.

Time would deliver that verdict.

7 WHAT THE?

olonists often turn up uninvited into the new worlds they are to inhabit in the future. So it was with the Senora College descendants. They were encapsulated into a life of youthful servitude under the banner of education with the catchcry, "Education will set your mind free". It was hoped that this would remain true; however, the original colonists known as the Cluids, who one day appeared out of the clouds and settled in the mysterious country they created, called Cluidinine, (Clu-id-di-neene), believed that control of the mind was essential for their survival. Over the generations, they developed their technical expertise in the hope that one day they could incorporate their country into the other world of Earth through educating their youth in Earth's ways and infiltrate into the population, gradually creating an earth-based Cluidinine. Their country existed in a parallel world; however, the leaders craved acceptance as a separate country and were seeking a host land to re-establish and populate.

This meant expulsion of the current living humans from that land and an influx of their people to establish their own enclave. The students sent on the exchange programs were to be educated in the ways of the locals and bring back that knowledge that would help their population blend in. Not all aspects of an enforced settlement would benefit the locals. The Cluid leaders wanted more students to be trained in their ways and to steal the minds of the local youth. The exchange program challenge about being the premier education institution was a gigantic ruse to grab some the best youthful minds and retrain them. Their population needed enlarging with control and the easiest access was via mental manipulation. It hadn't been proven beyond all doubt that the retrained minds wouldn't fail. That's why a time-line of existence had been inserted into each konnocker. It gave the leaders total control over who lived, who died and at what age, based on their whims or how valuable they were to the new breed of Cluids. Davidia and Slirander had both been konnock-ered; however, their timeline hadn't yet been determined based on the Cluid's technical know-how. They needed to be retrained first and their future usefulness assessed. This would determine their lifespan. Neither knew at this early stage of the exchange program that they were part of an ongoing permanent experi-ment. Imagine their reaction when they would learn that they were deliberately being trained for something that they both didn't agree to, enslavement and perhaps a shorter lifespan than currently expected. The full light is yet to shine on their day.

*

Next morning, Davidia was blessed with a visit from Miss Alpine. It was prior to the time of the first lesson for the day. Her square space felt full with the visit, yet Miss Alpine stood alone like a desert cactus. Davidia rubbed her eyes, not quite believing the sight before her. A yellow-tinged smile and an itching set of thin bony fingers dangling loosely by her side unsure of where they should be placed, framed that body. Davidia wondered if she was partnered – something that sour-looking must surely have an upside. She didn't dare hazard a guess as to what citrus she ate.

'Good morning, Davidia,' said a sweet-lilted voice laced with poison.

'Good morning, Miss Alpine,' replied Davidia, with the nor-mal everyday greeting that was used at home.

'Have you enjoyed your first day's lesson?'

'It was different to what I expected, but it was okay. It takes time to adjust to learning new stuff. Shall I repeat what I learnt?'

'There's no need to. I'm fully aware of the complete text.'

'To what do I owe your early morning invasion of my privacy?'

Miss Alpine winced. Her thoughts erupted into unpleasantness at having been questioned with what she understood to be impertinence. This was her school.

Davidia had never had anyone enter her bedroom without actually inviting them in. She felt it a gross invasion of privacy. At least a doorknock or bell warning would have been appreciated. She didn't appreciate being seen in night attire without any personal preparation for the day. As soon as she alighted from the bed, it disappeared into the wall and Davidia was dressed in full view. None of her personal anatomical belongings, especially the set where the boys might fixate a view, were visually exposed. It just happened due to the technology available. Grey was still the predominant colour. She was now upright, standing opposite her visitor. Davidia attempted a smile, but for it to materialise was like squeezing a lemon waiting for a strong sugar fix. Everyone loves the morning, don't they?

'You had an unwanted communication yesterday. Can you explain that?' said Miss Alpine.

Her colour hadn't changed and her stance was rigid.

'What do you mean? I don't control anything here. It's all automatic.'

Did Davidia think that she had discovered her thought chat with Slirander? Davidia absentmindedly palmed her scab and it let Slirander in on the conversation via her translated thoughts. It was a tense moment and already it was only the second day.

'Who was it from?' Miss Alpine waited.

'What was from whom? I have no idea what you mean. I've

been here all day and spoke to no one. I've been chained to my seat, so I haven't escaped to anywhere. Look, I'm still here.'

Miss Alpine was seething internally with anger at the unco-operative and strong-minded responses she was receiving. *This young lady certainly knows how to stand on her own two legs. She didn't need to prove a point anymore.*

'Who did you contact?'

It was like stretching elastic. Get to the point.

'I repeat. I don't operate the system manually, so how is it possible to contact anyone? You still haven't explained what it is you think I have done.'

The only indication of any communication was that solitary *"Help"* word which she thought was the cause of a faulty computer system.

'If you don't explain the communication truthfully, your study here could be jeopardised.'

'If you told me what it is you believe I am guilty of, it would be appreciated.'

Davidia felt hostility in the ether and, remembering Slirander's comments, tried to tease out her "communication guilt". The chameleon ethos lived well in Davidia. A leopard may not be able to change its spots, a final score in a sporting contest cannot change the result; however, a young girl associated with a chameleon attitude is certainly capable of adapting to what the situation requires when self-preservation is on the line.

Miss Alpine thought for a moment. Her modest body parts were experiencing an emotional tango of confusion in not being able to clarify her perceived predicament of obtaining the truth. *It had never been this difficult before with any other student. Was Davidia's friend this obstinate as well? She thought that troubled education may lie ahead. Mmm!*

'It has been reported that a foreign communication passed

through your computer yesterday. A security warning has been raised. Can you tell me what it was about?'

'How would I know if anything on my screen is foreign when I don't interact with anyone? I assume everything placed in front of me is part of the education process. If anything looks odd, then I accept it. As far as I am aware, nothing unusual happened.'

Davidia wasn't about to confess to an errant *"Help"* word. It had intrigued her too. Maybe someone did need her help or anyone's help and she was the unfortunate or fortunate receiver. Whatever it meant, there was no reveal today.

'Are you sure?'

Miss Alpine pressed. The poison-laced voice sounded threatening.

'There was one thing that was odd. The screen started flashing for a second or two, then it stopped. I thought it was a computer glitch and you guys fixed it.'

'Did the screen reveal a cross word or two?'

'It was over so quickly, there was nothing to read. Have I been hacked, or has your system been hacked? At home, it's a digital challenge everyone faces and once a hacker gets into your computer, in many cases, it's a digital Christmas for them. One hopes that your security system can avoid that tampering. Do you think your system has been hacked?'

'Our system is impregnable,' replied a huffy Miss Alpine.

The thought that their high-grade technology was hackable was almost laughable. If it wasn't from outside, then it must be closer to home.

'It can happen,' said Davidia. 'Is that it? Do I get a system change, or shall I continue with the same computer system?'

'There will be no change. If you receive any further screen quivers, please advise us and record what, if anything, is said.

It must have been international parallel world interference and nothing to do with the Senora College systems. It can happen from time to time in an educational environment.'

'We aren't being influenced by aliens, are we?' questioned an alert Davidia, grabbing the parallel world comment.

'Definitely not,' replied Miss Alpine. 'Please continue your lessons.'

Davidia couldn't help but notice that Miss Alpine had one finger longer than the others. It seemed that it had grown in her presence. It was curious though. She didn't understand why. Her room was silent once again. Her scab tingled. Big ears Slirander needed updating.

'Did you get any of that?' said Davidia. 'It was peculiar the way she questioned me as if I had created a problem.'

'Unfortunately, someone is unhappy here and your computer was picked as the recipient of asking for assistance. It is impossible to know the cause, but it must be plain luck that it was you. Nobody really knows that we are here except for the two teachers and a few security staff.'

'She asked if they were cross words that I had received. They weren't; however, I felt that was a strange comment.'

'Somehow, we have to explore this environment. My vibes are warning me.'

'What about my vibes? What are they telling me?'

'The same. It's lesson time. Good learning.'

Slirander timed out. She didn't want to spend any lengthy time on her thought channels in case they could be detected. One can't be too careful.

Davidia contemplated what would give them time to explore and snoop around their new educational environment. She pondered over the word *"Help"* and now cross words. Was there a connection and to what? She had no idea. A gong sounded. It was time to be seated at her desk. Sigh!

*

The Senora six were in a team huddle, like in a charity hug-a-thon, in the corridor discussing elements of their first day at Vlad College. They too had been mystified with the lessons given. They sat in open desks without being chained. There were other students to interact with. Outside freedom was foreign without being monitored. They lived off-site with other people instead of being alone in a square room. Each had a portable computer with an array of light pulsating games not allowed at school. It was more unbelievable than they thought. Would any of these new experiences hijack them from their trained objective? It was a problem fraught with temptation and often when temptation is available, the statistical chances of succumbing to it increase.

'How's it like going?' asked Miss Green, as she passed the group.

Casesix became the group spokesperson.

'Fine, thank you. Your school is quite different to ours,' replied Casesix.

Miss Green sailed past along the corridor to attend to her class which included Casesix and Casefive. It was almost time for the first lesson of the day. Each new Senora College student was given the names of Caseone to Casesix. Their naming or labelling didn't have any emotional attachment to it, so it was just as easy to number as name them. They had all settled well into their new classrooms, eager to absorb what education they could in their short stay of a few weeks.

'Remember to focus on our task,' affirmed Casesix.

They all placed their hands into the centre on top of each other and gave a short yelp. Their konnockers had been sent a reminder. Six sets of aching knees hobbled to their respective classrooms. Casesix's pain was so intense that she had to stop and place her palm onto her knee, pretending to rest. Connection to home was made.

'Are you all in place?' asked Miss Alpine, controlling their konnockers from her computerised establishment at Senora College.

'Yes, Miss Alpine,' replied Casesix.

'Have you made any progress?'

'We have all blended in as normal teenagers. The host families have made us all welcome. The education here is quite simple and not as difficult as we have learnt.'

'Splendid. Then all is going to plan. You have one more day before the procedure commences, understood?'

'There is a different feel about being here. It's a feeling of freedom,' replied Casesix, stating the obvious.

It was an innocent remark. The type youth often make.

This comment infuriated Miss Alpine. She increased the konnocker intensity and suddenly a pain-stricken female lay struggling on the corridor floor. It was switched on momentarily and then ceased. It was a warning.

'Let that be a lesson to you. I warn you, do not stray from your pre-determined task. Your future is under my control. Enjoy your day.' Communication ceased.

A few schoolgirls came up to Casesix and asked what had happened and whether she was okay?

'I slipped on the floor, that's all,' she said, dismissively.

'Your knee is rather red. Has it swollen?'

'That's where I fell. It will be fine. Thanks for asking.'

Casesix quickly flicked her skirt over the tell-tale bulge, hiding it from prying eyes before it become the butt of too many questions. The pain she felt was excruciating and she wasn't keen for a repeat. Learning with this pain had a bad edge. The balance of the class lessons was to enjoy. Tomorrow, without any pain, would not have that bad edge.

*

The Senora College school council were holding one of their tri-daily meetings in the Boardroom of the Wise. Apparently, that's a reference to the previous great minds that had trudged the hallowed hall. Only current teachers, instructors, managers and technical controllers were allowed entrance to the chinwag of decision-making. The main door was rigged with an electrical filter which acted somewhat like an X-ray. As each individual walked through the acceptance arch, it revealed each of their inner bodies to consist of a main stem (spine), but with no other obvious bones as we know that should exist. All their working parts were a profusion of water-based components. Their inner anatomy seemed to function like a constant electrical storm. It wasn't easily understood how they functioned properly without an all-over solid based structure. Without their outer skin they would all melt and become a puddle surrounding a tall icy-pole stick.

Each member, whilst seated, had to display their konnocker whilst sitting at the glass boardroom table called a Visi-flat-top. There was an individual electrical plug placed in front of each seat to which they were connected. This was a controlled sitting. If there was any dissatisfaction with matters under discussion, the chair Cluid tapped a switch to send an electrical message of rebuke to the straying member. Needless to say, all discussion point agreements were unanimous. Only a true Cluid could preside over these meetings. The school was in a virtual shutdown when these meetings took place.

Whilst this sitting was underway, all Senora College students were allowed to leave their squares for an hour with their personal escorts in tow. They could visit anywhere on campus and the portions of the town that were allowed. The opportunity to meet others was strictly guarded by the escorts. Failure in their duty meant replacement by more serious escorts. The regimentation meant that Davidia and Slirander had to con their escorts with their innocent girlish charms and rapier wit. They were headstrong and loved getting their own way. In Senora College, it was an essential trait if they were to survive unscathed.

*

In the evenings, the teachers also required their sleep and refreshment. They possessed their own specialty building where they could safely sleep at night. They slept in individually specialised and insulated body-shaped sleeping pods in a cool room that registered a constant zero degrees. It was like an overnight cryogenics' convention. It was actually an ice-bath bed where their parts all returned to a frozen water state. During their evening sojourn, they were constantly refreshed with a misty spray. They slept naked and the watered wash toned their bodies, renewing their skin.

An elite body of Cluid guards, called Cluds, looked after them. The power source for their preservation derived from deep underground where their active earth elements were constantly fighting each other, creating mass friction to be used as the power source. It is channelled to the surface by a conduit of stretched clouds (preferably cumulous from its outer layer) captured from the atmosphere and stretched like elastic to form a water-based channel.

Entrance was forbidden into these sleeping quarters. Cluidinine is a country of constant water disagreements.

If the power source was turned off, there was the potential for the teachers to stay in a suspended state, melt and disappear or turn into cross words, a dangerous adversary to good language. Their bodies were in a state of perpetual motion of angry ice particles.

If Davidia and Slirander could touch them whilst asleep, their warm hands could possibly melt them. Cause and effect need to be carefully considered before embarking on a program of destruction. They had to stay clear of any incursion at present until they had established what it was they were up against.

*

The Senora College students were well aware of the current new breed of arrivals. They had seen it all before. To them it was like another pizza delivery, except in human form. The new, brash, intelligent youth who had been gathered to experience education at its highest level, realised too late that the purpose of their education wasn't based on their current school curriculum. Once their lives had reached their education use-by-date, they were transitioned to another part of the country to work *en masse* as a human ant colony developing mind-training techniques. Needless to say, the country at present was still small and was learning various ways to grow its capabilities. Education was the main proposal put forward in its unusual manner. The country of Cluidinine was an evolving learning environment. Still, it was all about control, Cluid control.

*

Davidia and Slirander were about to prepare for the lesson of the day when it was announced that there was a council meeting and the students had an hour in which to roam "free". The girls weren't sure exactly what this meant. Davidia touched her scab and immediately Slirander had tingly toothache.

'Did you hear the news? We have an hour of freedom to explore our outside environment.'

'Yes. It's a surprise to me.'

'Can we meet each other under the changed circumstances? We can at least try.'

'There has to be some rules governing this time. So far, I'm not aware of any.'

'My room is still square,' said Davidia, thinking that there might be a change with the announcement.

'Mine is the same,' replied Slirander, who was thinking along the same lines. 'Walk towards each wall and see what happens.'

Davidia did as suggested. There were no wall protrusions at all. Nothing came at her. No kitchen, desk, table and so on. She passed her hand along each surface only to feel the coldness of a stone surface. It felt like she had been abandoned in a huge prison cell; no windows, no doors and not even the rudimentary round corner structure used for personal matters, existed. She was alone.

Suddenly, the whole shape began to close around her. The rear wall came forward, so she moved away from it. The side walls crept closer, so she moved to the centre of the smaller room. They also became angular and it was now a triangle. Was this part of the mathematics curriculum, the recognition of shape? The room further reduced and seemed to funnel her in one direction only as if she was being involuntarily pushed. She wondered whether grapes felt like this before crushing and producing a good vintage. She tensed for impact. Her eyes were shut. She had no intention of eyeballing the pain inducer, when suddenly she was greeted with two cheerful voices belonging to the Rrandys.

'Where do you want to go?' asked randy. 'We can escort you anywhere we think you want to go.'

A big smile with a fine set of canines, stood firm. The other Randy also displayed a fine set of canines. If sunk into anyone, Davidia realised the potential disaster of the pleasant warning. She still had her arm held tightly by her palm. She let go.

'That's an awful scab,' said Randy, who was the health fanatic of the two. 'That may need to be removed.'

'Don't you touch my arm! It's an arm pet and is healing well,' said a defensive Davidia.

No one was tampering with her lifeline.

'We are to act as your escort wherever you go in the next hour. It's the physical exercise element of the school program. It tires out most students. The fittest part of today's students, as we understand it, are their thumbs exercising on those small hand-held devices. Here, we prefer to walk.'

'So, I can go anywhere I like?'

'So long as it's anywhere we think you can go.'

'Can I see my friend, Slirander?'

'No. Known student liaison isn't possible, unknown is.'

'Are there any special classrooms to see?'

'No. Your square only is all that's available.'

'Can I visit the school hall or canteen or an outside area?'

'Not quite. The outside area isn't forbidden. We can take you there. Remember, you must only walk in silence, otherwise your one hour is confiscated and you will immediately be returned to your square. Obey the rules and any benefit available from compliance may be a reward.'

'Will I see any other students or anyone else there?'

'It's a possibility. We can't guarantee where other escorts take their responsibilities.'

'There doesn't seem to be much access to anything at all. No rooms or people. Do you communicate with the other escorts?'

The Rrandys' faces registered surprise. It had never been required or thought of before. Did they need to? Well, there was one incident when an escort, a single of a pair, attempted a subtle approach to chat to a fellow escort of a similar type. It was a male to female discussion with very simple dialogue at first. It was also a banned activity and those who flirted with the rules always engaged a disaster. The two companions were observed by Miss Alpine via her normal surveillance checks and she had heard uncommon words of affection, something which she wasn't endowed with. The two escorts were removed from duty and to make matters worse, each fellow escort of each pair suffered the same punishment. It was a painful electrical konnocker charge which rendered that leg useless. So it was that each pair had to support the other when walking with one good leg each. Their lives as escorts were over and they were given the benefit of another year to learn of the gravity of their crime before they were permanently konnockered from life. After that, no escort dared to achieve personal communication. The risk was too great. It was as if they were to be a permanent isolated pair with only each other and their charge to socialise with. Social contact was made as welcome as a lice plague.

'It's not allowed. Each other is sufficient enough,' said randy, wondering whether it really was.

Had Davidia sewn a thought of future discontent?

'Take me outside, then,' said Davidia. 'At least I can admire whatever view there is. I might even see someone else. I can't be blamed for that. If I see anyone, do I have to deliberately avoid them? Someone might like to meet me.'

'No contact and silence. They are the rules.'

'Okay then,' said a pouty-lipped Davidia.

She often didn't listen to excuses not worthy of following. She had her own definite opinions.

Suddenly, they were outside. The gloomy view was depressive paradise. The buildings and landscape were smothered in grey or black with no imagination in design in anything except the Senora College dome. The ground was devoid of any grass or soft underneath foot firmness. There was nobody around. It was a dark canvas of life. What in the hell was she going to do for an hour when two minutes had almost done her head in? Davidia was pragmatic and decided to make the most of the cesspit of fun on offer. One never knows in advance what might occur. A live animal might appear. Animation and imagination were on a treadmill of a workout. It was eerie walking and thinking in gloom town. The escorts were used to the procedure and it looked like they were actually enjoying the experience. Davidia wondered where they went when they were not guarding her. Did they have family? Did they live in a kennel? Did they share with friends and so on? She moved towards a small lump in the ground. It imitated a seat. She kicked it for curiosity. It didn't move. There weren't any growing plants or greenery anywhere. She sat down. Panic erupted with two stupid dogs barking and jumping up and down. She hoped that they didn't want to hump her leg in the excitement. Her escorts behaved like two normal pooches, but without chasing a felon.

'You can't sit there. It's private,' said the other Randy. 'Only staff are allowed that privilege.'

'It's only a rock. What's the commotion about? It doesn't do anything magical, does it?' asked Davidia.

She couldn't believe their silly outburst. The escorts might walk on their two hind legs, but the instinct of being a dog was enshrined in their DNA. They had behaved in their natural state for the very first time. It was an exhilarating relief for them. They both stopped as soon as they realised that they were making a spectacle of themselves. Humph!

'Randy, we will have to be more careful next time. I don't know what came over me,' said randy.

'I hope we weren't seen behaving in a common manner. I mean, we are a quality escort,' said the other Randy.

They both looked to see if they had been noticed. It was clear; however, that there were two dark wet-looking patches near the rock which had magically appeared. No one took ownership. It definitely wasn't Davidia.

'You both acted like dogs,' said Davidia. 'Did it feel good?'

'Remember, silence must be obeyed.'

Davidia thought that she saw two glimmers of a smile. Enough said.

8 WHAT NEXT?

In another space in the college, Slirander, with her hour of "freedom", was escorted by the two Bubbles who dribbled water profusely and expressed excess air. She didn't know where she would end up with her escorts. They were in a dark corridor, inside the building and not outside, like Davidia. Where did this long space lead to? Slirander was curious. She had no idea how she got there, only that she was.

'Where does this corridor lead to?' she asked one of the Bubbles.

It didn't matter which one. They both acted identically.

'I can't say. It's a forbidden area. We have never been allowed in there,' replied a Bubble.

Slirander thought for a moment. Instead of walking in the centre of the corridor, she accidentally on purpose, bumped a Bubble aside and now stood alongside the corridor wall. She moved closer with a Bubble frothing madly at the unexpected relocation of its space. Before any reciprocal action occurred, Slirander had placed her hand on the wall and ran it along rather like a kid with a stick on a sheet of corrugated iron, but without the din. Her hand felt gripped in a cold embrace. The wall vibrations were chilling. Her hand couldn't penetrate the wall, but her actions had been noted in the control room.

'What's behind these walls? A gymnasium or perhaps a pool?' she said quietly.

She had to be observant and on guard at all times. She was aware that she had overstepped the mark and was surprised by the tepid result, more of nothing. The wall wasn't divulging any information either.

'That is also off-limits.'

'Is there anywhere that I am allowed to visit?'

'Only outside. There's a square with the most fabulous views.'

'And blue sky?'

'Imagination is our trademark. There should be no one else there. Things are kept private here. It's like a meditation centre for one.'

No alarm bells rang inside their bubble heads. There was so much frenetic frothing it went unnoticed. Davidia was already in the square and joint space sharing wasn't allowed. Both escort sets would be in jeopardy if discovered space sharing. The girls couldn't have cared less. It was an opportune time to accidentally meet, if that happened. Who knows what dastardly words could pass between them during the "free" hour? In a flash, Slirander was in the same dull miserable square that Davidia was in, but at the other end. Fortunately, they couldn't see each other as they were disguised by the darkness of the place.

Slirander did wonder though how Davidia was enjoying her "free" hour. She tweaked her molar. It tingled. Message sent. Davidia's scab began to glow. She quickly covered it with her palm to ensure prying eyes hadn't noticed. They hadn't. They were too busy embellishing the story of the wet patch because that was a first for each of them.

'Where have they let you roam free?' asked Slirander, knowing full well it was an impossible concept.

'I'm in the dark square of misery,' replied Davidia. 'There's absolutely nothing to see or do. My escorts seem to be enjoying it. What about you?'

'I'm also in a gloomy square. It's nothing but bad vibes, dreary colours and the feeling of creepy everywhere. It certainly seems that it doesn't generate real happiness. It makes you wonder what a girl has to do for fun around here.'

'Bugger-all, I reckon. The whole place reeks of dullards and the feeling of sadness. I could be wrong. They might all be perfectly happy living under such oppressive control conditions. Maybe we could liven it up somehow? I sense that you are nearby. I'm looking down the square and there seems to be a few shadows there. Is that you?'

'It could be. Walk toward the centre and see what happens.'

'I'll ask the two Rrandys if that's permissible first. I wouldn't want to be obstinate now, would I?'

'You go, girl. I'll encourage Bubbles as well.'

Davidia turned away from her escorts and ambled toward the middle of the square, kicking at the ground, pretending to trace a stone with her feet. The Rrandys woofed to attention. She was on the move. There didn't seem to be any harm in an innocent walk; that is until there were objects noticed heading toward them. It was too late. A physical confrontation was about to explode. Davidia wasn't going to thump Slirander or vice versa, it would be between the escorts. It was forbidden to use the shared space and someone now had to pay. It was either the yappy dogs or the windy Bubbles that would be damaged. Each pair of escorts left their responsibilities and headed directly for each other. It had nightmarish apparitions as they closed in. The girls watched in amazement. Nothing to date in their time here had prepared them for the scene that they were about to witness. Even the control room was unaware of the outcome. It was also a first for a shared space episode. Tension was on a knife-edge or some other sharp kitchen appliance.

The Rrandys' tongues lolled about their mouths with saliva droplets suffering gravitational pull and ground splat. The Bubbles were passing wind quicker than the rev of an engine and revolving like a tornado. Disaster waited. The colour of the square hadn't changed. Suddenly, they met head-on. The Rrandys dropped onto all fours and performed a peculiar behavioural ritual. It was the sniff. Whoa there, air intake! The Bubbles frothed madly above their heads passing more aromas for inhalation. The Rrandys barked like ordinary pooches. They jumped into the air nudging the Bubbles as air balloons. The awesome foursome played together like a beach puppy quartet. It was truly an amazing act of natural behaviour. By the look on their faces and the extra Bubble wind-passing, it was a pleasure to watch. That dull, darkened, black square had a momentary ray of light and enjoyment. Davidia and Slirander saw it as normal behaviour. Miss Alpine and others were horrified at the gross display of pleasure.

Suddenly, four glass cages surrounded each of the escorts and entrapped them. Their behaviour was suffocated. They were last seen being air-lifted, still performing their natural traits and vanishing into the darkness. Where they were taken was an unknown. In a thrice, Davidia and Slirander were left standing alone in that depressive place. Before they could blink, each found themselves separated and spaced at the opposite end of the square to be alone and spend the rest of their "free" time alone. It didn't bother the girls. The time would soon pass and they would be returned to their individual soulless palaces. There was nowhere to place the rump, so they stood as if attending a classroom with a stand-up desk.

'That was entertaining. What next?' said Davidia.

'A return to our rooms after we are transferred out of here. Time to go, my tooth is aching.'

'My scab really hurts after a while too. Next time we'll keep it short to avoid any aches and pains.'

Davidia removed her palm and the glowing scab quietly subsided. It was deathly silent. Trying to estimate how much time left could have also been a mathematical component of the curriculum.

She didn't know what to expect next.

*

Casesix contemplated her task for tomorrow at school. It wasn't a homework piece to return, or an opportunity to make a real friend or re-file books in the library so that they wouldn't match with the correct filing category; it was the day of the konnocker and to introduce it unwittingly to some of the other students. She was on the reconnaissance team to sample a group of six students, enough to replace her and her fellow Senora College students and, hopefully, school numbers won't have changed or be noticed. She had the emotions of a young, teenage girl, but trained as she was, it was an oblivious thought; however, a few days at Vlad College had permeated her thoughts and she saw real freedom that she was denied at home. She was hungry for more and began to shift her thinking, much to her own peril. A knock on her bedroom door startled her. The sound echoed in the room. It sounded like scurrying rats in the roof, indistinct and scratchy, if she was guessing what they were. The sound repeated. She thought that it must have been either Rolet or Rotan. No one else resided there that she was aware of. She carefully crept toward the door. In her world, strange encounters were normal daily fare, but being well out of her comfort zone, each new experience was more terrifying. There was not the element of control over all things.

'Is anyone there?' she dared to utter.

'No. There's no one here,' a voice replied.

It wasn't dumb day, was it? A reply with sound coming from no one was certainly a brain teaser.

'Are you still there?' she asked.

'No. I'm still the same as I was with the previous question,' was the response.

'If you aren't there and we are talking to each other, how is that possible?'

'If you open the door, we can discuss it privately.'

Casesix knew of a few past events from her family's history, but with knowledge smeared so thin, nothing was easy to believe. Lack of detail always left a gap in her past of who she actually was. The rogue gene, that all Cluids were afraid of, may live in her and perhaps this was it visiting? Uncertainty crept into her mind like a strangler vine.

Once, many years ago, in a glimpse of perceived reality, or reality anyway, she remembered a visit as a young child from two strange-looking people who had very few similarities to her. They weren't from any Christian organisation, as they didn't exist, nor were they from a homeless shelter searching for tenants. She was only six at that stage and alone in one of the labelled educational squares. Hers was called Casesix. The two strangers sat down with her and spoke caringly about her future. The young girl listened. They were from the productive pool where children were fostered, no one explained how or who conceived her and that her future lay in expanding the education network of Cluidinine. She assumed that they were sort of surrogate parents. It took many years before she realised that they were her actual birth parents and the shock of looking so different was hidden from her to avoid any psychological impact. The word "looney" was known but never used in this context. Once born, she had undergone a physical transformation to look like the people she was to mix with in the future, hence Earth. The sossurge finger was an impossible trait to remove. At a young age, she was given to Senora College to be educated under the guidance of

Miss Alpine and Mr. Avalanche, the Cluid controllers. She had been well-educated during that time. Now it was time to transfer that knowledge, well she believed that was the purpose of her exchange trip, to the students at Vlad College, where she had been welcomed. What or whom had come a-knocking at her door? Was she in danger, or was it just her overactive imagination? She took a deep breath, which momentarily enlarged her confidence, and opened the door. The voice was correct. There was no one there.

'Thanks for letting me in,' said the voice.

Casesix couldn't see any visible form of any mass, large or small. No one at school had given her a hazardous substance, had they? She couldn't fathom another explanation. It was a mystery. She waited for an indication of something.

'Welcome to my space,' she replied uncertain of what she was speaking to.

'Tomorrow is an important day in your education and I'm here to cover any last-minute concerns before you go konnockering. Do you have any?'

'I'm familiar with my task,' said Casesix.

'Kindly explain it to me, then.'

'I am to nudge my konnocker against the knee of six students. That's all.'

'That's absolutely correct. Each of the six Senora College students will all repeat that motion to ensure that at least six konnockerings take. Failure is inevitable. That is why we have despatched six students to carry out this important task. The law of average suggests six will take and that is all that we need. Enjoy your contest. It will be interesting.'

'Aren't you going to introduce yourself, so I can see you?'

'You already have.'

The door shut. Silence returned. Casesix had no idea of who

or what she had spoken to. She hadn't noticed a minute spider crawl onto the top of the door and leave the same way. If she had, it didn't trigger any interest. She wasn't in the mood for a violent squashing, or hungry enough to eat "fresh". That may be the explanation. No others sprang to mind. Casesix changed into her night attire and raised one pyjama leg above her knee to admire her konnocker. It was quite beautiful for an imitation tree burr. She knew that it would bring the success she was sent to achieve. That night, her thoughts tossed like flotsam and jetsam, intertwining like spaghetti strands, unable to untangle a clear thought. She practised knee thrusts, groin kicking and special rubs. She thought that one of them would surely work. Finally, she fell sound asleep, only to be awoken by an abusive alarm clock.

'Shit,' she said, not to do, but to quote a new expression she had learnt at her new school.

It really was morning.

*

Davidia was alone in the dark square. Her escorts had been spirited away. Could she now roam free? She was about to test that theory when another impossible thing happened. She heard the heavy panting of another individual heading in her direction. How did anyone know she was even there? Had there been a leak in the Cluid information centre? She stood immobilised. There was nowhere to go anyway. The sound of urgent footsteps in small paces echoed on the stone surface. The darkness hid many a shape.

Whoosh! Suddenly, Davidia was kneed vigorously on her konnockered knee and sent reeling onto the ground in a crumpled heap. She only had time to sight a skirt disappear from view into a mist. It was an unescorted skirmish.

'Bitch,' she said, angrily. She wasn't a skittle in a bowling alley.

Students were never allowed to contact another, so how did this one escape, or had she? Was she a plant to test Davidia's intentions and whether she would be a disruptive influence? It was a tricky time in this new environment. Living quarters were kept secret from each other. Collusion of thought was not allowed. An independent bright idea might be too much to bear for the Cluids. Davidia scrambled to her feet like putting the egg back into its shell. She brushed her clothes of the debris that clung to it for excitement. Her hand felt an intruder in her palm. She hoped it wasn't a cypher to read what she and Slirander had thought shared. Whew! It was a slip of sticky paper which had written on one side the words "Bad language". She wasn't interested in learning filthy words or offensive expressions. Her present vocabulary bank was quite proficient. It had previously been heavily researched whilst at school. Living in a school environment is educational in many different ways.

She slowly unfolded the intriguing piece of paper, knowing fully well she could be under surveillance. There was strangely only one word written on the inside and, as she read, the paper disintegrated. Her hand was left with a sticky, sooty substance. She sniffed it, tasted it and rubbed it gently. It didn't reveal anything further other than becoming an annoyance on the end of her fingers.

'That was exciting,' she said, quietly.

The written word was once again "*Help*". It seemed that it was the word of the moment that wasn't allowed to be said openly. Davidia stood still, wondering what other oddball developments would arise. Her escorts had gone. A strange contact with a forbidden individual had occurred and Slirander was in the same rectangular space, standing alone like she was, albeit at a distance.

How were they to return to their spaces?

*

The morning dew patted the grass with a wetness, providing the day's moisture intake. A brisk few push-ups and leg stretches had Casesix primed for another school day. Rotan had been watching his boarder closely wondering whether her stay would eventually prove to be successful. He often had feelings of understanding of what others experienced. His warning radar had been tweaked with this young lady. There was something about her that registered his wary factor. He couldn't quite put a finger on it and, if he did in an inappropriate manner, his understanding might have been misinterpreted.

Casesix was rather ebullient with her day's expectations. This was her test day. She actually hummed the Senora College anthem, which was a mixture of melodious notes that soothed any nervousness. Its cheerfulness was in stark contrast to the normal drab existence of her daily education. Rotan had noted an improved behaviour pattern, which wasn't as abrasive as had been earlier when discussing her school. A noticeable change was that the length of her skirt had been raised to just below knee height with a hint of konnocker exposure, whereas normally it brushed her ankles with every swish. It provoked curiosity. She hoped it would create interest. Her hair looked as if it had been professionally prepped. A hint of lipstick, not normally worn, had been lightly applied as a bait lure to attract a matching set. The result of such an encounter was an unknown. She now looked like a modern-day schoolgirl with make-up, a short skirt, a modestly hugging shirt regardless of its fashion flare, an overweight schoolbag or backpack, and uniformly drab, standard shoes.

'Good morning, Casesix,' said Rotan, in his normal friendly manner.

Breakfast was the supposed bonding section of the day.

'Good morning, Rotan,' replied Casesix, with one of those normally forbidden smiles.

'You seem in high spirits this morning. Does it have a name?'

The suggestion was obviously referring to a male; however, that is not always the case whereby one can be confident, smile, and be in a good mood, without assuming a male was the cause. What would men know?

'It's school. I am enjoying the experience and today will be a special day for me. I get to express some of my talents in an educational manner.'

The school will wonder what hit them after her visit today.

'Is it a debate or sporting event?'

'Sport. It's a greet-and-meet sport that we have practised at my home college as a means of interacting with other school students. I believe it will be a first for Vlad College. I'm quite looking forward to its impact.'

Another one of those smiles spread across her face like an enlarging gap. The eyes, it's the eyes. They held a depth of fear within them. Rotan had observed the message without alerting her that he had an intimate understanding of observing fear. His background and years of tutoring gave him such insight. Breakfast was enjoyed. The Weet-Bix was eaten instead of played with. The creamy yoghurt slithered around as an uncontrollable snow avalanche. The toast crumbs played hide-and-seek on her ironed blouse. Rotan engaged in light banter. It was fun.

'Ready?'

'Yes.'

They drove to school in silence with each churning over a new supply of fresh thoughts. Every day resupplied them, so thought staleness never crept in. It was a relief that they couldn't be shared. Happiness might sometimes ooze from a marshmallow, but not today from a sixteen-year-old intent on konnockering her fellow students. Her thoughts were on active assignment. Rotan's thoughts were on puzzle-solving. The school gate materialised as a welcome visitor.

'Enjoy your day,' said Rotan, politely.

'I'm sure I will. You too.'

Casesix walked briskly away without an anger thrust as the car door shut. Rotan could see the development of another strong-minded teenager. He immediately thought of Slirander.

*

Davidia stood as a lone sentinel in the open square. She imitated an obelisk. If she was to feel loneliness in that place, it would be about now. Feeling abandoned in the gloom, she clasped her scab as a reassuring friend. It complied with a glow. Slirander was attentive.

'What's happening down your end?' she asked, with furtive glances in case she was spied thinking.

'The two stupid Bubbles haven't returned. Otherwise, it's quiet. Are they at your end?'

'We've lost our escorts, who have been spirited away for bad behaviour by acting naturally. I'm alone at present. I don't know how much of the hour break is left.'

'There won't be much. It's time to go.'

Contact ceased. Davidia was with her own thoughts when, suddenly, she was physically nudged on each side by something. To her shock, it was two schoolgirls about her age and height, but with a completely different complexion. Their grey, pallid skin seemed drained of any soft colouring. Their eyes were deeply recessed as if trying to hide inside their heads. Around them was a ring, not of confidence, but a dull red, hinging on purple. It made them stand out like bull's-eye targets. Davidia hadn't seen a decent zombie movie, but was she about to experience the "real" thing? They were dressed identically. The shoes were an interesting component. The ends were missing; however, there were no expected protruding toes. Had they had their feet shortened in the Japanese fashion of binding, had they been severed or rotted off due to frostbite? For the moment it would remain unknown. Davidia felt no warmth from their closely nudging bodies. She had once fallen into the family freezer when she was playing at home and remembered the coldness, which had almost numbed her fingers and toes. The two companion girls, or escorts, felt exactly the same way, like two cold ice treats. She wondered why they stood so close to her like support columns. There was no chance of her toppling over even without them standing alongside of her. She tried to push one of them to gauge her reaction. For a moment, nothing. Then, without warning, a hand flew upwards, palm opened and slapped her face. There was no emotional reaction with the free gift. Had she been accosted? Her two escorts stood motionless. They weren't robots, were they? It was impossible to move. Davidia was stuck in human quicksand. She wasn't supposed to use dialogue in the silent space, but, after the bracing greeting, decided it was worth it, whatever it would do; or should she slap the slapper, as she was now the slappee?

Words won the moment. Physical violence was not a problem solver, but a problem creator.

'Which one of you did it? Come on, own up. I won't take offence at your rudeness.'

Blank looks emanated. No movement was made.

'I have a good mind to slap you back,' she pretend-threatened.

Still, there was no response. At least her foot had movement. She lightly stood on a foot with her heel. No animation. She then decided to lift both her feet and legs off the ground simultaneously to be a human rod between two human poles. Amazingly, she was upheld and swung slightly like a swing. That action had no impact. Then she thought of her konnocker. What if she used it as a minor battering ram against a set of legs? It was on her left knee, so the nearest to her was to be the sufferer. She turned to face one escort and stared deeply into her eye recesses. For a fraction of a second, she thought she saw a light glimmer ever so faintly. It was a fleeting hope. The groin was too high to thump, so she rammed it into another knee. Other than the jolting stop to her leg, she had kneed an immovable object. She thought it was time to stop trying any type of strategy and just wait until it was time to return to her space. Nothing she tried had worked.

'I give up. We'll wait together until a signal to return is given,' she sighed.

The three girls stood together as a solid rock formation. Suddenly, Davidia felt a tinge of warmth emanate from the girl she had kneed. Nothing was said, but something had been in warm communication. There was no need for a reaction; however, the word *"Help"* flashed through her brain. *Was it a random thought, or had it been placed there purposely?* Before an intricate in-depth analysis could be undertaken, Davidia was startled by a few words of conversation. It was from the kneed girl.

'My name is Halp. The other girl is called Foll. We are sisters and your new escorts.'

'My name is Davidia.'

'Be silent. We move shortly.'

Davidia was amazed that either of them had spoken to her. Would they be punished for breaking the silence? A breeze whistled past disturbing any dirt particles into a rotating spout.

'We are here.'

'Where's here?'

Davidia realised that she was alone in her space again. Her escorts had disappeared and she was left to ponder the outside square experience and the strangeness of the events that had occurred there.

It was time for more lessons. The hour of freedom was over.

9 EXPERIMENT

asesix met with her Senora College fellow students before classes started to confirm that their day was to involve close contact with other students who might not actually favourably embrace the greeting they were to receive. It would be a hit-or-miss activity without full knowledge of any consequences. As all six were about to embark on their day, each konnockered knee suddenly lit up with a painful twinge. It was a message from Miss Alpine reminding them of their important task. No one dared disobey. A few fellow students walked by.

'You all look like you have seen a ghost. That's a painful look you each wear,' said a passing student, who politely used small talk.

'It's a bonding ritual we use each day. We use this expression to start the day and hopefully by the end of it, it has been replaced,' replied Casesix, who believed that each interaction required a reaction.

Ignoring anyone who personally spoke to you was the height of rudeness. Was Casesix learning new ideas unavailable in her beloved, or non-beloved, Senora College depending on a point of view?

Nothing more was said. Class was about to commence. The tightly-knit group dispersed.

Nerves were rampantly pulsating through Casesix's body. Her shape and looks were as attractive as any other female. Her blood was enthusiastically spirited around her body. This also triggered an emotional flow in parts not previously activated. There weren't any adult education classes at Senora College. Her internal turmoil caused some confusion. Her school shirt suddenly became sensitive massage material, which had others staring at her firmness. Other elements were alive but appropriately not reported on. The day had a somewhat different feel to it. The bell rang. It was time to focus.

At the first break, Casesix "innocently" sat to the left of a similar aged girl on one of those slatted wooden seats in the grounds that left a pattern on your backside when you stood up. Her konnocker was on her right knee. This was the first practice run. She sat close enough for a thigh to have slight contact and warmth of touch could be felt by both parties. The other student moved away. Casesix moved also until there was no seat space left, only a drop to the ground.

'What is it you want?' said the student, who was busily engaged in personal mobile phone pursuits.

'I'm new here and I don't know any students. I thought that we could be friends.'

'I'm over-supplied with friends, so just leave me alone.'

The student continued belting her alphabetic telephone console distributing, no doubt, words of wisdom to all her friends.

That answer went down as a nasty 'No'. Casesix slowly stood up and as she left, turned toward the student and kneed her on her exposed knee. Short skirts seemed to be the compulsory female school uniform. A few males would probably have preferred to have worn the same outfit; however, out of school hours was more of an appropriate time. Pain was etched on the student's face. It was a particularly nasty thrust and even Casesix's knee recoiled in pain.

'What was that for, you stupid bitch?' said an irate student, who suddenly slapped Casesix with a bruising blow. It was so strong that she fell over backwards, which exposed her sporting garments. Fortunately, no one else was near to record the sighting.

'Ouch,' she said, without a range of accompanying expletives.

She thought, *What a disaster*. Her next approach may have to be more subtle. The quadrangle was full of busy student relationship engagements. There was one noticeable male who seemed to attract a few selfless females intent on feeding his ego. If the girls were attracted to him, he must be of some importance. He could be a prime candidate for a soft knee cuddle. Casesix meandered over, determined not to attract any attention. She had let her hair down, camouflaging her well-shaped, facial features. There was no need to confuse the prey until she had honed in. She stood nearby waiting for a moment when he had shed the ego group and was momentarily alone. She seized her opportunity. She flicked her hair back and let it cascade down her shoulders and back. It fell into place like it does on one of those hair commercials. She had been noticed. Casesix stood face to face. He had been snared. The dialogue ensued.

'Hi there,' said Casesix, stroking her hair.

There wasn't anything else yet to stroke.

'How ya doin?' replied the male. 'Me name's Handfull.'

'That's an odd name.'

'Me dad calls me that because he says that's all ya need.'

Casesix had no idea what he meant. She continued.

'What are you studying?' continuing with the polite dialogue.

'You,' he said, with a smile. 'You want to feel me "guns"? Most of the girls do.'

Once again Casesix was a little lost on meaning. Handfull raised an arm, which hardened into a taut muscle ready to touch and admire. He was captain of the school rugby team. He beckoned her to come closer and grasp his taut muscle. Casesix did as urged. His gun was certainly in prime condition. She didn't "ooh" and "ah" like the other girls because she had another agenda. After she had run her hand along that smooth feature, she realised that she was standing at almost full-frontal touching distance with lips far enough apart to still speak unhindered. She wondered what to do next. The answer came quickly enough.

'What do you think of it?' said Handfull, still with his arm up.

'It's firm, isn't it?' she said.

'They is the best in school. Ya wanna touch the other one?'

'I'm fine with the first one, thanks.'

Without warning, Handfull placed his down arm behind her back in a surprise move and drew her closer. The surprise movement took her breath away. Her reaction was automatic. She withdrew a pace and raised her right knee to contact his right knee; however, in her startled state she missed the intended connection and slammed it into his groin with unnerving accuracy. Imagine her surprise when she encountered another taut muscle, which was unavailable for stroking in a public place! She wondered what it was doing there. Rugby must be a strange game to have firm muscles placed in all parts of the body, seen and unseen. Perhaps she might take it up as a sport? She didn't differentiate their use. Handfull let out a groan and crumpled to the ground, clutching his wounded anatomy. Casesix quickly retreated. She didn't want to hear what was said next. A few girls ran over to Handfull, all insisting on tending to his wound. Casesix had lost interest in the small gathering. She began to wonder how hard it was becoming to konnocker someone correctly. She had two attempts so far and two failures. The bell rang for classroom return. It gave her respite in her konnockering quest.

At midday, she regrouped with her fellow students to discuss their morning's attempts at engaging other students in their quest to be konnockered.

'I sat down with another student in the student library where you could sit opposite each other. The desks had access via an open space where it was possible to have physical knee contact. To ensure accuracy of knee placement, I had to check by sight under the desktop the range of movement that would be required for knee contact. The librarian noticed me looking under the desktop and quickly came over and put a stop to it. Forget the library to knee someone. It's too difficult,' explained Caseone.

'I stood behind a male student in a queue at the office waiting for a form to be issued for an excursion. He was taking a while to ask the relevant questions of the staff, when another staff member approached me to satisfy my request. I didn't have one at that time; however, I said I was just passing by and had now managed to stand at the front desk alongside the long-winded male with the slow request completion. I turned towards him and moved nearer for knee contact and to konnocker him, when a pushy bloody female placed her sizeable self between us and my approach was thwarted. I kneed the damn front office wall instead. This konnockering isn't an easy process,' explained Casetwo. 'Did anyone succeed this morning with a transfer?'

'I'm not sure,' said Casethree. 'I was in the gymnasium change rooms after the physical education routine and about to disrobe from Lycra back into my school uniform when an approach was made. I didn't know what to do. Another girl similar in age and height came over to me and began a conversation. She hadn't yet showered. Small perspiration droplets fell from her body as if it was coated in Teflon. She had the most interesting look on her face. She complimented me on various parts of my anatomy. Her hand reached down toward the floor and, fearing for my safety, I raised my knee defensively and it landed awkwardly on her right knee. Sparks flew. Well, they did in my head. She reeled backwards. She looked at me and as she stood tall, she handed me my towel that I had dropped by staring at her. This bruise on my face was the result; however, I think she was konnockered. Symptoms of transference will emerge in a few days' time.'

Casesix was proud to think that at least one of them had

a modicum of success. Casefour and Casefive had nothing to report. No opportunity had presented itself for them to take an advantage.

'Have you noticed that each time we knee someone, they return the affront in a far stronger manner with an act of physical violence? We have to be more careful and subtle to relay our message.'

The group spent the rest of the day scoping for opportunities. Their curriculum wasn't part of the school's curriculum.

*

Davidia palmed her scab and both Slirander's and Rotan's teeth tingled. Slirander felt it was time for a party line. They had to relay some form of message outside so that someone else understood the difficulty of their predicament or exactly what it was. Otherwise, they could become a lost commodity. Rotan was about to consume a comforting beverage when he received the incoming signal. A call from your daughter usually usurps any other activity, especially when she's "missing".

'Slirander, what's happening and where exactly are you? Your mother and I are concerned over your safety,' said Rotan, as a concerned father.

'I'm safe, dad, and so is Davidia. We are in some kind of training college. We haven't yet found out its purpose. There are so many strange and bizarre happenings. It's like a continuous Halloween nightmare. We have no idea how to escape or return home, but we will work it out as we find out more.'

'How are you coping, Davidia?' asked Rotan.

'I'm fine. It is an odd existence. I've never had so many strange events or ever visited a place like this before. We are confident of solving why we are here.'

Davidia felt it better to retain the full truth of their situation so as not to alarm others unnecessarily.

'Say hello to mum and not to worry,' said Slirander.

'Will do. Those exchange students from Senora College are rather an odd lot. Rumours are circulating around school about serious knee assaults. There is field of thought that they are the cause of it since their arrival. I don't know its purpose, but there is talk. Any ideas why?'

Slirander connected it instantly to the konnocker that Davidia and she had been impregnated with and wondered what the real purpose of it was, outside of the college. They were yet to learn its full implication for themselves and whether it was removable.

'It's time to go, dad. Lessons are recommencing. Bye.'

Slirander disconnected. Davidia was still tuned in.

'We aren't having any lessons, are we?' asked Davidia.

'We couldn't divulge too much to cause others to worry when we don't know the full story ourselves.'

*

Suddenly, their computers lit up with a demand for attendance. They were required to commence another day's learning activities. The desk protruded from the wall. It expected a visitor. Davidia sat down with the enthusiasm of a bored teenager. Wasn't there something else not to do? Slirander sat down with her enthusiasm linked to the "why" behind the messages on the screen. Today's lesson was mathematical in content at the commencement when subtle changes moved it from numbers to letters, mathematical letters. It was like sophisticated algebraic equations all teasing each other for a correct answer. It was confusing, to say the least. Neither Davidia or Slirander had been taught any of this advanced structure. It had to be advanced because neither of them understood it. Their eyes followed the patterns and they pressed keys in anticipation of an answer. Was that a square-root of something or an x-squared? Did a hyperbola cross paths with a fallen J-curve? Was that straight line deliberately placed in a horizontal position through the triangle to divide it into two unequal parts, and if so, what did the answer mean? Mathematics might be a skilled logical process, but today it was anything but. Behind all the eye-catching movement and screen changes, a calm, melodic sound was played through the earphones as if it had hypnotised their ears, if that was possible. Their brains only absorbed the sounds with their subliminal messages of control and subservience. The Cluids were tampering with their logical cells in an effort to mould them into to an illogical thought set. Every day, if this programming was enforced, both girls would eventually have a clean brain washed of any good thoughts. No one knew if there was another way to wash a brain. They can't just take it out, rinse it with a sudsy solution and then replace it in working order. The Cluids were experimenting with their minds and wondering whether they were susceptible to their flowing suggestions. It had to be proven. Girls don't often listen to who's filling their ears with literary wonderment.

This was day one of full-on mind bombardment. After an hour, it was a switch-in action. A five-minute break to observe the girls' reaction. The screen told them it was time for a break. Davidia removed the headphones and tried to stand up. Her legs had the wobbles for the first few seconds. She didn't feel well. Someone was delivering a migraine. It hurt. She visited the bathroom not for the usual, but a face-wash with cold water. The reflection in the mirror almost scared her witless. Who was it? Her hair was unmade and straggly. Water had splashed some of it to stiffen together; and that face – she remembered a familiarity about it, whatever it was. The Cluids observed the change in confidence of movement with their sensory technology. Miss Alpine felt that progress of mental impairment was occurring. Little did she realise the mental strength of an obstinate girl. It would be sorely tested.

'Is that really me?' said Davidia, after the mirror shock. 'I can't look that bad, surely not! What have I been fed? It wasn't food, so what was it?'

She felt like a retired person at that stage hankering for a short nap. Her eyes blinked just in time. The computer beeped for more attention. It was the mating call of a digital device.

'What now? More useless mathematics. Why can't it be geography or sport?' Davidia was mumbling to herself.

She assumed Slirander was confronting the same emotions and attitude. Slirander was able to deflect and distort the melodious advice that permeated her ears past the small mounds of wax yet to be removed. There wasn't time for a fingered exploratory. She was after reason and a sensible approach to make sense of anything. Her finely-tuned hearing picked up the actual words piped in. They referred to doing as one is told. Don't question the Cluids, especially Miss Alpine, and always obey the instruction given. It tried to form a sheep mentality whereby discipline of thought is obeying instructions without question. What if she disagreed, Davidia surely would? Being blind in a literary sense was dangerous for any "baa baa" follower. Leap into that raging river. Bungy jump without a chord. Lie to your parents. That third comment was less active than the first two suggestions, but as equally as dangerous for a survivor. Not all advice given by an adult has the hallmark of sense. Sometimes an own decision is required. Slirander was in complete control of herself. The melodic tunes, in her mind, were a senseless selection of repetitive slogans. Perhaps she could use a selection of expletives to form her own amusing answer? Before it became too deep in meaning, her digital advice emitted its digital mating call. Beep.

*

A few students at Vlad College milled together, which was the usual social ritual in the school grounds before the commencement of school. A point of interest – it was a few points actually – had them deep in conversation. The girls wore short skirts and the boys wore shorts, exposing healthy knees, no matter where one looked. The object of their interest was each other's knees, not usually the premier point of interest in either gender's anatomy; however, this morning it had centre stage. The cold, crisp morning emphasised the myriad of goose bumps that dotted the clean shaven and unshaven legs. A tallish male student had an arm directly pointed at a girl's knee.

'Is that a nodule growing there?' he said, pointing.

The perceptive girl took a close look and ran her hand over the suggested area of growth.

'It feels okay to me,' she said, confirming that there were no more than the normal bumps or undulations.

'It has slightly changed colour. It's orange.'

'No, it isn't,' she huffily retorted. 'It's my normal skin tone.'

Another girl, her closest friend bought into the discussion.

'It definitely has an orange tinge to it. You didn't spill any of your make-up this morning, did you?'

'No way. It's far too expensive to waste on camouflaging a knee. No one normally takes an interest that low.'

'Have a closer look?'

The girl reluctantly checked it. To her surprise, a small orange nodule had materialised overnight. It wasn't there yesterday. She felt it with a finger. It was solid, painless and looked out of place.

What was she doing growing an imperfection? It wasn't a wart, was it?

Casesix was in another group nearby and overheard the conversation. She smiled without saying a word. One of them had successfully konnockered another student. During the day there could be similar meetings and discussions.

'What about your problem? You didn't get that on the football field,' said a girl to another of the males.

'Get what?' he replied.

'That thing on your knee. It's not a bruised swelling, is it?'

The male took a closer look at his knee. It wasn't his normal area of anatomical inspection. It was a given that discoloration, swelling, cuts and abrasions form on or around the knees due to the nature of his sport. That sort of damage was taken for granted. Imagine his surprise when a tiny green growth imitating a squashed frog was attached to the side of his knee. It could be some sort of algae. He tried to brush it off. It refused to move. It was home on a host knee.

'I'm seeing the medical staff at lunch-time. They'll know what it is.'

The bell rang and the crowds dispersed. Casesix had the beginnings of a nice day.

The morning classes flew by. Lunch-time had arrived. The staff medical centre was always open during this time. It was the prime accident hour and the students were relied upon to fill in the time. The male student was there with his green growth and also the girl with the orange growth. One could be mistaken that they were from two different religions of Ireland with the orange and the green; however, today wasn't conflict resolution time, it was to learn about the growing predicament each one was in. Was it fungal?

'Come in,' said the medical staffer. 'Make yourself comfortable. What's the problem?'

The girl offered her knee first by raising it for placement on the bed.

'*My, what fine thighs*,' said the staffer to herself as she busied for an inspection.

'Can you explain what that orange growth is on my knee? It shouldn't be there,' she said, as the staffer eyed her nodule.

'It is interesting, isn't it?'

After a few prods, a knife was used to test the pain level. A sharp jab into the nodule made no impression at all.

'It's a solid little item. You felt no pain at all?'

'No. Can it be cut off?'

'I'm not into butchery yet, but I'll attempt to remove it. Lie on the bed.'

She thought how magnificent a nice pair of thighs looked laying perfectly still on her medical bed. It reminded her of when she was a young girl at school in her prime participating in any sport she could. Ah, those lost days, but the memories remained.

A specially hooked knife was used. A few silent saw strokes couldn't break the skin. It was an impossibility to remove. There was no way a swab or sample could be removed for testing. It was a real quandary. She decided to clamp it, twist and pull. It was as obstinate as its owner. There was no success in its attempted removal.

'You're next,' she said to the male.

He placed his leg on the bed and his bulgy node was green.

'Not very attractive, is it?' said the staffer. 'Is it causing any problems?'

'A few stares, that's all. Otherwise it's fine. It doesn't impede my sporting capabilities. It has only recently appeared and I'm sure I haven't fallen over to scar it or injure myself.'

He placed a hand on it and pushed it. It didn't take too kindly to being harassed. A small amount of movement occurred. At least that was something. The staffer imitated the previous procedure that she had tried with the girl. It too resulted in a "no" result. That small, so far insignificant, nodule was uncooperative. The examination was complete.

'I'm not sure what those growths are. Accessing them was impossible. My suggestion is to monitor them. If they enlarge and cause problems, then a hospital visit will be necessary. Enjoy your lunch.'

Both students didn't take too much comfort from the diagnosis. Should they be concerned? It was the colour that caused them discomfort. Other students clearly saw the orange and green growths. With the advent of social media and the pursuits of perfection, such growths seriously downgraded one's standing in that market. Both students shrugged their shoulders in resignation of "watch and grow". They were returning to class when Casesix saw them. She dashed over, appearing concerned.

'Are you two okay? I saw you leave the medical room. Is everything alright?'

'It's just a small issue with our knees. There's nothing to worry about. We have to monitor any change in the small coloured growths, that's all,' said the male, who sort of dismissed its significance.

The female didn't answer. There was nothing to discuss with the new girl.

Casesix knew that at least two of her group had been successful as shown by the different colours, one for males and one for females. Full transference would take a week or two and then Miss Alpine can incorporate them into her program. It would seem that the program was working. A few new konnockered recruits may go down well on Casesix's life resume when she returns to Cluidinine and Senora College.

She would only find that out when she and her fellow students returned.

Would there be any surprises?

10 HALP

The computer appeared unappetising for Davidia. It wasn't an intended meal at that moment, but she couldn't cope sitting in front of a digital device. She was half-zonked out of her brain after her visit to the square. Her logical section of the brain was being impregnated with messages through the headphones. None were really from any word selection set she would make; however, she was being mentally fed and intimidated. She became woozy and was at the danger level of succumbing to subliminal suggestions and, later on, these would be reproduced as her own original thoughts. *Enough,* her mind screamed.

In her hazy state, she slid a finger toward the console as a random selection, not fully realising her movement hit the one key in the alphabet that gave an independent reaction. It was the letter H. Her headphones scrambled any other messages and she heard the word "Help". This one word was becoming a recurring nightmare. Her wooziness took a quick trip to the insanity section of her brain and she suddenly reformed herself into Davidia, the schoolgirl. She shook her head and the headphones fell off. She leant back in her chair and steadied herself before a backflip occurred. Her eyes honed in on her screen. It was a scrambling selection of coloured dots all looking lost when, miraculously, the word "Help" flashed across the screen. She thought that this was insane. No sooner had the word disappeared than Miss Alpine stood next to her. She wasn't a mirage, so Davidia pushed at her to see if she was real. To her detriment, she was. Miss Alpine was splayed on the floor like a bumpy throw rug, caused by schoolgirl impertinence and soggy thoughts.

'I'm sorry, Miss Alpine,' Davidia stuttered. 'You shocked me by your instant appearance. I haven't been feeling well lately. Please forgive me.'

Davidia had the smarts to wheedle her way back from a bad situation to a tolerable one.

Miss Alpine's face really had a moment's distortion when she reformed into the nasty person she was – and her actions soon to become. She dusted herself down. There wasn't actually any real dust. It had been banned from the college by the formidable cleaning team.

'Have you been tampering with our equipment? You actually touched a key and it reacted. Why did you do that?'

'I have no idea. I was half-asleep when I moved. I thought that I was getting up from my seat and used the desktop for support. I hadn't taken my giddy pills. I must have touched it by mistake.'

'Who did you send a message to?'

'No one. I don't know anyone here and I don't have any personal email, Facebook or Twitter contacts. Who would I send anything to? You have total control over all of the equipment. Since being here, I have only followed your advice to the best of my ability.'

A pair of doughy eyes followed that comment accompanied by a wonderful schoolgirl pout. She could have used that lipstick that Slirander had been earlier.

'I'll have maintenance service your equipment. There must be a malfunction in there. It has never, and may I repeat, never happened before. Your friend next door is not experiencing any such problems. Is it only you and, if so, why is it only you? You haven't heard the last of this.'

A yellow twinge framed her face like a dull sunflower. Instantly, she was gone. Davidia thought that she certainly moved at a fantastic pace around the complex. At any hint of a problem, she appeared like a genie. There might be a secret hidden elevator or time travel capabilities or even hovercraft shoes. She realised that there was only a split second before an issue and an appearance. That meant a strategy of speed or a well-thought-out strategy before implementation. She palmed her scab. Slirander was signalled.

'I had that "Help" message flash across my screen again. It's becoming habit-forming. I still have no idea who, what, when, where, or why it appears. Miss Alpine is onto it like a shot. I feel like the turkey in a turkey shoot and it doesn't end well for the turkey. How are you coping?'

'I can't help at this stage because it's unknown to me. Perhaps in a few days' time, when we escape, we can search the surrounds,' said Slirander, with not quite a death wish but pretty damn close to it.

'Are you crazy? We can't escape from all of this.'

Davidia thought that her friend had visited one of those places where insanity is the norm. She wasn't visiting her if she was placed in one of those asylums. Maybe what she was experiencing was an educated form of insanity. Now, that made sense to her. Consider everyone else to be a nut case and retain your sanity. That coping mechanism might just work.

'For us there is no such word as can't. I have a plan of sorts. We'll discuss it later. I have another lesson to attend. I'm enjoying my time here.'

Davidia was perplexed. *How could Slirander enjoy being locked up?* She pondered for a moment and thought that really it wasn't much different to being in your bedroom alone with less electronic devices.

Suddenly, a stranger entered her room. It was becoming traffic central.

'I'm the service technician,' he said.

He wore stretch khaki-coloured pants with a large bulge where his konnockered knee resided. She could see a dark coloured outline and thought that it was larger than any she had seen before. It was impossible not to stare.

'Excuse me,' said Davidia, 'your konnocker looks black and is rather large. All others I have seen have been lighter skin-coloured and much smaller.'

'I'm from Africa,' he politely replied. 'Size doesn't matter; however, tradespersons have a larger one due to their heavy responsibilities. I need to concentrate.'

Davidia felt such a fool that she hadn't noticed his heritage. Next time, eyes wide open. A windy whoosh sound took her by surprise. She had been a single unit and now she was a triple. Her two escorts, Halp and Foll, were resting against both sides of her as if adhered by Superglue.

'What are you two doing here? I don't need a bloody escort to stand still.'

There was no response. The silent treatment agitated Davidia. The rudeness, lack of manners and absence of dialogue were feeding her obstinate and defensive streak. She thought that someone will pay for this appalling behaviour. The girls edged toward a wall, which opened wide and swallowed them like bait fish down a dolphin's gullet. It was as dark as a star-free cosmos. She remembered her parents listening to a tune decades ago called, The Sounds of Silence. She may not have been in the tune, but she was certainly experiencing its meaning. What seemed to be an indeterminable amount of time was interrupted by one single, solitary, four-lettered word, "Help".

'Yes, I know that's your name,' said a peeved Davidia.

'You didn't hear the correct vowel when I said it. It was spoken with an "e" not an "a".'

'Is this the forty-four-word crossword, is it, where I have to guess? How come we can speak in here? Isn't that forbidden outside of my space?'

'You are still in your space; however, this is a solitary confinement room attached to your space. In here, sound cannot permeate any wall, so it's safe to speak for the moment. We don't have long.'

'Can you give me some space? I don't mind bonding, but being attached to me is weird. If I wanted a threesome, I could certainly think of an alternative.'

'There is no alternative. We were advised that you were a threat and must be held under close surveillance every time that you leave your space. The Rrandys were loose. We aren't. We're tight.'

'Okay, then, what's with the word "Help"? What is it you expect of me with the constant taunt of it flashing on my screen causing me all sorts of complications with Miss Alpine?'

'We believe that you and your friend can save us. You are from the outside world, but you have the "Feal". It's an ancient custom whereby a true saviour arrives in the midst of a trouble-torn environment and saves it. Senora College is not what it seems.'

'How did we get the "Feal"? We've never heard of such nonsense. We aren't Wonder Woman and Wonder Girl, but we have been called wonderful before.'

The humour was lost in the darkness.

'Our konnockers have had their lifeline termination activated. See how they pulsate with a yellow glow. It means that we are of no further use. We want to exist, but not as fertiliser or a forgotten memory. The time left is unknown. It is enough that it has been activated. Everyone here has the same risk expectation. Only the true Cluids can exist forever.'

'I'm only a girl in Year 10. I'm here to learn a new form of education. Why should I jeopardise that? Once the exchange period is over, I can go home.'

'You may go home, but it won't be as you. We were told the same thing years ago, but we are now at risk of losing life at an early age and we never returned. We aren't your age. We're older, but it doesn't show. The process has kept us young.'

Davidia wasn't enjoying the knowledge-sharing experience. There weren't any positives in it. Even a toilet full of waste material (shit) had some positive aspects. She'd have to share this with Slirander. If they were to promote the Wonder brand, then they needed to be together.

'What should I do? How can I help?'

'There will be no more computer warning signs. We have spoken. You now know the predicament facing us. There is also the issue of other hidden family. Prepare the "family saviour" thesis. There are a few others with yellow, pulsating glowing konnockers. Those are the only trusty pulses you can trust in your new environment. We can't advise you of any action, but only inform you of the problems. Out fate is in your hands, delicate as they are.'

Davidia wondered what a friggin' mess this was. She was only an exchange student learning new skills and had been thrust into the role of saviour of a group of people she didn't even know and with no idea about where or who they might be. Talk about a puzzle.

'No more conversation. The wall is about to release us.'

A flash of light hit with such intensity, it startled Davidia. Her eyes were wide open like she had seen a fright. She had a throbbing head pain. There was no Panadol Forte available here. It was a drug-free zone like most schools? The escorts disappeared and Davidia again took centre stage in her own space. The service technician nodded goodbye. Davidia did wonder though whether he had installed the latest spy technology software. She thought that, from now on, she would treat her schooling with suspicion and she was an international spy. That mindset would help her cope with what she had been told. What a weird school it had turned out to be. Would it become any weirder? Vlad College was never this odd even though it had its moments.

*

Miss Alpine decided to collect the new exchange students from Vlad College and keep them together. It was most uncharacteristic of Senora College to allow such an event. She had the distinct impression that they needed to know, for personal assurance purposes, that each of them was fine and it may aid in the process of mental compliance from them. Dealing with the minds of youth can certainly be a stressful mental battleground. If all impediments were removed or downgraded, then success may be achieved earlier. It was all about risk-taking. A general message was sent to the six students that they were to attend a special meeting for educational improvements. It didn't mean anything to them; however, for Miss Alpine it was crucial. Her world was in conflict and new areas of influence were required quicker to stave off any foreseeable disaster. The six students were the current prime guinea pigs. It was intended that they would be the future emissaries of Cluidinine regardless of their past and family. It was a selfish and ruthless path to implement and follow.

Davidia's two escort sisters reappeared for transport purposes. Their knees still glowed a dim yellow. Slirander's two new messy Bubble escorts as replacements for the previous pair surrounded her with bubbles of excitement at the thought of future escorting. The other four students had different sets of escorts. One female, Rhonda, had a set of sheep. The other female, Jan, had a set of brightly polished shoes. One male, Rodney, had a set of javelin poles. The other male, James, had a set of hands without any body. The escorts were at random and there was no explanation for any selection. Whatever the task, it was performed. All escorts assembled with their student in the Meet and Greet room, once again devoid of any external light. The students were pleased to meet each other again. It was almost like a classroom reunion.

'How's the new accommodation? Are you enjoying your time here?' asked Davidia.

Before an answer was given, Miss Alpine appeared like an apparition. She was the conductor with the baton waving those long, thin, bony fingers on an elongated hand raised as a signalling device. Her hand looked like it was underfed. She stared at her charges. The yellow-tinged face was absent, so she was in calm focus. Her eyes were pellets, the size of sheep droppings, and they emanated such intensity, that to touch would cause finger burns. She was brimming with something, but it was doubted that it was good manners. She scanned the small throng, sensing any tension. There was none. She relaxed slightly by lowering her raised hand.

'Thank you for attending. Does anyone have any questions about the standard of education?'

No one answered immediately, then Davidia piped up with a response.

'Why is there no external light into any of the buildings? We work under artificial light and it's not good for our eyes.'

'Are there any other questions?'

'But, Miss Alpine, you didn't answer mine,' insisted Davidia.

Slirander sensed conflict. Miss Alpine began to yellow up. Confrontation with a student could be an explosive situation. Slirander moved nearer to Davidia and placed her hand on her scab. Their thoughts intertwined.

Now would not be a good idea. I sense danger, thought Slirander.

'I need to know. I'm not ruining my eyes for anyone,' replied Davidia.

Before any further thoughts passed between them, Davidia broke contact.

'In my school you do as instructed and that includes no back-chat from any student.'

Miss Alpine had them at her mercy anyway, so protesting was rather futile, but not for Davidia.

'I'm not ruining my eyes for anyone. I need daylight. Is there any here?'

'You are not in charge. I am. You are instructed to obey. Disobey and suffer the consequences. I will personally ensure your stay is uncomfortable. Privileges will be removed. Do you understand? I control your life and your very existence. Do not force me to konnocker your time.'

Her tirade of cross words took a pause. Miss Alpine's heart rate had increased tenfold. Her modest shirt size heaved heavily. It was as underfed as her hands. Davidia watched her change colour. It represented a sunrise. Her face was in full bloom like a fully-fledged yellow sunflower. No one had ever before seen such brightness shine from her face even though it wasn't for a good reason. She lit up the room. She certainly exhibited chameleon characteristics, even imitating a bright light bulb.

'That's the daylight I wanted,' said a goading, cheeky Davidia.

She had lit Miss Alpine's wick and the fuse was hallucinating with delight.

'Do not push me, young lady. I am your worst nightmare,' she threatened.

Davidia suddenly sensed a change in rhetoric and wisely toned down her obstinacy.

'I only said that I'd like daylight, that's all. I didn't think that it was too much to ask.'

'Point noted. In future do not cross words with me, otherwise you'll find that the alphabet is a dangerous tool. Pay attention. I brought you all here to meet each other and satisfy yourselves that being here is beneficial to you all. When you return to Vlad College fully-armed with the knowledge of what you learn here, you will all be a further credit to your parents. Learn quickly and appreciate the length that we, at Senora College, have undertaken to improve your knowledge. An appreciation will grow.'

Davidia felt an aching pain in her right knee and almost toppled over. Slirander noted her movement. A feint yellow glow throbbed from her knee. Miss Alpine smiled. She had a smile that all dentists love. Davidia noted the reaction. It was callous and non-emotive. She thought, *What a bitch to think that a slight knee ache would deter her from finding what the college is about and why they were really there.* She groaned like it was the end of the world. She hadn't lost any of her dramatic talent. Her knee stopped throbbing.

'Remember, I control you. Return to your spaces.'

Miss Alpine glanced toward Davidia. There was no need for any cross words to be said. It's in the eyes – the windows to your soul that tell the real story.

Whoosh! Home, sweet home, to a sterile space of four dull walls without a hug. Davidia had to rethink her strategy. She didn't have one readily available, but felt she might need one. It was difficult to plan for something that you didn't know about. Her space felt gloomy. Even Davidia with her sparkling personality, didn't improve its feel. She needed her real bedroom.

*

The escorts' "home" was located in a labyrinth under the main school building. It housed many different life forms and non-life forms. The life forms were made up of disappointed students unable to pass the grades set. Many possessed the rogue gene, a genetic formation of the brain that was permanently disagreeable to following orders. They did, up to a point, and when their inability to comply was discovered after a direction was disobeyed, there was a period of retraining. If this failed, then their time device located in their konnocker was switched on. A minimum of twelve months was allowed for any positive changes to occur. If not, then after that time it was a random process as to who was minimised and exiled.

Halp and Foll had not been able to comply with the rules. They wanted to escape their futile existence and that secret had seeped out when reported on by other succeeders. Their fate was to inhabit a slot in the wall, be fed by a tube and wait for recall as an escort. They had become tougher and, it was thought, on the road to redemption, when secretly they harboured real thoughts of escape. That thought could never be revealed to Miss Alpine or Mr. Avalanche, otherwise it was instant dismissal. Their life force would be lost. They lived a road rarely travelled. Presently, there were no other life forms like them in the labyrinth.

The other non-life forms had been conjured up by the Cluid Council to act as escorts without risking destruction of living matter, hence the Rrandys (not real dogs but presented as such), the Bubbles brigade, hands, and other objects which they injected computer movements into – mechanical staff that never disobeyed a directive; however, the two Rrandys somehow acted outside of their doggy brief by imitating one of their characteristics. Machines aren't always the perfect slave.

One day, when Halp and Foll were in their wall slot attached magnetically to their spot – they were always in an upright position – water seeped into their domain and, magically, they were detached and roamed free. Their magnetic field malfunctioned.

They walked the corridors of their home. They once had a real family, or thought that they did, and had no idea where they were. Traces of their existence were non-existent, or so they thought. All the other escorts they passed were in a state of suspended animation ready for that one task they were designed for. Above them was the vacuum funnel they exited their home by for instant delivery upstairs. The two sisters had the same delivery system.

The labyrinth was an ancient fortified system against inter-galactic attack, but that was long ago. It was now used as a prison, for want of a better explanation. There were traces left of some types of inhabitants and they seemed to relate to these objects. Suddenly, footsteps were heard dragging along behind them. It was Miss Alpine and Mr. Avalanche out for an invigorating exercise stroll. They were muttering about their future plans and what had happened to the other inhabitants on Cluidinine that they had relocated elsewhere on the planet as a useful workforce. They mentioned an area known as Cluff. The two sisters had heard of this place, but were unaware where it was, such was the tight control and security by the Cluids. They dreaded being found out away from their slots. They portrayed two stones to perfection in sight and sound. The danger passed. They quickly returned to their slots to wait to be summoned for further escort duties. They also had a mission of discovery – family.

With the arrival of the new exchange students, they felt that the "Feal" was alive amongst one of them. It was like female intuition, but far stronger. That's why they had to be Davidia's escorts to aid them in a plan of discovery. They had to seem impartial, whilst Davidia, with the help or advice from Slirander, undertook that task. It was a case of all care (advice) and no responsibility (to carry out the task).

They had learnt minimal computer-hacking skills as students

and understood the complexity of the Cluid system, which was believed to be impenetrable. Try telling that to a hacker! They were able to install a "Help" virus undetected into the system. In reality, the word "Help" only became apparent when someone from outside touched the H key on a computer. Security was so strict. Other new students must have pressed the H key occasionally without knowing for the "Help" word to flash across only on her screen the few times it did before she mistakenly pressed the H key and all hell broke loose with Miss Alpine up for a tanty (tantrum). That discovery meant the end of the virus and any future calls for help. Davidia and Slirander were now their only form of salvation, if they lived long enough.

*

It had only been a few days since the arrival of the new batch of exchange students and, in that short time, the serenity and smooth functioning of Senora College had been interrupted by the ructions of a few. Never before had any outside student caused any disruption. Now there was Davidia and her friend, Slirander, in prime student spaces to implement dissent. There was insubordination in the air. It was invisible to the eye, but, when it erupted, it would be led by a young female student. No guesses who? So far, Davidia had been the cause of any stir and questioned what it was she was learning which one would think was the normal workings of a curious mind.

'We haven't had such insolence before,' whined Miss Alpine.

She believed, in her world, that it was "Be seen and not heard", which is a somewhat, outdated adage.

'She has been somewhat of a pest, but maybe that's the type of personality that exists out there in the Earth world of today,' replied Mr. Avalanche, still out on the new student.

'Nobody has been the cause of losing escorts, answering back, equipment malfunctioning and ungratefulness for their new opportunity. We may have to use the Rectification Room if she continues to behave badly. I will not let her bully me. Her life is ours and her manners must improve, or the konnocker time life will be switched on.'

Miss Alpine was full of threats and treachery.

'Give it some time. I'm sure she will bend.'

Mr. Avalanche gave an insidious sneer that didn't compliment his face.

The college staff were gearing for a battle of the minds.

That evening, the Cluids needed a refreshing mist to calm their attitudes.

Tomorrow could be another interesting development.

11 SURPRISE

The solemnity of her predicament meant being alone wasn't the social Nirvana it sometimes was thought to be. 'If only I was left alone,' had a hollow ring to it in her space. She was actually left alone without any digital devices for outside contact whereby she could spread her digital thoughts and have interaction with others. Davidia was slowly succumbing to an appreciation of, 'I want out of here.' Her insides were on the boil like bubbling magma. It was a matter of when the whoosh would erupt. Here, there were no promises of a holiday, new dates, clothes or fabulous accommodation. It had been a real social letdown. She paced her space as if monotony was her companion. Miss Alpine would love to know what her current thoughts were. Perhaps it was better to share them with Slirander. She angrily palmed her scab.

'Shit, that hurt,' she said, not thinking calmly as she almost removed it.

She couldn't afford to lose that lifeline. Slirander's tooth tingled. Incoming thoughts. There was never just one.

'I'm fed up with this space. I want to get out of here. It's not healthy been cooped up inside without any real light.'

'My thoughts exactly,' replied Slirander. 'I've been giving it some thought on how to escape this incarceration.'

'How? We are technologically trapped. Somehow, we need to find out about this place without being seen. I don't have the invisibility gene; however, once when I fancied the new hulk at school, that bitch Sally, who hardly wore any clothes and looked like a "for sale" sign, had her skirt higher than her underclothing and got first bite. I won't say what she bit, but whatever it was, he didn't attend school for the next few weeks.' Davidia was beginning to ramble.

'Davidia,' yelled Slirander's headache thought, 'Focus. There are possibilities that technology isn't the guardian of all occurrences.'

'Rubbish. Our digital footprint is trapped in a digital room, inside a digital prison, inside a digital school, inside a gloomy city and inside an unknown town. Now, tell me we aren't caught like someone's favourite screen saver. One key press and we don't exist anymore. It's time to rumble. I hope Miss Alpine has a pain barrier on her backside. It's been a while since I kicked a football and I don't mean a goal.'

Slirander sensed Davidia's agitation. It was catchy. She felt a surge of optimism from her friend's thoughts. Had she thought through her evolving proposal? It was fraught with danger. Her delicate new self, if achieved, was only a swat away from extinction. Slirander wasn't into real violence. She wouldn't be stupid enough to threaten her manicured nails, a nice outfit or damage her standard school shoes; however, when confronted with the inevitability of an assumed short life-span, action was more necessary than a range of cross-worded platitudes. It was up to her to eradicate self-doubt and ignite her action plan. She decided not to let Davidia in on it, just in case she gave the game away. It wasn't a trust issue but a far safer option. If she didn't return, then only one of them was lost.

'Calm down. I might have a solution. If it works, I'll contact you. I have some preparation to do,' said Slirander, already thinking of her approach to their predicament.

'What can you do from within your space? I'd appreciate it if you could break me out of here. I need another environment.'

'Have you forgotten those pleas for help? I must go. The truth needs to be discovered. Keep in touch. Others are relying on us.'

Before Davidia could espouse further critical advice, her scab glow dulled to its normal colour. It still sat on her arm as a skin pet and hadn't deteriorated. It was hoped that no one noticed it hadn't changed for days. It could be a fake.

Slirander was now alone and that would turn out to be extremely resourceful. Her comrade-in-arms was restricted to her space barracks.

Davidia sat on her bed. She was exhausted. Her eyelids hit each other with a resounding thud, closing like a zip-lock bag. No light was escaping from them for a while. It was silent except for some rhythmic breathing from an inert life form.

*

No escorts were allowed in the solitary confinement room with a student, if it had performed a punishable misdemeanour. Slirander pondered over what problem she could create and be punished for. Being a normal goody-two-shoes, it was difficult to cross her personality with bad behaviour. Her space presented no immediate opportunity. Suddenly, her computer lit up. The demanding digital "child" needed accompaniment. She immediately sat down as she was trained to do without objection. Whilst seated, it dawned on her. This was her light bulb moment. Davidia had a shop full of them. Why not share?

'That's it,' she said, excitedly.

She extended both hands over the computer keyboard and carefully struck the H key after the Caps Lock was pressed. There was no "Help" plea across the screen as she expected. It had been removed because Davidia had extinguished that as a real problem because she had done exactly the same thing. Miss Alpine grimaced angrily.

'What in the hell is she playing at? Her friend suffered because of it. She might also need to be taught a lesson.'

Miss Alpine waited. A rat never takes the bait at first sniff.

Slirander moved her hands slowly above the keyboard. Was she computer divining? Was she confused what to do with them, or was it such a diabolically, cunning plan no one except her could make sense of it? It was a movable conundrum. Suddenly, her delicate hands clenched into two fists of steel and her face puffed up like a puffer fish. Miss Alpine was staggered at how her pretty looks were now misshapen. Without warning, Slirander thumped them down as hard as she could onto the keyboard much like Thor the thunder god with his hammer. A wild scream accompanied the bashing, believing it alleviated the pain of the thump. It didn't. It was only a theatrical moment. She let out a scream that no one could hear. The keyboard erupted into a dismembered digital mess. The screen became an arrangement of coloured dots imitating clashing atoms. The keyboard alphabet had reduced by more than half. Wires spouted spaghetti-like traits as they escaped their cage and dangled over the desktop edge. It was the furthest that they had ever independently travelled. Her room was in uproar. Apparently, the computer controlled more of the room other than listening to lessons. It was like a series of space invaders as her whole space reacted violently. The hidden walled items such as bed, kitchen, rest room and anything else, randomly moved back and forth in pretend attacks on Slirander. Her space now had more companion items than she'd seen before. Miss Alpine was outraged. Her face brimmed with the brightest yellow tinge ever seen. She had never encountered this atrocious behaviour before from any student. She wondered what she had been taught at Vlad College. It definitely wasn't subservience and good manners. She appeared in Slirander's confusing space.

'What a pathetic display of bad behaviour. You have cost yourself any hope of completing the course we had intended for you. Penance must be meted out. It's a stint in solitary confinement until I say you can be released. What made you do such a dreadful thing?'

Action can elicit different opinions depending on what side of the behaviour rainbow one lived. It was either control or freedom. Slirander wasn't going to apologise. Being imprisoned, as she understood it, was a bone to pick clean.

'I saw an arachnid the size of a dinner plate and I squashed it,' she said, as her excuse.

'There aren't any of those creatures living here. They are banned.'

Strangely, her fists displayed no damage and she experienced no pain. Both Bubbles floated in amongst all the confusion. They only added to the disarray.

'Where shall we escort you to?' they said.

'Solitary confinement, alone,' directed Miss Alpine.

The Bubbles retreated. They weren't required.

Slirander put up the 'but, but, but' protestation as an act of defiance, but it was too late. Solitary confinement swallowed her. She was alone, thankfully. Her space had to undergo major repairs; however, she had achieved her goal, aloneness. Previously, being alone wasn't considered a good thing, but when a definite choice is made about it, it became a good thing, especially in this instance. She now had time to metamorphose and enact her plan. Would she be destroyed? She tooth-tingled her dad.

'Slirander, great to hear from you. How is the new school performing?' asked Rotan.

'Terrible. It's a dangerous place. I need to change into …' and she explained at length her plans.

Rotan pondered for a moment.

'It's a risk.'

'There is no other choice. Davidia and I have to leave here with the other exchange students and to do that we have to discover the secrets of this college and its world, otherwise we are in doom land never to be seen again.'

'That bad, eh! The spell you need is …' Rotan quoted from an ancient Spell book of his forbears. It was rarely used. This was a special occasion.

The spell began,

It's a changing world of fly and wing,
Consider fate and change to bring,
Corner life in an object of flight,
Catch the wind with all your might,
May size deceive
The prize to be,
A flying titbit
That no one can see.

Slirander listened intently and repeated the words out aloud. She shut her eyes and imagined a change. Her solitary confinement room suddenly became a massive space. She almost felt lost in it. She wondered how she was exploring the space.

'My legs should be on the floor,' she said to herself. 'Where are they?'

They weren't there. Had she lost them? She wiggled her legs. That's odd. Many of them wiggled at once. Her arms had flattened into two thin wafers. There were things protruding from her head and she didn't wear braids. Suddenly she felt small. She was. Moving around seemed to be easy and wherever she wanted to go, due to her new size, it was a long way.

'The spell must have worked. I feel completely different.'

Her dad was still in contact.

'Dad, I've changed,' said Slirander.

'Be careful. The spell will last a short time, so when it ends without warning, be somewhere safe. Your mother and I want you all home safely.'

'Thanks, dad.'

The warmth of a parent's love wasn't lost on her. She was determined to succeed.

*

Slirander's time in solitary confinement lasted a full day only. Miss Alpine wanted a proper explanation for the destruction that she had inflicted upon their systems.

'Open the solitary confinement room,' boomed Miss Alpine's voice. It was laced with anger.

The room appeared, opened and disgorged an invisible flying, but beautiful, butterfly. Miss Alpine rubbed her eyes in disbelief. Where is she? A blank space greeted her. It was to be mayhem around that night's dinner table. The barbeque stopper question would be, 'Where is she?'

'Where is she?' she demanded. 'It's not possible for her to escape. Who assisted her? It wasn't you two Bubbles, was it?'

The Bubbles denied any involvement. They shed so much air, wind and bubbles they almost disappeared as mist. A quick search located the completely empty area. No one was satisfied with the outcome. No student had ever escaped before. In the meantime, Slirander had fluttered above the room and realised that, upon seeing her reflection (she was invisible to all others but not herself), she had become a graceful butterfly. No wonder she moved so easily. There wasn't much time. She alighted on Miss Alpine's head with such deft touch, it wasn't felt. She had never weighed this light before, ever. A thorough search of a few seconds revealed that wherever she went, she was gone. Miss Alpine visited Davidia and demanded to know where her friend went.

'I have no idea. We don't communicate (a little fib there) or have access to each other and are stowed in different spaces. What's she done? Disappeared, has she?' said Davidia as if the question was an ordinary comment.

'Yes, she has. Where is she?'

Davidia was totally surprised.

'You can search around here. I have no idea where she is. She's my friend. I want her found. I don't want to be alone in here without all my new friends.'

How did Slirander orchestrate her escape? A puzzle had been set. Miss Alpine left and returned to the control room.

'I'll find her. There is no way I can tolerate that attitude. She's dead meat or better still, dead student. No one does that to me!' Miss Alpine was definitely a glowing banana.

Slirander was safe for the moment. In the control room she observed all the buttons, colours, screens and the Cluids who operated them. She flew down to the console and the konnocker buttons registered activity. Various colours pulsated. There were the orange and green buttons and she wondered what the holes with the red outer ring and opening were for. It wasn't long before it became clear.

'I'll place that one in there for that damaged space. She'll pay. I could have gotten to know her. Her loss will be greater than mine.'

Miss Alpine's middle finger on her right hand started to lengthen. It was automatic. She didn't need a lie for it to extend. Her fully extended sossurged finger was a grotesque distortion of an angled bone covered by skin that appeared to be diseased. It acted like an insidious snake ready to curl around your neck and strike unexpectedly. Ugh! Slirander watched the slow execution of herself. Fortunately, when a red was actioned, there was a mandatory six months existence period where the subject couldn't be terminated. It was hoped that during that time any position of disagreement could be recovered. Miss Alpine took her time. She slowly slid her finger into the slot and wriggled it. It also turned a bright red to indicate that the six months had begun. Slirander noticed that her miniature konnocker engaged into a red pulsating action. Her size and invisibility meant it was unseen but it registered as active on the console. Doom had been initiated. The countdown was on.

'That's one lesson in six months you will forget.' Miss Alpine retrieved her finger. Its redness began to fade. 'Where is she?' There's that question again.

Slirander knew that she had to learn as much as possible, as quickly as possible and relay it to Davidia as soon as possible. Team D and S was taking shape. Even though Slirander was invisible, any wrong move landing on an engaged surface could be the squashing she tried to avoid. For her own safety, she did the ceiling walk by walking upside down with a firm grip by her sticky feet. From this vantage point, the overall control room could be observed. There was the complete plan of Senora College, the button for the area known as Cluff – the sleeping dormitories of the Cluids, the Rectification Room, all spaces of students and the general buildings surrounding the college. It was very intricate. The thin, bony hands of the Cluids mesmerised Slirander by their ability to function. The shapes of buttons had been grooved for touch. The holes available for insertion and ease of function were personally designed. The whole system had the college, town and country electronically mapped and controlled. Slirander memorised the total layout before contacting Davidia via her miniature teeth, which she retained during the transformation. A response was slow in coming. Davidia had been sound asleep. 'You've got mail,' echoed in her subconscious.

'Who stood on my brains?' she questioned, awaking with a jolt. There was no one there. Her arm began to vibrate. She thought, *Oh, it's Slirander.* She quickly palmed her arm. It was still there. It hadn't been stolen. 'What's annoying me now?' Davidia was tired and disorientated. She wondered if she was in a mausoleum.

'Davidia, answer,' said an urgent Slirander.

'Your thoughts are rather squeaky,' she replied.

'I need your memory. Open it fully.'

'What for? I don't fill it for everyone.'

'Just do it. I'm sending you the plans of the college and country. Record it. Delete those male files and all the cosmetic and clothing nonsense. This is far more important. I've also been konnockered for a final six months stay.'

'Where are you?'

'In the central control room. It's a technological Christmas. Vlad College could certainly use some of these innovations.'

Davidia began to gossip as most females do; however, Slirander cut her short. Someone had now stood on her feelings as well as her brains. That's not a good combination.

'I've just woken up. Say that again and slowly. Your squeaky thoughts aren't that clear.'

Slirander repeated everything she had previously said. Davidia nodded and noted the information. She cleared her memory. It was so full of unwanted clutter. Making a space was harder than she at first thought. It was filed under Senora. Slirander also implanted along with her sounds, an extra memory recognition sound that saved all details sent. They both now had a perfect set of plans of the college and country able to be regurgitated at whim. There was one last piece of the transport puzzle to be solved. How did the Cluids travel so instantly between any space? Slirander watched closely.

Suddenly, there it was, an object hand held by every Cluid. It was a palm bulge. It possessed a button and when pressed, it transported that Cluid to elsewhere. It was known as a Gizmic Transporter Device (GTD). It was so ingenious. It was almost a time travel regulator. Slirander's konnocker, small as it now was, was still able to allow her unimpeded travel access around the college and country with it, if she could move.

The downside was that she would be monitored by the control room. Every movement of her blipping konnocker would be tracked. The fact that she was invisible would test the Cluid's resolve to their frustrations at not locating her. That was the risk she had to take. Being a heroine held certain dangers. There was no free feed in the saviour world; well, that what it's thought to be.

Slirander waited patiently, still firmly attached to the ceiling. Her feet were becoming itchy. She felt the urge to move. Even insects react to upside down time.

'Davidia, I need to do something urgent. I have to do this alone. Only I can do it. I don't need any distractions. We'll "thoughts" later.' Slirander ceased contact with her friend.

Davidia wasn't going anywhere. Her head did ache with a fully-filed fresh load of information. She thought, *Fancy being used as a library bank.* Her head had cleared now and she still felt isolated in her space. Slirander would return her thoughts later. Vlad College appealed much more than her new "school". Was she missing school, real school?

Slirander observed intently the placement of the GTDs. Who used them? Did they leave them unattended? Were they carried everywhere as a personal digital companion? Suddenly, a Cluid in a fit of madness, left one unattended. It was a death wish when that occurred. There was no explanation as to why that could happen. If "impossible to do" is a trait of control, then this was a gross violation exception of that rule. What had caused such a mystifying reaction? On closer inspection, it was noticed that a few tiny moisture droplets had landed on its head and trickled down its face. It felt exactly like the night-time spray it enjoyed when refreshing overnight; however, these droplets had a yellowish tinge with an acidic flavour. It must have been condensation. There was no other ready explanation. Yet, inside the control room condensation was impossible.

Slirander had taken flight to right her from an upside-down position. Her urgency had escaped in the flurrying wing flapping and led to the embarrassment, if she could be seen. The mystifying droplets was Slirander performing naturally as an insect does. Her excreta followed the fall of gravity and the Cluid was directly under her flight path. It wasn't intentional and any rest rooms weren't visible. What's a girl to do? She couldn't apologise. It was her end if she did so. Slirander fluttered down and landed on the abandoned GTD. As she alighted, she wiped her itchy feet and miraculously the GTD began to shrink. A little leftover moisture had settled on her feet. She was new at this flying routine and hadn't mastered all facets of being an active insect. There were a few imperfections to iron out. With so many hairy legs, Slirander attached the GDT to a spare and flew off with the prize. It also became invisible having been attached to its new host. Now she had free unimpeded access to everywhere within Cluidinine.

Before she abandoned the control room, she wondered what had happened to the Cluid that she had unintentionally bombed. It wasn't a pretty sight. It had performed a series of staccato movements writhing like an electrified snake. A wet mass covered the floor. It had disintegrated. Miss Alpine was furious.

'I demand to know who did this?' she yelled, hysterically. 'Was it you, you, or you?'

She pointed her awful, arthritic-looking hands around the room half-expecting to skewer the perpetrator. There was to be no barbeque in the control room today. If only she could squash Slirander. That was if she knew exactly where she was. The Cluids were petrified of the dominant female force of Miss Alpine. She hadn't been in charge for years by being a wimp. She was one dangerous pack leader.

'Clean up this mess. Keep an eye out for that missing student. I don't know how, but I'm sure that she's behind all of this. I hope that it's a quick six months. Get out of my way.'

Miss Alpine left. No one was sure if she visited the sulking room or not. That wasn't on the official plan of the college. It was a sanctuary available for periodic disappointments. No one else had ever been there.

In all the confusion, not one Cluid had observed the console properly. Had they done so, a small constant annoying red blip would have been located in their midst.

*

'Psst, psst, Davidia, it's me,' said Slirander, having entered her friend's space. That was a banned action within itself.

Davidia was momentarily dazed. *No one pssts at her. Open your mouth. Use dialogue and not a sound that sometimes is accompanied by a fine spray.* She wondered who the annoyance is now. Her space was still vacant. She almost registered the same action before the persistent psst had her full attention.

'Where is the me?' she asked.

'Directly in front of you, sitting on your desktop. Can't you see me?'

This time Slirander was using her vocal cords and not palm-or tooth-thought sharing.

Davidia did an eye sweep and discovered that dust had congregated and gathered, acting as a social party for dirt particles. There were no other visitors; however, a tiny smudge blotted out the perfection of a constant dust layer.

'All I can see is dust and a clear desktop. If you are here, you must be invisible.'

'Correct. I'm the butterfly you can't see. It's a disguise. Miss Alpine can't locate me. We have to move quickly to discover the secrets of the college. I hope you have memorised the maps I sent. There may be one real issue. The Cluids can still follow me on their console, so we will be in constant danger. I need to find a way to make my konnocker inert so we can't be followed.'

'And how do you propose to travel around the establishment unseen and without two automatic escorts? Halp and Foll won't let us just up and leave.'

'They can come with us. They both dislike the college and are on borrowed time. Their hand has been revealed to us. They need their family connection, so we play the emotional card for their assistance.'

'That's all well and good, yet we're stuck in here. By the way, how did you get in here?'

'The Cluids have a GTD device, which I cleverly purloined. The "how" is irrelevant. One press of a button and whoosh, we can go anywhere. Remember, I am invisible. To avoid squashing me and putting me in immeasurable danger in my vulnerable state, I will need to sit hidden in your hair. I hope your follicles have been washed recently. I don't want to be covered in scalp snow.'

'Won't we be discovered as soon as we move? I'm not sure an incarcerated heroine is part of my school curriculum. That red blip you said you had is a tracking device. How about we try and stop it blipping.'

'You aren't going to amputate my leg.'

'Not at all. Why don't you re-visit the control room and tamper with their equipment. There must be an "off" switch somewhere. If they can reverse the termination process, there must be that "off" switch. You need to dismantle it so we aren't discovered easily whilst snooping.'

Davidia stood tall, stretched her lithe frame and, inexplicably, ran full tilt at where her door space should be. What coloured pills is she on? She landed half way up, feet first in a gymnastics movement that any *ballet de corps* would be impressed to introduce into their physical ensemble, and flipped feet first onto the floor. Suddenly, Halp and Foll materialised in a flash and stood tightly side by side to Davidia. The "triplets" had been born.

'You cannot leave this space,' said Halp, closely nudging Davidia.

'I had no intention of leaving. I was practicing a "keep fit" manoeuvre.'

'We thought that you attempted an escape.'

'I had thought of it. It's impossible, I know.' They couldn't read her thoughts.

Davidia gave time, not that she needed it, for Slirander to visit the control room and locate that bloody termination button. The console was huge and baffling to an ordinary butterfly, but this one wasn't ordinary. She fluttered closely.

An alert Cluid yelled, 'Intruder, intruder,' as they scurried to locate the danger. 'There's a moving red blip in here somewhere. That is just impossible. It's not a malfunction, is it? There was one of those in that new girl's space recently. It's not contagious, I hope.'

Miss Alpine appeared. There was something deadly strange

about her. Had she "sooked" long enough and was ready for battle? No alcohol or pill-swallowing was allowed in Senora College, so what was it? Had she finally realised that companionship was missing? It was none of that. She finally had a challenger. Someone of her mental ilk pressing her buttons like no other. Those two new students had enraged the serenity of her world. Chaos, a very long lost relative, had been introduced again. This time, the students won't be returning home, but first, she had to solve the current problem.

'Bring that student to me. The one that we know is still with us. Go, before I forget who I am.'

In an instant, the "triplets" were in the control room staring at a yellow sunflower. She hadn't spawned had she? thought Davidia. She looked much brighter than before, but not necessarily that bright that it bothered her. She had plants in her garden at home. This was an early bloom. Pick off her head and place in a vase, mmm.

'Where's your friend? There is a disturbance in here and it is she. Tell her to reveal herself or suffer.'

'I'm sorry, Miss Alpine, but I don't know anything about it. I would like to see her myself.'

'Then ask her to reveal herself. This is your last warning.'

Before she could answer, Miss Alpine had leant far closer to the "triplets" than expected. Her breath was rather offensive. It had a strong rotting-fish smell. It's strange what people sometimes eat. Who eats rotting fish? Amongst her threats, she had breathed over Davidia who had to refrain from puking, it was so gross. Where was the escape hatch? To avoid an extra inhalation, Davidia walked backwards dragging Halp and Foll with her. They ended up awkwardly on the console with three sets of buttocks resting on it. With their twitching nervous behinds, many buttons were accidentally pushed together. None were the victims of a tightening pincer movement. This caused digital panic. The console behaved like it had been breached with an unpleasant visitor – it had. The coloured dots all over the boards seemed to chase one another. In the mayhem, Slirander's termination button had been paused, which meant no more red blipping konnocker or tracking capacity. It would only be temporary, but would it be long enough? Technicians stormed in like dandelion seeds in a storm. Slirander alighted on Davidia's head. She was about to press her GTD when Miss Alpine raged at Davidia.

'You incompetent imbecile. This is your fault. When this is up and running again, you will be terminated. I cannot have digital distress in my college. Get out before it's an instant goodbye.'

The six-month time limit applied to that comment regardless of the veracity of its delivery.

'You need a good manicurist,' said Davidia, curtly.

She resented being verbally accosted. In a flash she was returned "home" to her space with the two clingers on. With the system down temporarily, it allowed the girls a quick word about the college. Halp and Foll, who they sort of trusted, were advised that they were going to search the college Cluff and find out the real truth about their "new education" and perhaps their family. It could be a treacherous journey. It couldn't be any bleaker than their surrounds, could it? Halp and Foll knew they were on borrowed time, had asked for their help and were now compliant in discovering what it is they would uncover. Heads nodded in agreement.

12 TRANSFORMATION

A few days had passed at Vlad College where concern was mounting for the students with the deformed knees. Their behaviour had a twist, which Casesix and her friends didn't see coming. The konnockered students began to behave irrationally. They ignored any guiding advice, took to light physical violence against their friends and verbalised the dictionary, repeating every cross word in there plus a few offensive and colourful adjectives added for effect. It wasn't the expected behaviour. The konnockered exchange students should have been polite, subservient and friendly. Those are three traits gladly accepted at any school.

'If you touch my locker again, I'll use you as a key,' said a male student, with the green throbbing knee.

He had tried to knee the offensive growth off by slamming it into his locker door. He winced in pain. It was futile.

One of the female students wrestled another to the ground screaming unpleasantries because another female student had sniggered at an unflattering remark which she had overheard. Scratches took place for any thought of a tattoo. Spats were sporadically erupting with the konnockered set. They weren't happy. Casesix sensed that something was wrong. She approached one of the wounded. That was done only once. That female remembered when she was kneed by Casesix on a previous day and suddenly Casesix was in the foetal position clutching a midriff muffin which had been forcefully kicked.

'Take that, bitch,' said the female, storming off, rearranging her displaced school uniform.

Confusion mounted. Casesix was so concerned with the outbreak of violence – there was a risk that the students would endanger the recruiting program – that she slunk away to a private place – not the toilet this time – where she palmed her knee for contact with Miss Alpine.

'Who the bloody hell is sending me an irritating message?' she screamed.

There was also confusion in the control room, which didn't blend into a nice attitude. It wasn't the appropriate time for pleasantries.

'Miss Alpine, it's Casesix.'

'What do you want?'

'There seems to be trouble with the konnockered students. They're behaving irrationally.'

'There's another batch here too,' she said. 'What are your lot doing?'

'Using physical violence against others. They are supposed to be calm and are anything but.'

'Failure won't be tolerated. You know the risks. Control them.'

Miss Alpine didn't answer to anyone; however, she had to share information with Mr. Avalanche, he being the other controller. She approached him with the news that there were a few issues with the process at Vlad College. He was also well aware of the damaging duo that was thrust in their midst. Both of those students weren't selected, yet somehow managed to infiltrate the college and the control room was in panic because of them. He wasn't impressed.

'Maybe the students at Vlad College are too big a challenge,' he said.

'Nothing is too big to overcome,' said a pride-driven Miss Alpine. 'We must find those two students and rid them from the college. Unfortunately, we cannot track them at present due to the enormous damage they have inflicted on the control room. Mark my words, it won't end happily.'

'Firstly, I think we need to send a messenger to Vlad College to assist Casesix and her group in their endeavours. We cannot let that experiment fail.'

'Hpmh,' said a boiling Miss Alpine. 'Send a messenger for observance purposes. In the meantime, I'll send in the Crisper to eradicate our little problem.'

The confident looking sneer on her face meant that she wasn't up for any form of romance or lip-locking conversation.

'Do you think it wise to send in the Crisper? It might be a step too far.'

Miss Alpine was concerned that the Crisper could be overkill. It was the college assassin. It didn't verbally desecrate the English language with adverbs, adjectives and nouns all in jumbled sentences, nor did it ruin any happy day if it existed; no, it was there to remove any uncooperative konnockered student who didn't conform to the Cluid's ideals. It was the removal of last resort when things actually became nasty. It was now that nasty moment.

Once, long ago, when there was a bad behaviour outbreak elsewhere in the universe where the Cluids had tried to assert total control, the konnockered process had been impaired with a behavioural impurity. The recipients refused to obey any Cluid direction. The planet of choice suddenly became a threat to their safety and continuance. Another location had to be sought; however, they couldn't leave behind any konnockered being if there was any risk of their secret being discovered. It was like a crime scene scenario where the evidence had to be removed to protect the guilty. Those life forms were doomed. The konnockers were turned on and the Crisper silently walked through the life forms tracing each and every one of them. When an active knee was throbbing in colour, the Crisper would approach its carrier with a palm outstretched in the form of a greeting. Its thin, bony fingers presented like a five-fingered fork. That outstretched hand skewered the recipient's hand as if aerating it. Whilst it had hold of that hand, its other hand was firmly placed on the konnockered knee and twisted it like a jar lid. Then it withdrew. The recipient had a sore hand and knee. When they looked to see where they had been touched, their kneecap resembled burnt charcoal with an escaping wispy smoke plume polluting the atmosphere. The knee lost all feelings and the leg joint could never ever again be bent. All recipients walked with a stiff leg thereafter. It wasn't a death sentence, but it definitely ruined that standard of life for those unfortunate to be selected for improvement by the Cluids.

Miss Alpine made her way to a heating pipe that ran diagonally across the floor. They were in a cross-weave pattern to distribute heat evenly. She placed a long, bony finger at the centre of the crossing and tapped impatiently – well, that was the impression it gave. A pinging sound flowed through the underground heating system generating force the further it went. A flush of anxious atoms collected together like besties ready to verbally destroy another group of disliked besties. The sound reached the depth of the inner core of magma that bubbled as the Cluid heat source. A thin, wispy moving mist emerged, representing the thin spirals a smoker leaves after exhaling a puff of unwanted breath. It travelled through the heating pipe system and emerged at the point of where the tapping had originated as a magmatic cloud formation with a smoky trail permanently heading skywards as its means of identification. That smoky wisp trail meant termination. It exuded an intense heat when summoned, rather like a glowing candle. The control room felt hot. The Crisper had materialised. Its eyes were two red-hot magma rocks. Its other discernible feature was an endless hole presumed to be its mouth. It had the ability to form into the shape of its intended targets with those thin, bony hands as its calling card. It was feared by all and was considered indestructible. It rarely spoke. A good listener has certain qualities often not obvious to those who don't listen.

'Crisper, I need you to rid Senora College of two exchange students, known as Davidia and Slirander and if you locate their escorts, them as well,' said Miss Alpine, as the teacher instructing the child.

An economy of dialogue was appreciated by the assassin. Its job wasn't to nursemaid the thoughts of any others. It had a duty. The sooner that began, the worse off it would be for some.

'Hear-me-roar,' it gargled from its mouth full of hot space.

The control room almost overheated. It disappeared into the space from which it had emerged.

'That will be the death of them,' said Miss Alpine.

The betrayal of her emotions was well represented by her yellow, frilly-fringed face. There wasn't a cross word that she could offer. Her mouth was frozen rigid with anger in the shape of two thinly made unlit, cheroot cigars.

Mr. Avalanche shook his head. It was his to shake.

'I hope that Crisper is successful. What about Casesix and the others at Vlad College?'

'I've changed my mind. They can handle it themselves. We have more pressing issues here with this electronic mess and those two impudent intruders who have put us at risk.'

It was difficult sometimes to differentiate as to who was the biggest A.

Would Davidia and Slirander and their escorts survive such a deadly assassin?

Was it possible to be defeated and how?

The questions become more difficult, with the solution becoming more of a shadow.

*

'There's no time to waste,' urged Slirander. 'We must make a move now whilst the system is down. They can't track us until it's repaired and fully functional. There may not be much time. Prepare for wherever we are transported.'

The "triplets" formed their escort stand with Slirander atop in Davidia's hair. Slirander pressed the GTD with a miniature leg. Suddenly, wind eddies and whirling spirals catapulted them through a dark abyss into the atmosphere. Their drop-off point was soon apparent. A desolate, black-rock mountain range emerged below their feet and, plop, they were soon on it. As far as the eye could see it was black misery. The rocky surface was unstable. Davidia kicked a rock in disgust.

'What a damn disappointment! I thought we'd at least see one actual living plant. It's obvious nothing has ever grown here. It's so bleak and uninviting. Mountain ranges are supposed to be beautiful and colourful.'

Davidia was belly-aching at the desolateness and dullness that they now stood on. Their faces flopped with skin-sag at their predicament.

'There must be an entrance somewhere nearby. The GTD wouldn't have given incorrect directions,' said Slirander. 'I assume this place is Cluff, where we wanted to go.'

'It's probably a malfunctioned SatNav system that now doesn't work, based on the control room fiasco,' replied Davidia.

'What do you two think?' Slirander asked the escorts. 'Is this Cluff?'

Their dark lined eyes blended with the landscape. They both

nodded. Were they tired or did they actually know where they were? The group were in the Enta Rockfields, a rockery for new rocks. Davidia felt an urge to release her anger. Normally, a good kicking at something did it, but this time she wanted to throw a rock. She bent over to pluck the lucky recipient amongst the rocks who would soon experience short air travel time and perhaps damage.

'I'll see how far I can throw this little sucker,' she said.

'I wouldn't do that if I were you,' said a dusky, throated voice that a lozenge wouldn't soothe.

'Who's telling me what not to do? I can do what I like,' said a testy Davidia.

'No, you can't. The landscape must remain intact. You could cause an avalanche if you remove us. It hasn't been done before.'

Davidia ignored the protesting voice and selected a palm-sized rock. No one was telling her what not to do. As she touched the rock her fingertips sizzled with pain. She almost had her fingerprints burnt off.

'What the f…' she screamed in agony.

She wrung her hands. The smell of burnt flesh filtered into her nostrils, which had reacted badly. She suddenly puked in agony.

'No, not on us,' shrieked another voice in pain. 'We thought that would never occur again. We're doomed.'

'Don't be such a sook. What is this place?'

'It's a rookery for inert rocks. We are never to move. Our stark environment was bliss before your arrival. Now, with rotted matter washing over us, we'll disintegrate.'

'Don't exaggerate. There's nothing here but a barren landscape. By the look of it, no one would ever want to visit. I'll cross this place off my holiday list.'

'Do not be so hasty in your judgement. Danger doesn't only commence with the letter D.'

Davidia still hadn't located the source of the voice. '*Halp and Foll weren't practising ventriloquists, were they?*'

'Does this place have a name? We're looking for Cluff.'

'You mean, Cliff. There's a whisper that the last visitor that made it to these parts came from New Zealand.'

'I'm not here to be teased. So, it's Cluff. Is it nearby? How do we get there? We were sent here.'

'Not by the Cluids, though. Listen.'

A rumbling sound neared them. Suddenly, a hole in the mountainside burst out of the rock surface exactly where Davidia had been previously ill. It had been weakened at that point. A magma burp was enjoyed by the mountain. It had been a long time between burps. Debris flew like tracer bullets into the atmosphere with white trails straggling behind as if scarring the darkness. There wasn't any danger to anyone this time.

'Wow!' said Davidia. 'What caused that?'

'You did.'

A cylindrical tunnel had been exposed with a gaping hole, beckoning entry.

'Where does this lead to?'

'To Cluff. It's inside the mountain.'

There wasn't any other exit plan available or elsewhere to go.

'What are we waiting for? Let's go,' urged Davidia.

She'd had enough of the blackness. Perhaps the perfectly cylindrical tunnel would be an improvement.

'I don't feel well,' said Halp.

'I feel worse,' said Foll.

'Move it. There is no choice.'

Whilst there was minor hesitation, the opening began to close.

'You two have to unhitch yourselves from me. Three won't go

into that hole. You both understand mathematics about space, shape and size? Well, the square peg won't fit into a round hole and at the moment, that's what we are.'

'It's forbidden to detach,' said Halp.

'It can't be any worse than it already is,' said Davidia. 'Go,' she yelled.

The girls detached with angst. They had never stood alone as an escort. It was a frightening experience for them both. They both stumbled at first, but with Davidia's insistence, they scrambled to the entrance like a wombat down a burrow without the large set of buttocks. Davidia dived and just made it through as the opening closed behind them. She never did locate what had spoken to her on the outside.

The tunnel was large enough for them to stand up and creep downwards. As they descended, the tunnel closed behind them. They were being sealed inside a mountain tomb, buried like the ancient Pharaohs, the major difference being they were still alive.

'Look out behind you. The tunnel is closing quickly. Move!'

The girls hastened their journey. Finally, after a few minutes, they emerged at the entrances to five identical tunnels. There wasn't an electronic device to guide them. For a moment, a puzzle had to be solved. Guesswork was brought in with logical thought. Slirander remembered Miss Alpine's sossurged middle finger and how it was triggered to determine her future demise. An imitation of the bird might be the answer.

'I wonder,' she said, 'try the middle tunnel. The others are dead-end, one-way trips. No returns from them.'

'How would you know?' said Davidia. Had a correct decision been made?

'It's logical. Besides, my aura, small as it may be in a butterfly, is being pulled in that direction. My antennae are also twitching irritably.'

There was no disagreement this time. The intrepid four entered the middle tunnel quite apprehensive about what might greet them. It was pitch-black with Davidia at the forefront and Slirander acting as a miner's light even though it was impossible to see. It was strange that they could walk in the darkened conditions without vision. Somehow, Slirander had endowed each of them unknowingly with the equivalent of night vision goggles without having to wear them.

'How come we can see in the dark?' said Davidia.

It was skill she didn't think she possessed.

'I secreted fluid from a leg gland that washed over your eyes. It's temporary,' said Slirander wondering whether the obvious question would arise. It did.

'You didn't, did you?' asked Davidia, concerned that she had been used as a waste receptacle.

'It's all above board. Can you hear that?'

Slirander diverted their attention elsewhere. They turned away toward a feint sound as they neared the end of the tunnel. The sound grew louder. It was a rhythmical chant, none of which was understood. It sounded like a dirge that would be performed at a funeral. Was it for them?

Halp and Foll acknowledged that they understood the sounds. It beggared belief.

'I understand those sounds,' said Halp. 'It's incredible. I've never been here nor can I remember hearing them before.'

Foll stood sullenly. Her head sagged in sympathy with the sounds. There was no pleasure in them. Loosely translated they said,

Shovel one, shovel two,
Sossarge me, sossarge you,
Push a button, push it true,

It's the end for me and the end for you.

They emerged unscathed from the tunnel, which closed immediately behind them. If that was an escape route, it was no longer available.

The scene before them revealed an assembly line of seated occupants all with a power source plugged into their konnockers. Were they dead, robots or zombies? They didn't possess human form; in fact, they were thin, transparent, water-based torsos full of animated atoms in conflict with each other and in a sossarge-shaped body. They had two pairs of protrusions, replicating arms and legs. Their heads consisted of three shapes in sequence when seated. There was the square head, round head and triangular head. The head shape designated the different tasks each had to perform. This was the electronic pulse of Cluidinine as the assembly line produced electronic equipment for delivery to Senora College.

Between each station, a team of Slugglers and Snooters with their square-backed shells, carefully transported each electronic component. There was no conveyor belt system. The process was delicate and slow. It was a monotonous existence. They were under a central control system high above that oversaw the process. It was tightly monitored.

During the processing hours, the power source kept the seated occupants active. At night, or non-processing time, the occupants slept in cylindrical holes within the walls and were sealed in. There was no power source for any activity. The sossarges' usage was dependent on whether they were plugged into the power source or not. It was like a battery workforce. Nothing was allowed any independent thought. It wasn't possible for Halp and Foll to find and identify any relative who might have any idea of who they might be. It seemed an impossible task.

'It looks like that they are controlled by electricity. Their kon-nockers are like plugs. I wonder if they can escape,' said Davidia, appalled by the imprisonment of so many sossarges.

The girls stood mesmerised by the event in front of them. They couldn't yet see the complete process and how it all worked. That was about to occur.

Slirander fluttered around the large space and landed high on the ceiling. It was exhausting arm flapping and covering a significantly large area. Everything seemed a long distance. Even the school cross-country course was a soda in comparison.

'What are they building? The components must go elsewhere from here,' said Slirander to herself.

Slirander observed that what she thought was a completed product disappear into a hole in the wall. The exit was open and in she flew. To her surprise, there was an identical work-force there, but they were all seated upside down directly underneath their above-seated counterpart, adding the fin-ishing touches. Once it had reached the end of the second line, the final product was sent downwards along another tunnel carried by the Sloggers – that had strong pincers to carry items – deep into the bowels of the earth. Slirander returned to the right side up room, relieved that she didn't have to fly upside down. Back in the central area, the girls were still hidden. She flew toward a large dial which impersonated a clock face, but wasn't. It was an observation and control post which monitored all work performance. It was the spy in the room. If a sossarge didn't perform (malfunction), wouldn't perform (if head shape changed somehow, it would be out of sequence), or lost their time competitiveness, they were eliminated by a mechanical tentacle that plucked them from their seat, disconnected and thrown into the useless pile on the other side of the mountain. Emotion of action was devoid. The sossarge community were obviously only objects of employment when useful, and even less when not.

Slirander flew back to the group.

'What are we doing here?' asked Davidia. 'It's obvious it's a highly technical mechanical workshop. I don't see anything of use.'

'Remember that control can't see or track us, so we should move safely and quickly,' replied Slirander, still trying to fathom what the real purpose of all this high technical equipment represented.

'To where? We are entombed in an underground cave workshop. Yippee! It's hard to see the bright side.'

Before an argument materialised, the two escorts screamed simultaneously. After all, they were twins.

'Our heads are changing shape. We feel awful,' said Halp, on behalf of the set.

It was true that their heads had undergone a sudden shape change. One became a square whilst the other became a triangle. Naturally, they were no longer identical. Davidia and Slirander rubbed their eyes in disbelief.

'Is that you, Halp?' asked Davidia.

'Of course, it bloody well is. Don't you recognise me?'

'Well, you do look slightly different to before.'

'So, would you if someone sat a box on your head.'

'But isn't that your head, the box, I mean.'

'So, friggin' what? Do you want to make an argument? Haven't you ever visited a beautiful square before?'

Davidia had in Rome and Paris, but that's not the square that Halp was referring to.

'It's a nice mathematical shape at least.'

There was no placating Halp's growing anger and disgust. Foll was the less belligerent of the pair, even though her triangular shape gave her a peculiar look as well. There were events happening that neither of them understood.

'Where have my breasts gone?' asked Halp.

They were only modest, but a proud shape to show anyone who glanced her way. Her body became streamlined, and with Foll the same event was occurring. She too was losing that feminine shape. It was a body nightmare. Before Davidia and Slirander's eyes, the escort twins had lost their shapes and were now two fully-formed sossarges like their counterparts, sitting along the assembly line. The only discernible difference was the shape of their heads, but they were still "identical" twins. Their throbbing konnockers could still be seen as a blipping wart on a smooth sossarged body. The twins were horrified with their new, latest look. It wasn't one for the hairdressing salon.

Davidia and Slirander had witnessed a living transformation. It dawned upon them that once inside Cluff, life forms must become exactly what they are.

'What's happening? We're becoming unhappy and scared,' wailed Foll.

It was her turn to express anguish.

No one could see Slirander; she was still invisible. Miraculously, Slirander's spell had run its course and she also changed back into her real self. Cluff had a magical effect on all it touched. Whatever life form entered, it left as it really should be. Davidia wondered what Miss Alpine and Mr. Avalanche would look like if they were here. They'd transform too into their real selves. What could that be?

Slirander was pleased to be herself again. She approached Davidia and gave her an unannounced and invisible hug. Her konnockered knee throbbed as it should have. Davidia felt something touch her. In fright, she performed the "wax on, wax off"

Karate Kid movie arm movement and an automatic knee jerk caught a girl unawares.

'I'm being attacked. Back, back, I say, or you'll get more of the same. I've got a black belt and I'm not referring to the one that matches my latest outfit.'

'It's me, Slirander. I'm myself again. Can you believe it? No more butterflying.'

'That was you, wasn't it? I didn't recognise your movement. It hasn't changed, has it?'

'It is me. This place has changed us back into our real-life forms.'

'I liked me better when I looked like you,' said a tearful Halp.

Halp and Foll now looked like terrific candidates to be a prime beef sossarge on a barbeque plate. They weren't happy at all with their life change form.

'Now that we all are wearing our happy faces, what next?'

'I believe that all products are sent to Senora College as maintenance parts to ensure the smooth technological programs and all other equipment operate at optimum capacity,' said Slirander.

'And how do you know?' queried Davidia.

'In the control room there was a well-used S button and it can only be assumed that's what it meant. Besides, by the size of the products, they appear to be small component parts which have replacement sizes all over them. What we need to do is tamper with a few of them and cause a massive malfunction somewhere.'

'Okay, genius, what's the idea?'

'Replace two of the sossarge seaters with Halp and Foll who are exact replicas of them. They can then rewire a few of the products by reversing the wiring the previous sossarge completed. I'll visit the control room. Be ready when the line stops.'

Slirander went to the control room unseen. She watched the process of what buttons were pushed by someone and noted those that were less touched. Bravely, she pressed the less touched buttons and mayhem erupted. The lines shut down temporarily with enough time for Halp and Foll to sneak up to the assembly line and act as shift replacements. They stood silently behind the two to be replaced. When the line halted, they quickly unhooked the two stunned workers who became inert without their power source from their station and lay them down in their inactive state. They sat down next to each other so that they could make changes by an electronic alteration.

'What changes are we supposed to make? We don't have much time,' said Halp.

Foll was the more experienced techno head and took control.

'That part there is part of their sleep pod station controls. If you move that wire there to there in reverse, that section will wear down quickly overnight and malfunction around half-way through its operation,' said a confident Foll.

'How can we guarantee that it will work?' asked Halp.

'By twisting that wire into a coil, it will slowly unravel, touch the other wires, wear down its outer covering by rubbing bare and the current will be automatically reversed. I learnt that when I was in class. Not many students learnt the negative electronic process. Quickly, overlay that with that. Done. Excellent. Each of the completed units will be delivered by the Wisp Express Line direct to Senora College as replacements.'

'Let's hope our tampering will prove successful.'

Halp and Foll had interfered with four of the component parts. It was time to leave before they were discovered. They replaced the operators, reconnected them and re-joined the girls.

'Well done,' said Davidia. 'We've got to leave before we are discovered.'

The lines suddenly recommenced operations. The controllers weren't any the wiser that product tampering had occurred.

Life resumed as normal after an ordinary operational hiccup. Slirander returned and told them to follow her. They descended into the bowels of the mountain to the ejector area. She had seen where the operation depot was located.

'Those delivery pods are ready for transport. Replace a component with each of us,' said Slirander.

The girls were edging to go. The four female missiles were ready for expulsion from Cluff.

The pods were earmarked for Cleef to transport unwanted sossarge members and not to Senora College as expected.

What a surprise!

A red coloured scarf that appeared as a scrape on the landscape had just missed their departure. Apparently, there was more to their journey than their escape from Cluff.

13 CLEEF

The four pods moved silently through the darkened atmosphere like four miniature scratches across the sky's surface. They were sealed tight and there was no indication as to where they might end up. Their expectations were spiked on one location; however, their journey had taken an unexpected detour. They also had no idea they were being stalked by a deadly adversary.

Each pod was reusable. It was actually the mode of transport between Cluff and Cleef for the transport of the sossarged inhabitants as workers going on a one-way work journey. They never returned. How that was possible for Halp and Foll is the stuff that legends are made of. The entry depot was as busy as a beehive. At the extremity of a cliff face the depot opened to receive and dispatch cargo.

The area of Cleef was a desolate place. Misery, unfortunately, seemed to be the dancing companion of the inhabitants here too. The country of Cluidinine held little joy for anyone. Life was lived in its various formats inside the mountains. The outside was nothing but rock and blackness. Davidia and Slirander had yet to see one living green plant or organism. With the lack of sun and warmth, nothing grew. Maybe, inside Cleef a welcome surprise might greet them.

Whoosh! Thump! Screech! The pods had landed. When opened, the sossarge workers back-flipped in amazement at the two strange movable life forms that emerged. Before any harm could beset the girls, Halp and Foll stepped forward and instinctively performed the greeting salute. Both their middle fingers instantly enlarged. They crossed them and nodded simultaneously, holding them out in front for a greeting touch. Once contact was made, they subsided. It represented peace.

'Where in the hell are we?' said Davidia, as she looked around and couldn't believe she was standing amongst her dad's favourite barbeque items.

She hoped that these didn't sizzle that well. They weren't that appealing as an edible food source. It would possibly be considered cannibalism if she undertook to eat this life form. Ugh! Thankfully, it was only a private thought.

'Halp and Foll seem to know them,' said Slirander, who was now visible.

The pod journey had removed her invisible status. Things had a way of changing back to normal in Cleef, a place that was obviously, not normal.

'Who are these life forms? They look exactly like you two. Do you know them?' Davidia asked Halp and Foll.

Davidia was curious to know where she was and what was staring at her. She was beautiful, but that wasn't the reason she was eye candy for the current masses. They couldn't discern what her shape meant, nor her well-shaped facial features. She and Slirander were the oddities of the day. Nothing else looked quite like them and the sossarge group had never seen a collection of moving items constructed as they were. The two sets of opposites stood staring at each other. This time it wasn't considered rudeness or bad manners. It was a surprise.

'How do we speak to these life forms?' said Davidia.

There was no point staring endlessly at each other, nice as that may seem. At school they had language classes to at least enable the learning process of another language. Halp and Foll instinctively knew what to do once again. It was like their DNA was connected. It probably was. They looked exactly like the other life forms. Once again, but this time all five fingers on the right hand only elongated to an oversized glove mitt. This enabled the fingertip-ends to become an easy touchable size. Halp and Foll approached their counterparts holding out the right hand and engaged in tip-ending by touching each of the five fingers. It was a communication connection.

'We are Halp and Foll, emissaries of Senora College,' said Halp.

'Welcome to Cleef, the source of workers,' said their leader. 'What are those two objects? They are so strange looking and with an unsightly growth on their tops. We've never seen their coverings either. Are they dangerous and what exactly are they?'

'They're harmless and friends of ours, but that's not important. Foll and I are seeking any inhabitant who might know us. We're twins you know.'

'That word is not known to us. This is an incubation and growth colony supplying workers for the Cluids. That is our sole purpose.'

'What about our parents, brothers, sisters and cousins, our family? Surely there must be a descendent of them who can tell us who we really are?'

The leader took a closer look at Halp and Foll. The silly trolley must be in there somewhere. As sure as an egg is an egg, they looked identical to every other life form present. There's nothing different to tell.

'None of those names are known. This is a worker's sossarge colony. We create sossarges for work consumption. There are no other known names here. We work. That's it,' replied the leader. 'Whatever family is, it isn't known.'

Perhaps Halp and Foll had been converted by the characteristics of their human conversion as escorts that they had learnt a sense of belonging?

Davidia and Slirander waited patiently for verbal progress. They weren't too sure what was being said because they couldn't understand the communication.

'Those strange objects are impurities to us. We sense strange bacteria from them. They can't stay here. They must be sent first to Senora College in the next transport and the two pods that they arrived in must be destroyed. Survival is a safety factor.'

*

The processing procedure for the sossarge group was carried out inside a mountainous cavern via a complex series of unseen equipment and base ingredients. The beginning of the life of a sossarge was a hidden and undiscovered secret; so much so, that even the narrator has been denied access to that knowledge.

In the early stages of life-form development, at the pod-popper stage, each new life form is placed in a cylindrical shape for a period of time whilst its outer covering and shape are determined. A series of wall holes hold the new hopefuls on the beginning of their journey for a future productive working life. After their incubation period, they emerge from their cylinders all as identical oblong shapes. Were Halp and Foll really twins or the result of two identical pod sossarges whereby any of them could be twins, triplets, quadruplets and so on up the same family chain? Nobody had different discernible features.

In the next stages the pods pass through a series of addition tunnels with body components being added on the way, such as head, eyes, legs, and so on, until finally they experience the electrical force that enables mobility. All newbies with their fresh set of everything are then placed in pod holders standing upright like a forest of sticks in a field waiting for service. The final addition is the all-important dreadful konnockers added at the last moment to make them fully operational and capable just prior for despatch to Senora College. It is a proud moment when they realise that they have become a proper sossarge capable of good things in service.

*

Halp and Foll withdrew contact and told the girls the details of their conversation. There was no need for any further communication as they had now found their "family connection" for whatever it represented. Their forebears were sossarge workers.

Halp and Foll tip-ended for the last time. It was a sad moment for them to leave the place of their birth. It was unknown why they were selected as escorts because no written records were kept.

'You can't stay here any longer. It's time the two oddities left. They represent danger. I can almost smell it. Do you two want to stay?'

'No thanks. We must fulfil our duties as escorts to the end,' replied Halp. 'Farewell.'

It wasn't that Halp and Foll were ungrateful for the invitation to stay, but they preferred to return to Senora College and hopefully regain their human form shape as escorts which they were far happier with. Nothing was guaranteed.

The four individuals were loaded into the transport pods and gladly sent on their way.

It was a moment of good timing.

*

Suddenly, Cleef had an invasive visitor. The leader could see a red streak heading their way. It was an unusual phenomenon. The colour that dominated their lives was black.

The leader waited patiently. It gradually began to feel as if its skin was tanning and parts of it were turning black. Heat had preceded the red streak. Cleef was experiencing global warming which wasn't man-made. The leader looked around to see many of its fellow sossarges beginning to split and their insides leaking out. It struggled to feel the others skins as they hardened into a stiff covering. They were being fried without an ounce of oil, fire or a nearby barbeque. It was chaotic.

A simmering, volatile mass of red-heated magma had landed. It was Crisper. The heat increased with its anger.

'Where are they?' demanded Crisper.

'Who?' said the leader, barely audible. Its vocal cords were almost fried.

'The students that have escaped from their educational training. Tell me quickly or you will all be blackened and unable to move.' Crisper wasn't into niceties.

All the leader could do was to point a thin, bony finger in the direction where the four pods had been sent. It then fell over as stiff as a board or a badly burnt sossarge, its finger now pointing in a different direction from its prostrate position. There were no more directions to give. Crisper had certainly lived up to its name. It left Cleef in a hurry. The red streak headed in the trajectory of the pods. They were headed for Senora College. Had he waited, there would have been no need for the chase because they had returned to the scene of chaos. It wasn't impressed travelling in a circle. After a while, it naturally lost some of its heat and needed recharging. That effort could have been saved. The sky was full of red anger displaying a most magnificent sunset, if one was to occur in Cluidinine.

The inhabitants of Cleef were left to clean up as if a brawl had erupted at a family barbeque. Many inhabitants were replaced and life went on as normal. Halp's and Foll's relatives would survive in the new batches yet to be produced.

*

Davidia was tightly wrapped in her pod. She never had her doona wrapped so tightly around her at night, nor was that fresh hug she received recently at school from a male cultivating his sensitive side, that tight. She had a moment of reflection without any mirrors. She wondered what would happen next and whether they could manage to escape their re-education at Senora College. It was guaranteed to be a hostile reception when she met Miss Alpine and Mr. Avalanche again. The one thing that she did notice in common with Halp and Foll was those thin, bony fingers. Did they hold a deeper meaning not yet discovered? It was curious though. Time alone allowed the mind either to play tricks on the psychic or clear the mind for rational thoughts.

Halp and Foll pondered over the visit to their relatives and would have to rethink their position once they returned to Senora College. They might be meted out a serious form of justice for failing to stop the girls on their damaging travels. Would they be able to return to human forms? Was it possible to reconnect as a proper escort, or would their konnockered time be hastened to be extremely short? Whatever the actual result, they were pleased to have met "family".

Slirander was planning their escape from Senora College and Cluidinine. She didn't know exactly how that would be achieved, but her sleuthing thoughts needed sharpening if that were to occur. She was unaware what the dangers were ahead, but expected a basketful of nasties. Miss Alpine wasn't the apologetic or excuse-accepting type. Did she need another of her father's spells? It might be a perilous time ahead.

The transportation to Senora College was uneventful.

*

Entry to Senora College cargo depot was guarded closely by abandoned escorts as punishment for failure to carry out their escort duties faithfully and to Miss Alpine's satisfaction. The cargo depot was a permanent prison, only to receive and despatch pods to and from Cluff (parts) and Cleef (sossarges). The inhabitants at the depot had no other contact with any other living Senora College inhabitants.

The four pods arrived simultaneously. Halp and Foll emerged first. They were thought to be two more of the same with no particular skills. They were ushered to one side for movement to their next post. Davidia and Slirander emerged next.

Suddenly, a great 'ooh and ahh' erupted at the unexpected female duo. This was a first. Not ever had anything else been transported this way. It was normally impossible; however, Davidia and Slirander were two girls who didn't understand the meaning of impossible. There were some familiar faces among the greeting crowd.

'Been touring, have we?' asked a tallish, tail-wagging life form with a large, pink tongue lolling about for a good licking.

'Is that you, Randy?' said Davidia, astonished. 'I thought that you'd been terminated.'

'Not quite. This is now home. Say hello, randy,' said Randy.

Both of them barked together. They once again left a wet patch of enjoyment, but this time it was a known. The last time it was a surprise.

'This is my friend, Slirander. We've been visiting a few places not on the College's normal curriculum and now we must return unnoticed. Can you assist?'

Suddenly, the two Bubbles burst forth and wet Slirander with their best mist and made their best sounds. They hovered around her much like a pair of halos. They had shrunk a little, but, other than that, they were still full of bursting air.

'Great to see you again,' said Bubbles. 'We thought that we'd never meet again. Once here, we are isolated from everything except pod despatch and delivery. It was much more fun being an escort.'

'Thanks. We are in quite a hurry. We've upset Miss Alpine and made a mess of their control room. They don't know where we are. Can you keep a secret?'

The escorts' "retreat" hadn't had this much excitement since they ceased being escorts. They were given an extra responsibility by two strange life forms who had treated them well. A favour deserves a favour returned.

'What is the secret?'

'If I told you, it wouldn't be a secret anymore; however, tell no one where we have gone if you are questioned. We are trying to change the educational programs of the college,' said Slirander, 'where everybody receives fair treatment. No more escorting, living in singular spaces and breathing life into the planet.'

It sounded like a manifesto of good, but their achievements may fall well short.

'Does this mean we no longer have to despatch pods and can do the normal things our life forms are supposed to do?'

Davidia and Slirander gave them the nod of confidence. It was, 'Yes' all around.

'The two sossarges, Halp and Foll, are our escorts and need to come with us to avoid suspicion that we have been detached,' said Davidia. 'Slirander needs a new set of escorts, which we hope to attract when we return.'

'How will we know if you are successful?'

'You will know. That's all. How do we get to Senora College from here unseen?'

'That's easy. Stand over there in that wall space, cross your arms and shut your eyes.'

The foursome did so. A strange light enveloped them. A moment or two later they were returned to their individual spaces. Had they been tricked? Davidia and Slirander were alone again. No escorts could be seen. Were they trapped? Davidia walked around her space toward the walls, but nothing happened. Slirander did exactly the same with an identical result. For a moment, confusion reigned. It was short-lived. Davidia walked toward the west wall, whilst Slirander walked toward the east wall and before any exclamation of surprise, they met each other. The electronic wall spaces had disappeared except for the appearance of the four walls believed to be impregnable. Was it an optical illusion or delusion? There was no written explanation. Had their control room tampering rendered useless the spaces in which students lived? The blank looks of surprise on the girl's faces said it all, duh?

'We aren't imprisoned any more,' said Davidia. 'Does this mean that we can move freely throughout the complex without discovery?'

'It seems so, doesn't it? That control room fiasco has certainly eased restrictions on our movements. We don't know how long that will last. I wonder if we can regain entry into the control room unseen. Maybe we should send Halp and Foll in their new form pretending they are lost or have been misplaced? I'm not sure what's next,' said a pensive Slirander.

The girls were still unaware that they were being trailed. Whilst thinking of their next move, a howling wind sound entered the corridor outside their spaces. It was feint at first and gradually grew louder. They were sure it was an upset breeze. The girls froze like icebergs not ready to be cast adrift from their ice-shelf. The sound changed meaning the closer it came toward them. It wasn't a happy sound. It reminded them of a sore loser on the sports ground.

'Those exchange students are finished. They will be rid of the college when they are located. Their rudeness, nastiness, insubordination and lack of manners will be quashed like an insect under a bulldozer. How dare they infect my college with their mental disease of intelligence? I've never suffered such obstinacy before. I don't like it, nor will it be tolerated. Why does my head hurt? They have caused me intolerable migraines. Get out of my way,' she said to the void, as an obviously mumbling, hyped-up, upset Miss Alpine, who acted as if she was experiencing a mid-life crisis. If she was, it was a bummer.

The girls waited for a moment and then ducked outside their spaces to see Miss Alpine's form diminish into the distance. Halp and Foll didn't immediately attach this time as escorts to Davidia and they didn't change form into two twin, human, female sisters. They stayed as they were, surprising themselves. Their automatic change into the form they were as escorts was absent. Something had changed; however, they were to act as escorts in their real form. The girls discreetly followed. In her cross-worded angry state, Miss Alpine didn't notice or didn't care at that stage. She had another fish to fry and this was also an intimidatory action. The girls followed until Miss Alpine disappeared into a small sanctuary space. It was her special hidden space. Davidia and Slirander and the two escorts crept along the floor like four Ninjas without a sound between them. Following a set of someone else's buttocks could lead to an imaginary encounter. Miss Alpine had unintentionally left a gap in the door space, so the girls were able to peer in. She wasn't expecting company. Tension was on the menu, not as an entrée but as the main meal, causing heartbeats to slow down. The sound thumped through their bodies as if they were hollow echo chambers. Miss Alpine began to undress. Her over-garments were removed first. The girls were wondering whether it was impolite to observe another of their gender undress in front of them, especially one that appeared to be an older-aged individual; but amongst their own age group, nah, that thought was not followed. They didn't know how far this would go. What should they do? That was answered almost immediately, nothing. Miss Alpine had only taken off the over-garment. Whew! It was relief all around. She raised her arm directly above her head as if to admire the cleanliness of her most recent hair removalist maintenance. Davidia noticed the rounded tattoo that she had also seen on Mr. Avalanche in exactly the same position.

She whispered to Slirander, 'I've seen that before. It's been expertly applied. I don't know what it means. Mr. Avalanche has one too.'

'Maybe she's embarrassed about her body art being seen. She is a teacher and sets an example to students to follow,' replied a whispering Slirander.

Before they had time to speculate and create a rumour, like they might have at school, Miss Alpine had finished patting her armpit and lowered her arm by her side. She then placed a hand under her armpit and produced an armpit fart. The sound was irrelevant. The result was surprising. Before their very eyes – both sets now as large as satellite dishes – a station, a tram, tramlines and a human-form student appeared out of nowhere. The tram sign said "Vermont". The girls were stunned. Had they suffered an electric shock?

'Did you see that?' asked Davidia.

She rubbed her eyes, blinked, rubbed again and stared.

Slirander nodded. She was more into close observance.

Miss Alpine strode forward to the student and whispered a few brief instructions before she boarded the tram. It departed and the whole scene before them disappeared as if it was make-believe. The yellow-fringed look on Miss Alpine's face said it all. She had dispensed an anger management episode that Vlad College was to experience, especially Caseone to Casesix. It was time for further removals. The unsatisfactory evidence bag of failures was being mopped up. Miss Alpine allowed herself a sneer, the equivalence of a Cluid smile.

'That's how we leave Hildsbridgeburg,' said Davidia. 'There doesn't seem to be any other way that we've discovered so far.'

'You may be right,' said Slirander, who thought that Vlad College might be in danger.

The student sent had its konnocker impregnated with the removal element, with a live exposure of one day before that expired.

'We better leave before we are noticed,' said Davidia.

The group retreated to what they thought was their space; however, a surprise lay in store for them. What was it?

*

The despatch depot was still fussing about the excitement of having met their previous escorted subjects when the dull, grey misery of their environment suddenly brightened, but not for good. The red flash Crisper had arrived. Fortunately for the life forms, the journey it had undertaken had exhausted a supply of its red-hot heated material and instead of frying them to a crisp, reddened their bodies to a sauce red only; yet they survived. It was a day of firsts for the life forms. Was it going to get any better?

Crisper cast a red-hot eye around the hopeless life forms before him. Randy wasn't wagging his tail and randy certainly wasn't wagging his either. Bubbles began evaporate. The other life forms began to imitate red capsicums and faded beetroot. Even the sky had a shepherd's pie hue; however, the weather pattern wasn't about to improve. Crisper raised a thin, bony hand which dribbled with heat creating red rock welts on the ground's surface.

'Where are they?' growled Crisper, whilst hissing heat.

'To whom may you be referring?' replied Randy, who was the polite conversationalist.

'Those two students and their escorts. I demand to know where they are.'

'They aren't here,' said Randy, whose tail began to stiffen.

His hairy covering was being singed. He didn't relish the thought of appearing on the menu of some Asian countries, if he knew what they were.

'I'll ask once more. If you don't give me the answer I need, your usage will cease. Now, where are they?' demanded a real hothead.

Crisper raised both arms outwards from its body ready to swathe them through the atmosphere and obliterate the despatch depot's former escorts. Fear emanated from each life form present. It might not seem to be much of an existence, but it was still an existence. Randy's throat felt like a fire had been lit. He attempted a response which sounded like a weak yelp. No one else was offering any verbalism. They were all too afraid.

'They have been sent to Senora College to resume their education,' said a shrill Randy.

His eyes showed that if he could bite Crisper, he would; however, he thought it nicer to have friends.

'Not again. Each time I close in on them, they manage to elude me. This is exhausting. They are back where I started this journey. I'm not happy. Travelling in a circle is unpleasant and a waste of time and energy. Ugh! It won't be long now.'

Crisper, as an assassin, always had to demonstrate unpleasantness, display no fear and lord it over his domain as an aggressor, so before he left, he swathed his arms through the atmosphere and gave the former escorts a series of burns as a reminder never to cross it again. Their faces represented squashed strawberries. Their bodies were scarred with unsightly red, bumpy welts like body acne. It was a let-off. Randy was sad that he couldn't warn the girls of their impending fry-up.

Crisper left.

Would it be successful in frying the girls?

14   CLEAN UP

'Those students like require like detention,' said an agitated Miss Green. 'They have been like deliberately disruptive creating like unpleasant learning experiences for their like classes. The principal like needs to be made like aware.'

Miss Green was quite tetchy, having to attempt to impart the importance of educational literature to a few who had no particular interest in learning at all. The students in question had been konnockered by Casesix and friends. They had become the class disturbers and the whole room operated in a non-harmonious manner. Even their language had a cesspool quality about it. It was extraordinary that students knew this style of speech. It might be news to the teachers, but not to the students.

'Why am I here?' questioned a knee-throbbing male whose green knee was thought to be winking at an orange knee nearby.

'To be educated and like take a place in like society as a like useful and intelligent like member of the community,' said Miss Green.

'It's so tedious collecting all this so-called future knowledge. Isn't there an app for it?'

'It's called time,' replied Miss Green.

A female with an orange throbbing knee suddenly stood up and swore.

'That bitch there, the one with the implants, touched me where she shouldn't have,' she lied.

'I didn't know anything was off-line,' said the male. His smile was creepy.

'As for you, if you're not careful, the school will know about late after-sports training and what you really do to work up a false sweat.'

Threats began to seep across the room. It was obvious that the tenure of conversation was heading below naval height. Miss Green had to arrest the situation and restore a modicum of good manners. Students are often influenced by their peers and today wasn't a good example.

'You two, out! Principal Jones needs to have a discussion,' said Miss Green, in plain speak, without liking every third word.

It was a day of shocks and contrasts, bad language and attitude from some tempered by the enhanced speech from others. Was Miss Green cured? It certainly seemed so? The students were escorted to the main office and told to wait for the principal. They couldn't have cared less where they were. They could fill seated space anywhere. Miss Green returned to her class and the behaviour from those remaining had improved considerably.

Casesix was fully aware now of the inoperable success of the konnocker program. That behaviour wasn't part of her program of recruiting students. Perhaps they might need medical treatment? If that occurred, the konnocker would be unexplainable. Something must have been tampered with, incorrectly programmed, or eaten a virus. Was she and her fellow students at risk? That night, Casesix decided to contact Miss Alpine for direction.

'You two again,' said Principal Jones. 'In the past few days, your impeccable school record had been blotted by these bouts of unexplainable rebellion. Do you have any explanation?'

Principal Jones was worried that the name of Vlad College as an educational institution would be brought into disrepute by the actions of a few. Indiscretions had to be kept in-house. Could he discover the base of the problem? As he stood there wondering what action deemed to be appropriate, he glanced down at what he thought he saw were two flickering lights. The female thought he was being offensive. The male wasn't sure.

'Watch ya perving at, Principal? I could have you arrested for sexual harassment,' said the female.

The male stared back.

'What are those green and orange winkers on your knees? You each have one.'

'You ain't touching mine,' said the female, emanating aggression.

'It's odd that they flash. Have you both hurt yourself recently? You both have a sightly enlarged kneecap. What happened to them? They are rather unsightly. Is it a medical condition?'

Principal Jones was showing genuine concern, not that it was understood.

'Mind your own business. It's my new trick to latch onto the guys,' the female continued. 'You're too old for me. You could be my grandfather.'

'Wait here.'

Principal Jones visited the medical section.

'There are two students with the most peculiar knees,' he said to the attendant. 'One flashes green, the other orange.'

The medical staffer recognised the issue. It had been inspected before with no outcome of what they were.

'Principal, they have both been examined and I cannot offer any conclusion. They resemble giant warts, don't they?'

'Yes. It's peculiar, really. It's the first time I've ever encountered such an oddity. Do you think anyone could give a proper prognosis? I feel there's more to it than a Christmas light display.'

Both staff stood still momentarily in a pool of muddled thought, or was it a gigantic lake?

*

Slirander felt the beginnings of a toothache and pressed her communication molar to her father, to ease the pain. It was a psychological pain, which told her that she needed to warn the students at Vlad College that a catastrophe was arriving by tram. She couldn't personally be in attendance and had no idea how or what any plan had been sent by Miss Alpine with the lone student, female, of course. Her father responded.

'Slirander, it's been a few days since our last contact. Are you two safe?' asked Rotan.

He missed his daughter. He'd say the same about Davidia, but he wasn't her parent.

'A student has been despatched from here via tram to school. Something terrible is going to happen and we don't know what it is. Can you meet the student at the tram stop and divert whatever the action is? It's important. I fear for the new exchange students. They are in the barrel for an unpleasant roll,' explained Slirander.

'How will I recognise this student? There would be so many there that I could be accused of stalking someone, or, even worse, be falsely accused of approachment. It's a difficult protectionist legal framework that schools must surround themselves with these days. I'll take Rolet and make it a look like a parent visit pretending to search for our daughter, who we believe had caught that very tram and had not been seen since. That might disguise the truth.'

'She will be wearing a longer dress than normal, have a yellow tinge around her face and her hands will look thin, bony and aged. You can't miss her. She looks sixteen. If looks could kill, she'd make the front cover of Time magazine as a serial killer. She's wearing our school uniform. Under her dress are two, yes, two, konnockers that have a decimating message. It's not written, it's transferred by a knees-up double prong attack in a knee pincer movement. We don't know the reaction it will generate.'

'Is this part of your education at your new school? It's a rather peculiar outcome of learning new skills. How will this help you pass your exams?'

'It won't. There's much to explain, but not now. Find that student. Give her a hamburger, drink or something to attract her attention, but do it now. Time is running out.'

'How's Davidia? Is she coping well?'

'She's as well as can be expected. There are six exchange students. You already know one of them. Keep her under observation in case she's approached. All six are in danger. Bye.'

Rotan quickly contacted Rolet.

'Meet me at the Vermont tram stop. We have someone to meet. Hurry.'

Rolet was rather relaxed about rushing anywhere. Time evaporated and passed regardless of the speed people anticipate hurrying will do. Saving time is only a saying. It actually can't be saved for reuse later on. She did wonder, though, what was anxious about meeting a tram. It wasn't a heritage design. They'd gone long ago. Who was she to meet? Slirander had been away a while and her current replacement had proven to be quite abrasive at times. Youth develops its own behavioural patterns and when Rolet remembered her own youth, she nodded and said, 'Yes, I've met that girl before.'

Rotan and Rolet arrived at the tram stop. It was empty. There wasn't any villainous youth loitering for destruction of the safety glass, just a single young girl thumbing a smart phone emanating words of wisdom. Rotan and Rolet approached her, smiling.

'Hello, there,' said Rolet.

Female to female contact produced a greater non-confrontational comfort zone between parties. The young female looked up and feigned disinterest. Her phone was more important.

She didn't respond. Meeting strangers can make one wary.

She flipped her long hair around her face as camouflage, yet she wasn't coming out of prison or being interviewed by the press. Rolet persisted.

'Hello, there. Have you just arrived by tram? Are you waiting for someone?'

The young girl peered from beneath her head blanket. They looked harmless.

'No. I'm waiting for the next tram to arrive.'

'Has any other tram passed through during the past ten minutes?'

'There was one,' she said, 'it was weird. It came from the opposite direction and there are no tram tracks. I'm texting my friend who believes in aliens. She'll understand it better than me. The really strange thing is that only one schoolgirl got off. There were no others. She went that way.'

The young girl pointed in the direction of Vlad College. Rotan and Rolet headed off in hot pursuit. They even developed a jog. It reminded them of their youth when both competed at school for various athletic prizes and, instead, won each other. The cement footpath was littered with elevated ruts intent on tripping an unwary user. Tall gums had elevated the pathway as they explored the moisture highway via their roots. The undulations made footholds quite tenuous when a puddle had pooled as a committee gathering of raindrops. This time the committee system worked a treat. Splash! And pooling had to be done all over again. Imagine the overtime.

In the distance, they gradually caught up to a single schoolgirl wearing a long dress, exactly as Slirander had described it. They pulled alongside and glanced at her. She was well-proportioned for a sixteen-year-old. Her shoes and legs, that could be seen, appeared normal. Her face was a pallid grey and not a fringed yellow lily as thought. She had focus. She never paid them any attention. Each step was perfectly proportioned, identical in every movement.

Rotan accidentally bumped her as he and Rolet accelerated in front of her. It wasn't a marathon but a short sprint. The surprise movement moved her sideways, but her feet never missed a beat, as if adhered to the footpath's surface. That was noticeably odd. Rotan stopped. He turned around and faced her as she neared.

'My apologies,' he said, politely. 'The path is so skinny I missed allowing sufficient space to pass safely.'

He waited for a moment. The girl stopped. He was in her direct path.

'Sorry, I was deep in thought. It's a cavern in there.'

'Are you returning to Vlad College after a late lunch?'

'Not really. I haven't been well and have missed a few days from school. I have to make up some classes and, unfortunately, my tram was later than I thought, so I'm still walking.'

'My name is Rotan and this is my wife, Rolet. Our daughter attends Vlad College. Her name is Slirander. Do you know her?'

The eyelids thinned into a periscope mirror, the face began to tint yellow and, fortunately for the parents, the shock that appeared on her face wasn't meant to be viewed. Her body tensed slightly.

'Brrr! It's chilly here. I'm sorry I don't know the name as I've recently transferred from another school. I'm relatively new here.'

She was aware of the name and its damaging companion, Davidia. She had been briefed by Miss Alpine before departure about the troublesome exchange students; however, she was trained not to react poorly to surprises.

'Vlad College is nearby. Can we join you for the last part of your journey?'

There was no response, just silence.

The distance took five minutes. Rotan held out a hand for a

courteous handshake as good manners require, but was ignored. He noted that her hands were awfully thin. They parted at the school gate. It didn't oppose entry. The thin, wire-braced fence dotted with a rust collection along the top of it, designated the school boundary into two parts, inside for education, outside for public usage.

The young lady didn't look back. Her mission was inside the school premises.

'What do you think?' said Rotan, as his gaze followed the young girl.

'She was rather cold, though trying not to be. We didn't make a friend there. I'm not sure that the day will end well. It's just a feeling I have,' said Rolet, as she too gazed after the student.

The day will bear out a result, but the outcome was unknown.

*

Davidia and Slirander wondered what was next on the agenda; escape, destruction or being lost. They didn't have to wait too long.

'Where have Halp and Foll disappeared to?' asked Davidia, feeling vulnerable without her escorts. She was becoming accustomed to them being nearby.

'They were here moments ago,' said Slirander.

She knew that they wouldn't desert them without a good reason.

The area that they thought was their space was actually a rectangle of mathematical lines criss-crossing a floor in evenly numbered squares. Was it a chess board, scrabble platform or an intriguing domino surface drafted to confuse? It didn't make any sense. The girls were actually on one side of the space and there was nothing that they could see on the other side. Suddenly, the area began to reduce and they felt buffeted by an invisible feeling, like two big airbags putting on the squeeze. The last time anyone tried to put the squeeze on Davidia, it was one of her classmates at school, intimating she couldn't afford lunch. After a verbal "guilt trip" beat-up – your parents are wealthy and so on – Davidia finally caved in. She passed over her lunch money, only to find out later on that it had been used to purchase cigarettes, which was shared with a male of interest to her. She wasn't a lemon and didn't like being squeezed. At least she found out her emotional interest smoked, which she wasn't aware of before. Was it lunch money well spent? It was a good thing she didn't hand over her credit card.

'What's happening?'

'We are being silently pushed toward that square for some reason,' replied Slirander.

She was thinking of calculus, trigonometry or algebraic equations to understand why? It wasn't a flat Rubik's cube, was it? Dimensions had become distorted in Senora College. Whilst they were being pushed closer together, there appeared on the other side of the square, the other four Vlad College exchange students with Halp and Foll, who had gone off in search of them. Everyone waved at each other. It was a moment of pleasure in dim-lit land.

Suddenly, the girls weren't being pushed anymore; however, they were trapped and didn't know it. The only way out was to cross over the squared floor to the other side. Davidia took the first step onto a square. It reacted like jelly as her foot submerged below floor level. She quickly extracted it and incredibly it was all still there. Slirander did the same with an identical result.

'We can't cross it. We're trapped,' wailed Davidia.

Instead of creating a scene, Slirander went through her mind into her father's Spellabook to see if there was a spell to show them the way out of their predicament. Alas, there was no such spell. The girls were lost for reason. In anger, Davidia screamed in anguish.

'Bastards!'

A first line of floor squares immediately changed colour to blue. Davidia tentatively stood on it with a foot and it remained solid. There were eight lines of squares to cross. She tried to stand on line two. It wobbled to the touch like slow moving molasses. *I wonder,* she thought.

'Shit, I can't cross that,' was her second comment of dissatisfaction, upset at being caught in a trap.

Once again, the second line of floor squares changed colour to brown, representing the colour of the word mentioned. An idea dawned upon them. Each time they said a cross word, a line of squares solidified into a different colour.

'Maggot,' called out Slirander. It was her turn.

The third line of squares changed to white in theme with the aforementioned word.

'Crap.'

The fourth line of squares changed to light brown as a previous comment had already soaked up that darker colour.

'Bitch.'

The fifth line of squares changed to red, representing a crimson complexion a female's complexion may change to when called by that word. It was usually venomously said, hence the colour accompaniment.

'Bugger.'

The sixth line of squares changed to yellow as it was a word of frustration and increased the anxiety level of the speaker.

'Cretin.'

The seventh line of squares changed to green as it can be

associated with making people sick by merely calling them such an offensive word.

'Arsehole.'

The last line of squares changed to black, blending in with the local colour scheme of Senora College, the environment and how the girls felt about their visit.

They safely managed to negotiate their way across the rainbow squares by use of cross words not normally popular in their vocabulary. To know and think is different than to think and say.

It was a crossword of cross words.

Once they had negotiated their crossing safely, there were hugs all around, even though each set of two hadn't met the other sets before. Halp and Foll were hugged by all.

'We need to leave this place and return home,' said Davidia.

'How? We've no idea,' said one of the older students.

'We think there is a way; however, we must remain together so we leave together.'

'Who put you in charge?' said the oldest male student, who felt he had right of management being the senior student.

Davidia thought carefully before answering.

'Listen, pal, we've experienced what this lot here have in store for all of us: enslavement. Now you can whinge and carry on all you like, but we're leaving here and we know of a possible way out. You can stay and disappear if you want to never see Vlad College or family again. It's not my choice. This is a dangerous place. Ask Halp and Foll, who, by the way, are my escorts. If you have a better plan than the one we don't have, let's hear it.'

That confused the senior student, who had the sense to realise that the junior grades at school certainly had some feisty personalities. He didn't have a plan either, so it was a stalemate for the moment.

'Where are your escorts?' said Slirander. 'Have they abandoned you?'

'We've never had any. We haven't left our spaces since we've been here. Those two sossarges are the first escorts we've seen. They aren't edible, are they?'

Halp and Foll smiled. A meal indeed! Perhaps there's more to education than looks. Before they engaged in a deep and meaningful discussion, a rushing sound was heard from along the corridor. A hot wind blast was heading their way. Hot air was its introduction.

'Slirander, do you remember the map of the college? We need to find a safe space. Something is stalking us. It's a feeling. I'm not sure what it means. If we decoy from the others, it might be easier. Halp and Foll, take the students to another space. We are heading toward the special sleeping building of the Cluids. Why, I don't know; however, it seems to be appropriate. We might be safer there. Slirander, you need to guide us. Quickly, it's getting hot in here.'

Slirander wasn't pleased at the anxiety her friend was creating. Pressure had a way of backfiring on good intentions. Then, she remembered that she still had the GTD in her pocket where she had placed it for security once she returned to girl form. What a bonus! She took it out and it was still operational. She palmed it by pressing a button and simultaneously thought of the Cluid sleeping quarters. The link between thoughts and the GTD enabled directions to wherever it was she wanted to go. It was thought controlled. She had to link arms with Davidia so they could be transported as "one". Before she knew it, they were on their way. The instantaneous heat they had experienced a moment ago was gone and a cool atmosphere had replaced it.

Halp and Foll secreted the other students safely in another space, just in time, whilst the girls headed toward the sleeping building without knowing why or if they were being followed. Emotions can flag an array of directions and sometimes it can be quite confusing which course to take. There was the time when Slirander had met another student at school and they discussed architecture and origami. It was the crossing of two fertile minds. She was pulled toward origami based on the doe eyes of encouragement of the fellow student; however, she chose the more practical course of architecture as it seemed to offer better longer-term employment and career prospects. It was purely a practical decision and not one based on emotional feelings. Mmm!

The chef of their next course on the survival menu had arrived, agitated and fuming, seeking its ingredients for desecration. Crisper halted in the corridor. It sniffed the air, spat out a few chunks of red-hot lava, which sizzled on the floor, and scanned the area with its fireball eyes.

'Where are they? This isn't a game of tag. It's war.'

Once again, some of its power had diminished in the chase. Its unhappiness was clearly visibly expressed by constantly missing its quarry by whatever margin. This time there was no one available to threaten or provide details of where they had gone. Had its quest ended? That was most unlikely.

*

Rotan approached Principal Jones, who had just dispensed with the two aggressive students with the winking knees. They had returned to their classroom to engage in mind pursuits. Their behaviour wasn't controllable as deaf ears do not want to hear what is said. Trouble may brew with a growth in anger. It was a waiting game.

'Principal Jones, it's Rotan, Slirander's dad.'

'Yes. What can I do for you?'

'I think you may have a new problem that has arrived at the school some minutes ago.'

'This place is full of problems. What's a few more,' he said, feeling exasperated.

'This one is deadly serious, with the emphasis on dead.'

'Is there some sort of threat? Is that what you mean?'

'I met a young female student outside the main gate not long ago and she has been sent here to eradicate six of your students, those new exchange students.'

'Preposterous. It's unheard of. There aren't any assassins in my school and you say a young female student. I don't believe you. What proof do you have? This is idiotic.'

Principal Jones took it as a personal affront that someone would suggest that his school was unsafe and its safety record challenged. It wasn't America. His heart rate pulsated erratically. He wasn't preparing for a stroke, was he? He blustered and stalked his office space as he digested the comments. Unbelievable. Was Rotan a crank, an annoying parent, or was there some truth in what he had said? His day was worsening. Firstly, there were those knee-winking students and now a man relaying serious threats. There was only one option if he believed Rotan.

'How do you know of this threat?'

'My daughter, Slirander, told me. She contacted me from Senora College and warned me.'

'How is she enjoying her premier education?'

'Let's say it isn't as good as here. She has expressed interest to return home. Premier education as presented has created a few obstacles for her and Davidia and now they wish to return as do all the exchange students. It wasn't such a successful experiment.'

'You mean they prefer being educated here? That's terrific. I'll summon all the exchange students to my office immediately and sort out any nuances.'

Principal Jones used the school intercommunication system, requesting all exchange students from Senora College to attend his office immediately.

Caseone to Casesix were surprised to be called up. They hadn't transgressed into bad behaviour or caused any misdemeanours, so why were they summoned? There were seven students who became available, which was a surprise. It didn't matter to the seventh student that she would be discovered. Her mission was the only thing of importance. Sacrifices have to be made, but not by those in command. She was prepared for her one-way trip. There was no return ticket.

The students were identical in their youthfulness, uniforms, hairstyles and height. There were three male and four female in attendance, but wait, weren't there only six original exchange students and not seven. Principal Jones knew his mathematics was excellent and there were seven in attendance. How did that happen? Rotan eyed the girls suspiciously and recognised the student that he had met in the street. He was about to say something when Principal Jones took over. He was, after all, the principal.

'It has been brought to my attention that the cheese isn't as tasty as it should be. There is also a bad taste happening and it's not being shared, or is it that there is a dangerous intruder amongst us? You all look so innocent.'

Principal Jones had difficulty confronting a serious situation with simple straightforward dialogue. Casesix recognised the threat comment only too clearly. Before any other student reacted, she was beset upon by a frantic, knee-high, double-legged kicking student who knocked her to the floor. She tried to double-prong Casesix's konnockered knee by trapping it between her own set and set off the pre-programmed chain reaction to termination that would ensue, if successful; however, Casesix had observed other female students in the schoolyard and learnt how they protected themselves if an unsavoury advance was made. She swung a leg into the midriff of the assailant who was stopped momentarily, but her anger and aggression didn't abate. She rolled over and tried again. If it wasn't such a deadly attack, it could be misinterpreted that one of them was pretending to be a male in a compromising position.

Rotan knew a thing or two about unruly daughters. He stepped in and dragged her off Casesix, who hadn't been damaged. A yellow-tinged face full of fury and rage spluttered obscenities at him. Apparently, Senora College students had access to a dictionary as well.

He grappled with her. It was like trying to hold an elusive seal. Her thin, bony hands scratched his legs, leaving red welt lines like tracer bullets heading toward his knees. He didn't have any konnockers to be tampered with. Suddenly, all her clothes fell off. She was stark naked, yet in a pleasant way. Her body had reverted to the shape of a sossarge where all her female attributes had slid south into a smooth cylindrical shape with no discernible features that a normal female possessed. She had two winking lights at knee level that were to decimate her fellow students. Suddenly, they both shot forward simultaneously headed once again at Casesix. She certainly was the target of some aggressive and unpleasant behaviour. It wasn't revenge or a spat over the best sauce to be shared with was it? No, she had been specifically targeted. One of the other male students nearby who had seen the art of cricket played during a recess, swung an arm in a flat bat style and smote both winking lights back at the sender. They hit with such force, her skin was penetrated and she began to leak her life substance. The agony etched on that face was impossible to describe, but it was a ferocious end to a deadly assassin.

Principal Jones had beads of sweat swamping his usually crystal-clear forehead. Casesix and friends were relieved that they hadn't been terminated and Rotan was pleased and exonerated at handling what became a naked girl sossarge. A last light zap flashed between the winking lights as they faded having sent their last message.

Miss Alpine was buzzed. She felt the impact of the loss. Her anger was gradually developing into an obsession. How could her student fail her? It should have been impossible to defeat it. The humans are a formidable but not an undefeatable force. She still had six to eradicate; however, the pleasure of those two girls would be satisfaction enough. Her thoughts weren't printable, they would create paper burn. Her world had been seriously tampered with and rectification needed application. Her mind hurt. That pain needed to be transferred elsewhere. She thought that Crisper should have more success, after all, it was the premier assassin.

15 RISK

The control room, which had caused the major blackout and lack of observation throughout Senora College, blipped back into life once again. The panel was fully-lit with coloured lights cascading over its surface in a symphonic light display. Miss Alpine eagerly sought the pair of damaging students who had caused her a massive hiccup. Now where are their tracker lights? It took but a moment before her eagle eyes sighted the blipping pair.

'So that's where they are,' she said, slyly, 'and where are those imbecilic escorts that were entrusted with attachment and surveillance?'

Another moment passed and they were also located. She nodded slowly. Her neck muscles weren't in need of a workout; however, they were synchronised with her thought patterns. Remedial action was always instantly dealt with, but for some inexplicable reason wasn't meted out this time. She thought that she needed those escorts to be reattached to Davidia, with a fresh set for her fellow student, Slirander. That way, there was no chance of fouling their assignment. She was giving Halp and Foll another chance as she had no idea what had been happening whilst the tracking system was stuffed. Caution isn't a dirty word, yet to tread carefully is a recipe slowly followed and eventually a slow cooked meal will appear.

'What have they been up to in the darkness since I lost track of them?'

*

Halp and Foll had located a safe space that they considered secure. Mr. Avalanche wouldn't find them there, so they thought. It was too dangerous for all of them to remain together so Halp and Foll instigated a plan. It was up to Mr. Avalanche to seek them out. Miss Alpine didn't always do the dirty work. It was a shared responsibility.

'We can't stay with you,' said Halp, with a hint of agitation.

'Are you abandoning us? We have no idea where we are,' replied the senior male student. It was his time to shine.

'No. We will be located by Mr. Avalanche, who might deal unpleasantly with us. We are supposed to be attached to Davidia as her escorts. We have broken the rules. That usually means the end for us. It is better we spare you that ghastly moment. Stay here. You should be safe. We must follow Davidia and resolve a few issues. She might need our help. Do we look like twins to you?'

'Identical,' said the male student, who was aware flattery goes a long way and the two female sossarges needed a dose of pick-me-up right now. They were risking their lives to join Davidia as part of the "triplets".

'That's settled, then. Take this and do not lose it as if your life depended upon it. Without it we won't be able to find you again.'

Halp handed over a mini receiver purloined from Cluff amongst all the electronic equipment. Its signal could only be transmitted to Halp, so if termination was her fate, so it would be for the four older exchange students. These were dark and strenuous times.

Halp pressed the GTD device and they were on their way to meet, was it Davida, Slirander, Miss Alpine or their maker? The sleeping quarters of the Cluids was their destination, a place they had never seen before. It had the feel of a thrill, the chase on a GP motorbike and the trepidation of doom. Whatever it was, they felt alive. Bring it on!

They had also inadvertently signalled to Crisper that they were on the move. It had felt the vibrations activated by their GTD device.

'So, that's where you are heading,' said Crisper, still spitting out molten rock, albeit in far smaller pieces.

Its throat burnt badly with all the conversation it espoused. It was time to end the chase and return deep underground to be reheated and reinvigorated in a magma sauna. Even the baddies need to feel good sometimes. At last, it felt near the end of its journey. It wasn't a failure. By proving how bad it was, allowed it to continue in full employment. Whoosh and it was on its way.

Miss Alpine watched from the control room the meeting of the blipping lights. There were two girls, two escorts and one evil assassin. It was to be one mess she could be proud of. To rid Senora College of two impudent female students and their two untrustworthy, in her eyes, escorts, who deserved no better than a short life span, would be a satisfactory achievement. Her face said it all. It was time to revel in being nasty. It was show time.

*

'What do you think we should find at the Cluid's sleeping quarters?' said Davidia, as they travelled through dark space. It wasn't a distance thing but the feeling of time.

'I'm sure whatever it is, there won't be a welcome mat. We aren't important personages to whom that privilege would be given in this environment. It will probably be as black as everything else is about this place.'

They both had no idea what awaited them.

Halp and Foll enjoyed the experience of movement in the dark. They were accustomed to this type of travel; however, they were concerned for their safety as the other four exchange students were now their sole responsibility. Was it a burden they could cope with?

'I wonder if those parts from Cluff have been delivered; you know, the ones we tampered with,' said Halp.

'They should be there by now. I don't know who installs the updates. We may get the chance; after all, we rewired them,' replied Foll, pleased to contribute to the conversation.

'We should pretend to be the service staff and replace the parts.'

'How do we know which parts are the damaged ones? I can't remember them. They all look identical, just like we do.'

'I marked them with small letters h and f, so no one could identify them as other than the norm. We need to locate those parts first before we achieve any heroism. They should have a storage depot. We'll head their first.'

Halp had high expectations of achieving change, but knew that anything done was at risk now that they were unattached escorts and threatened control. They veered off-course slightly toward the depot which was based directly under the sleeping pods, much like a mechanic in the pit with the cars raised above by a hoist. Often their best work is done in that space.

Miss Alpine couldn't discern whether the blips were on a collision course, but she did notice the slight directional change of Halp and Foll. She didn't think too much of it as they would soon encounter Crisper. She had every confidence that the day would end well, with Senora College returned to normal and life would continue with its black heartbeat. Who needs a holiday when total control of a black paradise in under your fingers? Confidence is often misplaced. Has it been swallowed sufficiently this time?

Davidia and Slirander suddenly landed with a thump.

'They ought to improve these transport devices. If that were an airline pilot in training, he'd have run off the runway and been scolded severely for such shoddy roughness.'

Davidia rubbed her rump, which had taken the brunt of their seated landing. Slirander took a moment to focus. She looked around. They were in a huge space with feature columns separated equidistant apart and standing alone as individual sentinels. Each reached the ceiling and had a design chipped into their base for identification. They could be walked around. It would take a few body arm hugs joined together; they were so huge. Schools with student quarters this size certainly didn't exist at home. The girls crept along quietly and as they neared the first column, in much the same manner as in their own spaces when they had first arrived, it seemed to move closer to them. Were they magnetic, imagining it, or did they really move? They both blinked. A good eye wash might be a prelude perhaps to hallucination. They pinched each other hard enough to recognise minor pain and realise that they had all their senses.

'Did that column move?' questioned Davidia. 'It seemed like it did.'

'I'm sure of it,' replied Slirander.

The small, thin, wispy hairs on the nape of her neck stood erect as echidna quills ready to prick an attacker. Her aura was combobulating.

Davidia felt the tension. It was a moody-feeling place like discovering ancient dungeons where foul play was meted out by an upper class of control freaks to the hapless slaves. It didn't feel good. She hoped she wasn't going to be set upon by a trident wielding maniac intent on puncturing a perfectly good body. She took a step closer and didn't gain any ground. She took another step and once again it moved away. Had she got close enough so no further closeness was achievable? Davidia signalled to Slirander to walk around the opposite side and for both to take a step toward the column and see what happens. The girls were in position.

'That is an unfair advantage. One step is fine but two steps would be too intricate to outmanoeuvre,' said an unusual voice.

It sounded as if a gravel grater had been drawn across its vocal cords and the sound resonated sadness. Was it because everything was black and fed a depressive atmosphere?

The girls were shocked. It was a talking column. Diamonds might speak a language of their own, but a tall stone column was very doubtful. The girls waited. Well, who's going first? Davidia stepped up for an oral display.

'It's fantastic that you can communicate with us. Have you ever met a girl before?'

'Is that what you are called?' was the reply.

'You look so tall and strong and we wondered what the inscription is at your base. It might be your name. We can't read it from here. We can't get close enough to read it.'

'You can't come any closer. Intruders are banned and expunged quickly if they represent danger to a Cluid.'

'Is that what you are, a Cluid?'

'No. I'm a Clud, one of the guardians of this area.'

'What exactly is this area? It seems lonely. Have you any friends here?'

'We have fellow Cluds. Each of us guards a column. Please leave before you are terminated.'

'That's rather drastic. We're peaceful. How dare you threaten us?'

'It's not me that threatens you. Have you noticed how warm it is becoming? We are all under threat.'

'Who threatens us? I'm not aware of any danger.'

Davidia thought that it was an excuse to force their departure; however, it was becoming noticeably warmer. Slirander tuned in a fine ear and held up her hand as a silent gesture of quietness and not as an exercise to force blood through her fingers for warmth or quicker movement. A whooshing sound emerged in the distance. They could see the space being lit by a moving fireball. It seemed to crawl along the ceiling with the adherence of a fly's feet. It spread like a spilt, red, runny sauce bottle coming closer. As it did, a transparent substance began to gather around their feet.

'I told you that you are under threat. Now, do you believe me?'

A glug, glug, sound gurgled on the floor. The Cluds were actually invisible skirts around each column, restricting entry. The heat from Crisper, because that's who it was ceiling-crawling and space-filling, had melted their resistance and left each column vulnerable to attack. The girls definitely didn't want to be fried, with or without oil.

'It's too hot here,' said Davidia. 'We must escape the heat.'

'That inscription is a name. Read it out and push that design with a finger; why, it just flashed into my brain?' urged Slirander. 'I'll defend you until then.'

'Against what? Sunstroke?'

'Just do it. You may surprise yourself by taking advice.'

Davidia scowled. Begrudgingly she complied. She still bristled against taking advice, but as she grew older, she could give out more than she received. That was a slow mental march.

The inscription read Cluid-Big-A-F. Davidia put her slenderest finger into the small indented hole and waited.

'Great bloody joke that is,' she said. 'Absolutely shit, nothing.'

It was becoming hotter like the inside of a pizza oven. The girls began to wilt in the heat. It affected their dialogue. Two large, red, ruddy, magma eyes spotted them and they had brightened considerably. It was nearing the end of its quest and that well-earned rest, a magma sauna. It still spat out lava refuse, welting all it landed on.

'Those students will pay for the agony they have put me through,' said Crisper, feeling confident. Nothing could or ever had withstood its heat, its most endearing feature.

Unfortunately for it, plans can have a tendency to be destroyed, re-routed or forgotten about. As it neared, an amazing sight greeted it.

'Davidia, the column is falling over,' yelled Slirander. 'Get out of the way, you could be crushed.'

True, the column was tilting like the Leaning Tower of Pisa; however, it didn't stop there, it continued until it was level with the floor. A door had also opened and Davidia walked through it. She noted the enormous amount of inside space available and called out to Slirander. She ran quickly. It was cool inside. The heat of Crisper couldn't be felt any longer. It was a short reprieve.

They had entered the area of the Cluid's sleeping quarters. It was a most private area. In the centre of the space lay a large, open pod, the length and shape for a fully-grown human body. The floor was transparent and underneath was an open work space, which ensured that if any maintenance was carried out it could be clearly seen by whom or what. Imagine, a pod suspended on a transparent floor. Well, that's what it appeared to be. Above the pod, a system of suspended water pipes intertwined with minute puncture holes in its length, which allowed a constant soothing, misty vapour to brush over the pod overnight. This is how the Cluids refreshed their skin, by being lightly misted. They weren't necessarily like a snake shedding its skin, but certain similarities couldn't be overlooked. This was an essential daily treatment for the Cluids aka Miss Alpine and Mr. Avalanche. It was their sacrifice that to lead Cluidinine as Head Cluids, they had to endure this routine. Occasionally, on special occasions, they could last a few days only before replenishment. They were trapped forever on their planet.

The girls searched everywhere for a pressure button to turn on the water just to test it. There were none to be located. They weren't sure what they had found. It was intriguing. There were also no seats available to rest a weary torso. Davidia sat on the only place that offered rest, the edge of the pod. Suddenly, she was wet with a light mist.

'Who peed on me?' she yelled. 'It's too early to take a bath and definitely not in here in front of whoever can see me.'

Her clothes had been slightly wet and there was no need for the hysterics that often accompany a surprise; however, excitable youth was prone to outbursts on occasion.

'You turned on the water,' said Slirander. 'It must be operated by getting into the pod.'

Slirander also sat on the pod edge on the opposite side and once again, a light mist fell. It covered the complete pod and the excess dribbled onto the floor, only to pool in small gutters around the edge of the room. This meant a completely wet floor overnight.

'I don't think I want to lie in a watery mist all night. I wonder what happens if it's turned off.'

'I suppose we won't know. I don't have any intention of staying in here for a sleepover.'

The mist had become rather heavy with the two modestly weighted, seated females. Water spread everywhere as expected. They had discovered, unbeknown to them, that the water was the secret ingredient to the long life of a Cluid because without the refreshment of the skin, the disaster that awaited them was horrific. The word "shrivel" would be implemented.

Before they had become too comfortable, a sudden flash of heat entered via the door. Crisper had arrived to menace and terminate them. It hadn't counted on tough resistance or unfavourable conditions. Once inside the sleeping quarters, the door closed behind entombing, if there was no escape, the three of them. Its eyes glowed with anger, frustration and delight. It had cornered its prey. It opened its mouth as wide as possible and blew as strong as a storm. The heat it ejected was laced with hot magma rocks that normally would devastate anything in its path. They flew across the room as flying debris to sizzle them. Fortunately, the girls, being quick of mind, both jumped inside the pod, causing the mist to revert to a heavy downpour due to their extra weight. By the time the magma had reached them, they were stone cold inoffensive rocks that flew past the pod landing harmlessly against a far wall. Plop. Plop.

Crisper blew up into a rage.

'There's no escape. You are doomed,' it boasted.

Davidia sometimes had a mental death wish and provoked Crisper to come closer and get a good look at what was about to defeat it. The last look before it was "lights out".

'What are you? A red embarrassment pretending to be some sort of demon. We aren't afraid of you. I dare you to come closer. You're no match for us. Our school has the most intelligent females ever. No one bests them.'

'What did you do that for?' said Slirander. 'It's going to decimate us. It's too hot for us to handle.'

'Don't worry. Have you noticed how much water is swilling around? It will dampen its enthusiasm for a contest. Watch this.'

Davidia instantly stood tall. She was now an easily hittable target. Crisper breathed in again and let fly with more nasties. This time they hardly made it to the pod. The strong mist was swamping its abilities. Davidia raised her arms, as if to say, hopeless. Crisper hadn't moved at this stage. It had remained near the doorway. Its next step was an unmitigated disaster for it. Its long, red tail dragged along the floor and a huge sizzle erupted, reducing its tail of length and power to expel from its mouth. It couldn't ceiling-crawl as it was too wet. The water flow didn't abate. Crisper was shrinking. Those magnetic red eyes full of menace began to fade. Its whole body began to shrink in the damp conditions. The thin, bony fingers it possessed imitated burnt tree twigs ready to snap off. The large mouth was closing. It wasn't so threatening anymore. There was nothing Crisper could do. Water was its main enemy and, added to that, two rude schoolgirls with attitude was an inedible feast. Davidia took the unprecedented step of striding out of the pod and splashing her way toward Crisper, who by now was in agony. She stopped within throwing distance, took off a shoe and dipped it into the water and threw it over Crisper. It shrieked in pain. It reminded Davidia when she played splash at the beach with her brother when she was a small girl. No guessing who won and never cried in the salty water. Davidia repeated the process. Finally, the all-conquering termination assassin of Cluidinine had faded into a mass of cold rocks bereft of any further danger. It had been soundly defeated. The girls were saturated. Slirander climbed out of the pod and the mist stopped.

'How did you know that would happen?' asked Slirander.

'I didn't,' replied Davidia.

'You certainly took a risk.'

'I'm glad that's over.'

*

Miss Alpine had registered the loss of Crisper's blipping light, not believing it had faded out, and yet, those two other bright lights belonging to the girls continued to blink brightly. Even the escorts continued to blink. How could that happen? It's impossible. Crisper had never failed before. Its excuse to fade from the control board needed a damn good explanation.

'Check that those signals are working correctly,' yelled Miss Alpine.

Mr. Avalanche was normally in control of his outbursts. He usually delivered his opinions in a softer but no less deadly manner. Miss Alpine's shrill voice was high alping, far louder than any yodeller. The control room staff were flushed and harried to confirm her horrendous fears. Failure wasn't in her dictionary of usable words; however, there were many more that could substitute for it, also beginning with the same letter.

'Is it true that Crisper's beeper has ceased, malfunctioned, gone off-line, or is that control panel in denial? What is it? Give me an answer quickly.'

A staffer stuttered in fear. Miss Alpine's body shook with anger as she swayed with disappointment. Her patience suddenly erupted. Answers to her questions weren't flowing quickly enough for her liking. The staff ran around like stunned ferrets, not knowing which rabbit hole to enter. She quickly made that decision for them. Her face, once again, had the yellow fringed menace around it, signalling something disagreeable. Her hands had grown twice their normal length. Ten sossurged, thin, bony-fingered structures with arthritic parents, were rammed mercilessly into a confused staff member unable to satisfy a quick answer for a hungry mind. A limp form with a twisted expression slid silently to the floor to become a mess for another to clean. She ran an alert eye up and down her fingers ensuring everyone present observed its meaning.

'Get that out of here. Next?'

'Crisper's light has ceased. It's not a malfunction but a termination of it,' said a nervous staffer, not wishing to become another pin cushion.

It waited to be aerated. Was its answer quick enough? Tension was simmering.

'What? Who dares to tell me that Crisper is kaput?'

Mr. Avalanche had held his tongue to date as it was rather offensive if you held someone else's. He could see an unrestrained maniac unleash, without any rational balance, on those nearby when staff were a required support team in troubled times and not to be expunged as an enemy. He raised his arms, not as a sign for prayer but as a calm warning "stop" sign guide to Miss Alpine. Even a woman scorned wasn't a patch on this angry life form.

'Miss Alpine, I think that we've established that Crisper has, unfortunately, failed in its duty and we need to rectify the situation to our advantage. Those other four blipping lights have had free reign for some time, so it's time to eliminate their freedom. I suggest that I confront them, gain their confidence and teach them an educational lesson that they will never forget because they won't be alive to remember what it was they were taught. How does that sound to you? I almost forgot. There are the other four who also have no need to return to Vlad College. We'll retain them too. It will be some going-away party,' said Mr. Avalanche, sounding quite like a confident salesman planning a Christmas function with him playing the part of Santa.

Is it party time or something more sinister? Who is going to burst whose balloon?

Miss Alpine was still hyperventilating at the thrill of her recent termination. She had tasted destruction once again and was angling for another feed. She walked around the control room acting as an executioner does selecting the desperate and the ill for transportation to a better place without them having knowledge of their destination. Besides, there were plenty more staff where they came from at Cleef, which was a permanent supplier of rotisserie-rounded sossarges. Even in her state of high exhilaration, she had sense to listen to a voice of reason. Her mood changed to amiable. The strange thing about her torso this time was that her ten hand digits stayed twice their length. Normally they receded to regular size. Had an irreversible body transformation been triggered by the intensity of her anger?

'Are you suggesting that you extract revenge on those intruders into our sleeping quarters?' said Miss Alpine, with her mind engaged in a dangerous pursuit, whilst eyeing Mr. Avalanche's eyes for the same intensity. They were a match.

'Yes. They really haven't had any dealings with me and I may just get under their guard. It's worth a shot. What do you say?'

Mr. Avalanche could certainly speak with a silken tongue as a Don Juan who charms his lady into submission. Miss Alpine wasn't totally convinced he had the balls for the job. She didn't have any real ones; however, she was quite capable of acting treacherously without them. She agreed that he should have the first opportunity and, upon his failure, if that materialised, she would ensure that the f word was crossed off her vocabulary list. It was a word requirement and reminder she didn't need.

It was time to move forward with the male plan.

Was it any different to the female plan?

What treachery and danger were the girls and escorts to confront?

Could they bat any threat to the keeper?

A game of skill was about to erupt.

16 CONTEST

'Where are Halp and Foll?' questioned Davidia, now that Crisper was no longer a threat.

'I'm not sure,' replied Slirander. 'They must be with the other four students because that's what we told them to do. I hope they listened to instruction.'

'This is an interesting place with those sleeping pods. They really are just a watery bath. I wonder how the whole system works. There's water everywhere, but for what purpose?'

'It is incredible to think that a place like this actually exists. This probably isn't the only room like it. There aren't any other connectors that I can see from up here; however, down below seems to be a huge open space that life forms may travel along. It's probably a secure space. Let's move onto another room and investigate if there are any similarities.'

They returned to the door and popped their heads outside. There wasn't a guillotine above them to lop them off, but one can wonder in this strange location. It seemed as before; a massive space filled with impressive individual columns. They moved onto the next one.

'Entrance is forbidden,' said a voice.

'Why so?' asked Davidia.

'Entrance is forbidden,' said a voice a second time.

'Why so?' asked Davidia.

'Entrance is forbidden,' said a voice for the third time. 'Can't you hear? Are you deaf? What is it you don't understand? Thrice is sufficient mention of a situation. There is nothing further to say. I'll repeat painfully, for the fourth time, entrance is forbidden. Please leave.'

Davidia thought that the conversation wasn't elevating anywhere useful.

'Are you a Clud?' seemed to be the obvious question.

'What wants to know?'

'I do. I know you can see me, but we can't see you. You are an invisible skirt around the column, protecting it from intruders. We aren't intruders, we're visitors. Mr. Avalanche has given us permission to enter as part of the Senora College educational program. It's important for us to learn about saving water and its multitude of uses. Apparently, there are special uses here that we don't even know about. We're his personal student tutorial group.'

'I don't care. You will not be allowed entrance regardless of dressing up a reasonable reason.'

'See that inscription on the base there, it reads Cluid-Big-A-M, which I believe is his personal sleeping pod. Is that correct?' queried Davidia.

'That information is private and banned for anyone but him. Entrance is forbidden. That phrase is becoming obnoxious. I won't repeat it again.'

The Clud went silent. Its task was to guard and protect. Those were its integral and important tasks. Anything other than that was peripheral and an unnecessary distraction.

This time there seemed to be no chance of gaining entry. Slirander had listened carefully and had observed how the Clud reacted each time Davidia spoke. It couldn't be seen, but she felt a warble and wobble in its skirt the more it conversed. The sense of feeling she possessed was a special ability. Could Davidia wear it down by talking to it constantly? That would tire out most talkers. It was worth a try. Slirander whispered to Davidia about her idea.

'And you tell me you are the intelligent one. That's a daft idea. What should I say?'

'You gossip about everyone at school, so it should be right up your alley.'

'And you don't?'

'You are far better at it than me. That's all.'

'It's not a very pleasant back-handed compliment.'

'What else can we try? Kick it instead. See how that works.'

Davidia was sensing anger and lashed out with a solid right kick. It hurt. Her foot suffered shock. Pain danced all the way up her thigh. The Clud skirt was immovable. She didn't want to deal in any more pain, so reluctantly agreed to talk it to death. Her fellow classmates had often had to endure unwanted advice or otherwise about her intending emotional exploits, which usually left them exasperated and worn out giving her advice as they sorely looked for an exit. It was verbal torture, but not seen as such. Davidia reconsidered the physical violence aspect. Talking was less likely to cause a dangerous reaction.

'I was once a small column. I pretended with my brother that I lived in Rome where the rest of my family lived. When I was under construction and on the way up, they built me at an angle and when completed, moved me to another Italian City, Pisa. Guess what they called me?'

'A column.'

'Not officially. I leant so far over that I pointed to Rome with my column lean. It was thought that it was a direction finder like a compass point and a homesick signal, so I was transported back there and I didn't lean anymore. You know, I was made from a single piece of marble and, to this day, there has never been another piece found anywhere else in my known world. I'm unique. That was after I was found underground. Guess where I was found? I'll tell you. You would never have guessed it anyway. It was in a snow-bound country known as Icepick, where ice caverns and crevices as large as small islands abound. It was on a speleology expedition that reflected light bounced back at the holder of the light. It almost blinded them. They did have difficulty removing me from that landscape. The terrain was altered specifically to remove me. A series of subterranean caves were destroyed by widening and removing the debris. They built a small mountain called Davice after me in an effort to rearrange. I believe that they now have a winter ski resort there, it is so large. Now I live in sunny Italy to be admired endlessly by every visitor. I stand at a place called the Colosseum. Do you know how many visitors there are annually in Rome? Of course, you don't, because you haven't travelled. Well there are …'

Davidia droned on and on. She spoke non-stop. Slirander felt the frustration of the Clud having to contend with the incessant nonsense being served up as interesting dialogue of which it wanted few words. It couldn't escape. A captive audience is a godsend to a poorly rated comedian. It was entrapment. The Clud suffered in silence. Slirander felt its stiff collar shudder and the slightest movement of wilting. It needed a rest from the onslaught.

'Davidia, it's working. I feel a softening of the skirt. Keep talking.'

'My jaw aches. This is much harder than it sounds.'

'Not long to go. Tell it about your latest emotional interest. That should be a highlight for it. If I fall asleep, I'll apologise in advance.'

Slirander allowed herself a snigger. Davidia might reveal who she is interested in at school. If she revealed that, then that would avoid competition if she also had an interest in that same student.

'There was this guy at school from last year who I thought had the makings of a really close relationship. He made the school uniform sing with interest. When he walked past, the cologne he used was so aromatic some girls couldn't attend class. They had to take a rest break and refresh their reddened faces with cool water a few minutes later. His torso bulged from under his shirt. There were so many undulations it was embarrassing to stare at them all. I fancied him a little and one afternoon he walked by, I gave him the eye, in fact, both eyes, but not an eyeful. That was usually reserved for a more intimate setting, if one arose. You know, the bastard ignored me. Well, if that didn't light an anxiety complex. No one ignores the come-on from me. Well, do you know what he did? Of course, you don't. You haven't met him. He smiled at me with a rounded mouth as if it had just finished sucking a banana. I learnt later that is exactly what he had been doing. He was a plantation worker. There was a school report about unsavoury grunts and noises coming from the boys' restrooms and he was later expelled. Apparently, he did more than suck fruit. Does that happen here; misbehaviour that shouldn't? I wouldn't think so. You can't leave your post, can you? Where would you go if you did? You aren't allowed to access anywhere in this place without control. I like my freedom.'

Davidia took a deep breath, preparing for another verbal onslaught. Slirander signalled to her. She felt that the Clud had collapsed with exhaustion. It couldn't hold any of the words said and it didn't understand most of it. No wonder it had a minor collapse. It had a bad case of skirt sag.

'Davidia, there's a gap in the skirt. I can feel it. Follow me,' said Slirander, as she ran her hands around the perimeter and found the break. 'In here, quickly. It may recover once you have shut up. Even I found it hard going. Was that true what you said about that student?'

'Who cares? It was part truth and part imagination. Which is which, I can't say. I did as asked. So, it worked. Great! Shall I place my finger in the indentation like I did with the other one?'

'Yes. Go ahead.'

No sooner had Davidia inserted her finger, the column lowered itself horizontally to the floor as the other one had done. It was a pattern of the design to enable the occupant to sleep flat in their pod and not sleep standing upright, otherwise the water treatment wouldn't work correctly. They pushed through the door and found themselves inside Mr. Avalanche's personal sleeping pod. It was like entering the bowels of someone's privacy. Once again, they were unwelcome intruders. The space was identical to Miss Alpine's with a few noticeable exceptions. The sleeping pod was slightly larger and the base of the pod had special indentations for anatomical parts to nestle without squashing. Apparently, the female Cluids slept on their backs whilst the male Cluids slept face down. Proper engineering was required for sleep comfort. The girls sat on the edge of the pod and, sure enough, the mist surged from above exactly as before. They patrolled the perimeter and satisfied themselves that there were no other surprises, but were there?

Mr. Avalanche had triggered his GTD and landed outside his own personal column. He had never before seen it lie horizontally. It was a shock. Nothing had ever entered his private space either. He seethed with anger. It seemed that it was an ever-increasing popular emotion in the Senora College environment and who would have been the cause for the dissention? He almost tripped over the Clud who reacted more as a worn garment than a stiff skirt base. It struggled to communicate.

'It was those two strange life forms. They out-educated my verbal abilities. I offer no other excuse. I'm exhausted,' said the weary Clud, fully expecting replacement.

'I understand. They are a force, aren't they? Rest and prepare to guard again.'

Mr. Avalanche was almost conciliatory, which was a surprise;

however, he had to mentally tune in to a softer approach to gain the girls' confidence. He didn't want to be their friend, date them, raise them or compete at sport with them, but he wanted them at his mercy, which wouldn't be given anyway. He pushed through the door, and there silhouetted against a watery glass window pane stood the two protagonists. He paused nervously, moved his sets of thin, bony fingers in an exercised rock–paper–scissors motion and moved side to side like a lilting vessel. He glared daggers at them. They eyed him suspiciously. Inside the pod, the occupants needed to tread carefully. Inexplicable reactions could erupt without knowing the sensitivity of the equipment involved if a wrong foot or action was invoked. The girls had no idea, but Mr. Avalanche was the wary one. He knew the pitfalls and needed his pod to stay safe and secure, that's why he needed the girls out of there. They were a great danger to it and him. A silent stalemate ensued. It was eyes at forty paces. Who was to speak first, make the first gesture, or move from where they were standing? The girls strangely stayed quiet, which must have tested their resolve not to burst out.

'I'm Mr. Avalanche,' said Mr. Avalanche, eyeing his protagonists.

The opening gambit had been made. There was hope yet for non-confronting dialogue.

'I'm Davidia,' said Davidia.

'I'm Slirander,' said Slirander.

'Do you know where you are?' continued Mr. Avalanche.

'Standing exactly here in front of you,' said a smart-answerer Davidia.

'I meant, this place, this room, this area. Are you aware of what this space is all around you?'

'It's a bathroom without a secluded change room. Anyone can see in. It's not very private,' said Davidia.

Slirander remained quiet and was quietly assessing the situation. She was alert to any movements, changes in body language and voice elevations. She was the research hub, whilst Davidia was the orator with a penchant for the occasional tirade.

'This is my private sleeping space and there is no need for cover because no one can see in. It has one-way transparency,' replied Mr. Avalanche, softly.

'One-way glass. I get it. What's this space used for?'

'It is a bedroom, but not as you would understand a bedroom to be. Cluidinine has different forms of quality for attending to different life forms. They may be strange to others but not to us. Take that sleeping pod for instance, it has a wet side and a body shaped space for comfort to match the anatomy of the sleeper perfectly. All pods here are designed in the same format to the sleeper's requirements; however, in your world I understand your sleeping arrangements are on a flat surface called a mattress and you adorn the area with coloured cushions, doonas and so on. You sleep dry. We sleep wet. It's only a point of difference, but sleep we do.'

The girls' understanding had increased slightly. They weren't sleeping wet for anyone.

'I suppose we can leave here on our own, can't we?' asked an inquisitive Davidia, who had noticed that Mr. Avalanche had blocked their exit.

The GTD devices didn't work inside this space like it was electrically barren. If there was an exit strategy, it wasn't speaking. Slirander contemplated a physical affront, but their opponent was physically stronger. *What next?* she thought. *Is this bath thing the way out and if so, how?* She leant over to Davidia not to whisper sweet nothings – they were mates that's all – but suggest that they part, stand on opposite sides of the room and lean backwards against the wall. They did so with the walk of stalk. Mr. Avalanche's darkened eyes followed them. He hadn't moved. What were they planning? Did he see any dangers? It was currently a blank canvas, but the girls had intentions of colouring it red, the colour of strength. It was a stand-off like that which preceded the O.K. corral shootout of the past wild-west cowboys. The girls stood like two stallions chomping at the bit, hearts heaving, gearing up for an onslaught of epic proportions. All it took was a wink, which eye didn't matter, it was the signal. Simultaneously, both girls rushed at the bath and leapt over it, slamming into the opposite wall, protecting themselves with arms crossed. The whole room shook, shuddered, and they felt like they stood on stilts of plastic needles. It had that sensation. Mr. Avalanche was shocked watching two stupid girls try and damage two perfectly good walls. Before he could react, they did the reverse, not running backwards but repeating the process. They appeared to be flying. Bang! Into the wall again! The floor became jellied and see-sawed from his end, not the girls' side. Mr. Avalanche suddenly felt his body slip toward the bath. It attracted him like a wet magnet. The girls did a third run and the room was chaotic. The sleeping pod undulated rapidly. Mr. Avalanche lost his footing and fell into the bath on his back, a forbidden position for males to sleep in. He stuck fast because the bath shape was different from that side. His GTD device became unattached and malfunctioned with all the water now washing over it. The girls' antics had proven a disaster. To their horror, they saw a ghastly transformation as a life form struggled for freedom. The water shower reacted differently as he lay in this strange position. It saturated the room, and slowly Mr. Avalanche returned to his former self prior to being a senior Cluid, as an ordinary sossarge. His skin wasn't replenished, it was removed. It was unbelievable. The girls didn't believe it either. He could be a relative of Halp and Foll. A bloated sossarge now filled the sleeping pod, unable to move. Its powers had disappeared. Mr. Avalanche disintegrated and slid down the plughole as bathroom waste. It was an unedifying finish to an unpleasant life form.

'Did you see that? What a mess! He just disappeared,' said Davidia, amazed at what she had witnessed. Her fellow students wouldn't believe her if she told them.

Slirander realised that with the loss of Mr. Avalanche, their chances of escaping had been reduced by fifty per cent. They needed Miss Alpine alive and undamaged, if they were to escape. They may have created their own dilemma and now had to preserve someone intent on their destruction. They'd have to give some serious thought to their next proposal. That armpit of Miss Alpine's had to be saved and initiated if they were to escape. The only problem was how.

Miss Alpine had seen the dimming of Mr. Avalanche's light on the control room panel. She became incensed. Her anger exploded like a firecracker, the big bunger type. The control room staff fled. She had no excuses for anybody anymore and confronting her was a death sentence. Were the girls that brave or stupid?

They now had a huge problem. Like they didn't have one before?

*

Halp and Foll had arrived at the cargo depot of parts used for the maintenance of all sleeping pods, located underneath in a separate area. Access was allowed wherever a repair was needed. The handlers of the precious instruments were fellow sossarges so suspicion wasn't immediately aroused by their arrival.

They utilised their cross finger greeting to allay any threats that may have been felt.

'We are the replacement staff,' said Halp.

'We weren't aware that there are any replacements,' replied the head life form.

'It's a recent new edict from Miss Alpine and it seems she has unfortunately not passed on the details. We can assure you that under no circumstances would we interfere in the smooth workings of the maintenance group; however, to keep everyone alert and up-to-date, the new system of replacements has been introduced for work experience for when the colony expands and there is an immediately trained workforce to cope with any growth. It's called forward planning.'

'I've never heard of that one before. Do you know how to operate the system?'

They'd be lying if they said they did, so they lied.

'As part of the work training program we have already been inducted at the Cluff facility and, to follow through, we had a few pods of parts sent and labelled with the letters h and f so we could identify them when they arrived. It is a trial instalment for us. It has been impressed upon us to use those parts only that we have prepared, otherwise we could fail our training and end up in an unpleasant elsewhere. You don't want to be responsible for the failure of the pet training duo of Miss Alpine, do you?'

Halp had embellished the thoughts sufficiently to breed fear into the life form.

'Certainly not. How can we help?'

'Those pods with our initials on should have arrived by now. There should be four.'

'They might be over there. We received a new delivery not long ago from Cluff.'

After a short search, the pods were located. Halp and Foll made sure that nothing had tampered with them. Satisfied that it was all good, they took the four pods to the main area and prepared them for assembly and insertion. A keen-eyed fellow sossarge noticed a difference in the wiring technique that hadn't been seen before.

'That wiring is incorrect,' it said.

'How so?' replied Foll, adding a few words' worth of dialogue.

'Those wires are coiled. That's never been done.'

'It's a new technique that Miss Alpine had us prepare for her personal sleeping pod. It has secret elements that enhance her life form without electronic side effects. Innovation is the new terminology.'

'Wow! We only install the equipment. I wish we could create it like you have.'

'You need the right contacts and association with those in the know. Kindly show us which pod belongs to Miss Alpine. This will be a pleasant surprise for her when she next sleeps. It would be something we all crave. In time, if this trial is successful, the intention is to expand the program as part of the Senora College educational curriculum. Wouldn't that be exciting?' said Halp, knowing she had an attentive audience.

The truth was smeared in there somewhere.

'It's that one down there, about four along. The one with the smooth shape that hangs down like two half-moons at its lowest point. The replacement section is at that end in that open space where the feet rest. Can we observe how you install the new trial wiring?'

'Surely, you must understand and respect the need for privacy as it is Miss Alpine's personal pod. We are her personal specialist pet duo entrusted with this particular task. Secrecy is of the utmost importance. If it became known that we had shared this secret, once again our end would be unpleasant. I'm sure that the next installation will be your responsibility if this trial is successful.'

The head life form felt a sense of pride in its flat rounded chest as it dreamed of the next installation. Halp turned to Foll and signalled it was time to go. They collected all the components and headed off toward the preparation of an impending disaster.

'That was close,' said Foll.

'I'm glad they haven't been as well-educated as us, otherwise we would not have made it through.'

They stood directly underneath Miss Alpine's pod.

'Does she really have that shape?' questioned Foll.

'She does in her present life form. I wonder what life form she originated from.'

Before they wandered off into wispish land, they set to work installing the new wiring system. It was the negative electronic process, which simply meant that an electronic current when applied to the pod would react in the opposite manner, the ramifications of which were not known. In trial terms, it was definitely a trial. When Miss Alpine next retires overnight, only then will the full impact of the trial be understood.

Halp and Foll had done their work and now it was time to reconnect with Davidia and Slirander.

An ill feeling was felt throughout Senora College. Miss Alpine was on the march.

17   DECISION TIME

avidia and Slirander having witnessed the demise of Mr. Avalanche, retreated from his sleeping pod back into the main area. Once they had exited, the flat column reformed as an upright column. The area resumed normalcy.

'We have to find our fellow students,' said Davidia. 'They must be fraught with fear being abandoned in a dark space. Somehow, we must leave this place together. I doubt if Miss Alpine will see it that way.'

'She won't allow an exit path. We must have an alternative plan. My dad can help,' said Slirander.

'What can he do here? Nothing. It's impossible to visit,' said an annoyed Davidia, because she couldn't think of a solution.

She's now got a competitor for problem solving. Maybe she should express a few cross words for her frustrations at this point in time.

'I think that we should return to the others with Halp and Foll and determine what to do. In the meantime, I need to contact my dad. He'll know a way of leaving here.'

'Do what you have to,' said Davidia, resigned to the fact that it wasn't her idea.

'We need Miss Alpine. She is the only one who can allow us to leave and she has the means. The only way back is initiating the existence of that tram. Remember how she did it.'

'She did it by an armpit fart on that tattoo on her underarm. It looks like a darts board. It certainly is a strange place to have a tattoo. How are we to gain access and get her to flap her arm by cuddling a hand?'

'I have an idea. That's why I need to speak to my dad. Incidentally, have you noticed that none of our konnockers are blinking anymore? I hope that doesn't mean our end. Miss Alpine could have inflicted pain on all of us if she had wished us harm. She must have a more personal reason not to. I don't trust her, and that yellow fringed sneer which masquerades as a smile needs to be wiped off by her arse.'

'That's rather nasty even if I agree with you.'

'It's time to step forward, again.'

Slirander pressed the GTD into action and once again they were transported through the darkness. During the flight, Slirander contacted her dad by molar interaction.

'Slirander, are you okay?' asked Rotan. 'We've had an incident at the school involving the exchange students. An assassin was sent, but fortunately has been despatched. Those exchange students are certainly an odd lot. How are you faring?'

'We've had a few issues as well; however, I need another spell from the Spellabook to carry out my next task.'

Slirander explained the details. It was a dangerous transformation that she had selected. Rotan was concerned with the bad choice, but, once again, it made the most sense. It could mean her demise with only five students returning instead of the original six, or it could mean success. She thought that the risk was worth the effort. There was no other way that she could see. Rotan opened the Spellabook and searched under the small change spells. He selected a magical poem titled Itchy.

'Remember, this is a one-use spell. Failure to implement it properly needs no explanation. I wish you would reconsider.'

'Dad, this is my decision. I'm old enough to make choices to save my friends. Read it out.'

Rotan sat down on a soft bean bag and began rocking

rhythmically as if in a trance. He moaned at the anguish his words would inflict.

Itchy, witchy and tickle too,
Change an itch into a welt or two,
Make it fast, flat and quickly too,
Scratch the bitch that angers you,
Make it short and make it sharp,
Arm the past with a tickle part,
Watch it grow and irritate,
Too late the cry to shut the gate.

Once the poem had been read, the Spellabook page enlarged as if the letters were escaping from the page. They acted like a puff of dust and resettled. Rotan held his head in his hands knowing that might be the last time he ever reads to his daughter.

'I remember when she was six years old and … ,' his voice trailed off.

Slirander didn't feel any change. She was accustomed to being something she wasn't.

Davidia suddenly landed in the space with the other four students with only the one thump being heard.

'Where's your friend, Slirander?' asked the older male student. He seemed to be the most talkative.

Davidia was dumbfounded, but she was becoming used to her odd friend. She shook her shoulders in a non-committal manner. The older student thought he saw more movement than two shoulder blades. He filed that under his mental dating app for when they return to school.

'Where's Halp and Foll?' asked Davidia. 'They should be here with you.'

'They left looking for you and your friend. Did they find you?'

'No, we haven't seen them. I wonder where they could be.'

'They left us this mini receiver and said to use it if help was needed.'

'Push it then.'

The older male student did as suggested. The signal was sent. Halp and Foll received it clearly and instantly set off on their return journey. They said goodbye to their fellow sossarges and blip, they were gone.

'They must be in trouble,' said Halp.

'Mr. Avalanche may have located them. I don't like their chances if he has,' replied Foll.

They were unaware that he was no longer in existence.

Miss Alpine had observed the gathering of the winking lights and knew where to meet her problems and extinguish them together, once and for all. She had no compassion for their families' losses. They were a means to an end even if it wasn't a happy one. She pressed her GTD; she was on her way. Those sets of large, thin, bony hands twitched incessantly. It was like they were itchy.

Slirander was still with the group, but in a small formation that made her almost invisible to the eye. Davidia's hair was an excellent hiding spot regardless of its seemingly unhealthy nature. It hadn't been washed for days. What's a little offensive odour when saving lives? There's nothing to object about on that basis.

Two more thumps and the whole group was now intact. They were either pigs in a poke, sheep in a barn, cattle in a stall, or turkeys in a shoot. Whatever the collective noun, together they made one large and easy target. Their fate and destiny were yet to be determined, but there was interest in it being determined in someone's favour.

Miss Alpine was the last of the cast to appear. It could be a one-act play without an encore.

The sense of soft goodbyes didn't feel that they were present, nor were there to be any pleasantries to be shared as party cakes.

Miss Alpine surveyed her prey with a feeling of ill-will. Those two female students had caused her untold damage, the school and the planet of Cluidinine, and also to have two escorts prone to following orders like religious zealots disobeying her directions, was tantamount to mutiny, with the only course to follow: execution. That space they mingled in wasn't a feel-good situation. The other four exchange students from Vlad College were ignorant of the true situation. They thought that they were to return to Vlad College together even though the circumstances had a feeling of danger and discomfort.

'How do we return home?' asked the senior male student.

'You don't,' replied Miss Alpine. She stood symbolic of a piece of granite.

'There must be. We came here by tram, so I assume we return the same way.'

'You cannot return. That pathway is closed. You must remain here, forever.'

'But we want to return home. Our families and the school will miss us. I insist that you send us home,' continued the male student.

Miss Alpine shook her head. It was an ugly shake. Her manner was engaging on the horrid. She raised one of her enlarged hands and prodded the male student. It stuck like a nail into a piece of softwood. It drew blood. She lifted her hand to her mouth and slowly wiped her finger clean. The male student winced in pain. The jab had pierced his skin sufficiently to warn him of any further objective comments. His body convulsed with the shock. The others supported his ungainly balance.

'Who is next?' said Miss Alpine, who was drooling with deliciousness of deleting those before her. Even though she wasn't cannibalistic, she gave the impression of someone that bad. Her eyes noted the fear. Her plan was working perfectly. She wanted it to last, such was her sadistic side. No more "nice Miss Alpine" the educationalist.

Suddenly, she began waving her hands around like a windmill attacking an imaginary adversary. Something was prodding her, which displeased her. She accidentally stabbed herself in the face and fell over with shock. She momentarily passed out.

'What's happening?' said Davidia.

Slirander buzzed close to her ear.

'It's me, Slirander. I have to return to the control room for some unfinished business,' she said.

'What in the hell are you this time? You scared the shit out of me when you disappeared and now you are leaving us to cope with this female maniac.'

'It won't be long; besides, she will be out for only a few moments, sufficient enough for me to return. I can't tell you what I am. It's part of the risk that I'm taking. Be safe.'

Slirander hit the GTD device and headed toward the control room.

Miss Alpine lay prostrate on the floor, momentarily dazed.

The four students with Halp and Foll stood together like a rugby pack not knowing from where the next attack would materialise.

Davidia didn't join in. She was thinking.

*

Slirander couldn't understand why Miss Alpine had left the control room to personally engage the group she was now tormenting. It was so simple a task to have increased the pain threshold of the konnocker to "unbearable". It would have solved her issues with the group and especially her and Davidia. Perhaps the pain level wasn't sufficient for termination and it had to be a personal task. Whatever the decision, the situation that now confronted them needed a solution, one where the group remained safe.

The spell that had Slirander change her form and seemed to have her physically disappear, had transformed her into an annoying mosquito, the bane of many a human. She didn't quite know what effect she would have on Miss Alpine or her staff of sossarges. She was now a ridiculed pest with bad habits. Danger lurked everywhere by the sound she made. It included the damage she inflicted and the germs she carried that no one wanted to share. She was in one tricky, dangerous situation. There was not a living friend who would come to her aid because she was a mosquito. She had to survive for Davidia and the group to have any chance of escape. The control room beckoned.

The ceiling was the safest spot to land and observe the movements below. The control room was in full flow now that the errors of malfunction had been corrected. It was difficult to recognise the meaning of all the moving lights; however, observing larger operation buttons gave a far better chance of understanding. Slirander was far too small to be physically able to press any button herself no matter what weight she put on it. Her plan was to encourage one of the staffers to do her bidding. It wouldn't happen by asking a question. It had to be done unknowingly. She had to risk her life for that to happen. Firstly, she observed what buttons were oft used, those less used and those hardly touched at all. From her vantage point, it became a game of patience. She reasoned that those less touched were the buttons that required activation and strangely enough there was one large purple button with the letter R on it. She noted that no one went near it at all. Every other button was pressed often as if playing and placing poker machine bets. What are the chances, she mused?

Could it be the reverse button to deactivate the konnockers and would it react on every life form, human or otherwise, that had been konnockered? Without knowing, a risky decision had to be made. There were no other obvious answers. Just as Slirander was to fly into operation, a staffer suddenly began pressing an array of buttons at random.

'Miss Alpine's instructions are to tell all konnockerees that a mass gathering in the square of darkness needs their attendance.'

'Does every button get pressed?' asked an uninformed staffer, who was on the job training.

'Not the one with the R. It's the reversible button for the human life forms. That is never to be touched. Only Miss Alpine and Mr. Avalanche have that authority. If pressed in error that would mean the end for whoever pressed it and that won't be me.'

That was the clue for Slirander. The problem now was how to manipulate its activation? Once pressed and activated, the reversal was forever and could not be reinstated. That would save the humans, but what about Halp and Foll?

'What about any other life forms? Do they have a reverse button?' asked the trainee.

'They do, but that's not to be known. We don't want outright dissention if they knew.'

'Which button is that, so I can avoid accidentally pressing it? I don't want to be terminated either.'

'It's a double click on those two pink buttons next to the red R reverse button. Stay away from them at all costs. Remember, tell no one. You have a responsibility to retain that knowledge and that is why you have been selected to be in the control room. Very few receive that privilege. Don't waste it.'

The trainee acknowledged that it needed to abide by the secrecy rules. It had no choice.

Slirander now had her answer. Her size was a problem, but

not the size of her brain. None of the control room staff had ever seen a mosquito before, let alone heard the sound of one. Slirander left the safety of the ceiling at risk of being squashed. She had no choice either. Her droning sound suddenly had the attention of all those present. She was so minute and moved so swiftly, she was impossible to see. The control staff stood motionless listening to the invasive sound. Had their equipment malfunctioned? It wasn't that. An annoying adversary was on the loose. Slirander didn't want to actually jab anyone with her proboscis and suck blood. That wasn't her purpose. Besides, how disgusting would that be? Her purpose was to wreak havoc and, in the uncertainty created, have the reversal buttons pressed. There was no set plan. She had to wing it. Her personal safety was ignored. She flew directly between the legs of the staffers, then around their heads and their ears where she tickled them with her many feet. Arms and legs flayed helplessly as the squeaky drone zipped, zagged and whizzed everywhere. The staffers began to get angry with the constant noise. How could it be turned off? Their ears weren't well-tuned for that sound. Slowly their thin, bony fingers began to enlarge with anger. This made them ungainly and a dangerous weapon when waved about.

'Where is it?' yelled an agitated staffer.

'What is it?' said another.

'Turn it off,' screamed another. 'It attacked my ears.'

Suddenly, the sound stopped. Slirander retreated to the ceiling. It wasn't to rest. She observed the scene below. Every staff member had doubled the size of their hands. Those thin, bony fingers would become a problem. There was no way that they could control hitting any buttons accurately. Slirander took off again, drawing more angry responses. She landed on the large red R button. Her tiny frame was clearly visible. She droned extra loud to attract attention. It was noticed. Without thinking, an exuberant staffer intent on becoming a hero, tried to swat her. It missed the mark, but accidentally activated the reverse process for the humans. It gasped in fear. What had it done? It looked around for respite. There was no support forthcoming. Before any retribution was meted out, Slirander had landed on a pink button. Once again, the staff wanted cessation of the infectious noise. A group of them slammed their hands onto the control panel and pressed the pink buttons at least twice, whilst Slirander made a desperate escape. She felt the wind of death brush past. Her heart rate was zooming. Once again, she escaped to the ceiling for a rest. The control room was now in chaos. The reverse buttons will create havoc not seen before in Senora College. The control panel which was once lit up like a Christmas tree was losing its appeal as lights went out. Slirander felt a surge in her leg. She checked. Her konnocker light had gone out. Her leg now appeared normal. Had she succeeded? There wasn't time to wait and dine out on her success, she had to return to Davidia and the group to see what problems there were with Miss Alpine.

There was no purpose in waiting in the control room as there was nothing else to achieve.

*

'I feel strange,' said Casesix, as she absorbed the threat that had been perpetrated on her by an emissary of Miss Alpine, and being a fellow student from Senora College, no less. 'My head throbs, my knee aches and my body is changing.'

'It's not diarrhoea, is it?' asked another student standing nearby.

'I don't think so. It's more serious than that.'

'You're pregnant?'

'It's not that either. I can't explain it. It's the first time that I have had these feelings. They're completely foreign to me.'

'Who have you got a crush on then? It's not the head sports champion, is it?'

'That would be nice, but no.'

Casesix was still in Principal Jones' office with all her fellow exchange students. They were aghast at the attempt to terminate them. It was a time of reflection. Were they to be in constant danger whilst at Vlad College? Rotan, who was a sensitive new older guy, a snog and not a snag, sensed the atmosphere was plagued with uncertainty. His emotions were being tampered with in an uncertain manner. He realised that in his midst something strange was occurring. He showed his concern by walking over to Casesix and supporting an arm. She appeared to be tilting.

'Sit down for a moment,' he said, as he escorted Casesix to a nearby chair. In fact, it was Principal Jones' chair, which was met with a brief grunt of disapproval, but in the cause of student care, nodded agreement.

'I feel faint,' she said.

As she sat down in the chair, her skirt was raised above the knee-line, not to attract any unwanted attention, but dragged upwards as she sat on it. There were suddenly a few 'oohs' and 'aahs' from her fellow students. It was impossible, wasn't it? What was? Even Casesix hadn't been treated to such pleasure of appreciation before. She was a little lost for words. Suddenly, a thin, bony finger pointed at her knee, the konnockered one. Where was it? Where was that blinking light? More importantly, where was her konnocker? The other five students all held their collective breath.

'Your konnocker has been turned off. It no longer blinks. That's never happened before. Has something occurred at Senora College? Miss Alpine would never voluntarily turn off anyone's konnocker,' said a fellow student.

Casesix ran her hand over her knee and was surprised it had shrunk. There was no tell-tale residue of a knee burr at all. It had become a normal knee with its natural bulges and odd shape. She was stunned. It took a moment before any realisation of what the true meaning meant. She had no idea if it was an aberration, real or permanent. She continued to experience excruciating pain, which she didn't understand. Before long, there were six exchange students with similar symptoms.

Rotan didn't understand it either; however, he had noticed changes to their hands and their bodies begin to alter significantly. Then a bird thought flew into his brain. Bang! There it was. Each exchange student was turning into the shape of the girl he had manhandled in the most appropriate manner earlier on. They began to look identical to her. Before there was mass panic, Rotan took Principal Jones aside and suggested that the exchange students present needed a change of clothing and could he organise it. He'd stay as the adult to oversee the operation. Having Principal Jones removed from the situation, Rotan was alone with six exchange students experiencing a change of life. He didn't want the other students to be aware of the situation in case it freaked them out. He had to save them somehow. In a pensive moment, he accidentally pressed his molar and sent a signal to Slirander. She was mid-air on her way to save her friends.

'What now?' she said out loud. Her tooth tingled. 'Dad, what is it? I'm in the middle of something.'

'Slirander, the six exchange students are changing into another life form and I don't know what to do.' Rotan wasn't panicked but gravely concerned.

'What shape are they taking?'

'They are, I hate to say this, but they're turning into sausage-like shapes.'

Slirander realised that the buttons pressed in the control room had worked and each life form was returning to its original form. There was no need to worry; however, her school friends might not understand as well as her. She had to extricate them from the school.

'Dad, you have to take them all to the Vermont tram stop and wait there until the tram arrives from the opposite direction. There will only be one. They must all board together. That is the only way to save them. They have become what they always were, sossarges of Cluidinine. I'll explain when I see you next. Hurry, you don't have much time.'

'What about you? When will I see you next?'

'When the tram from the opposite direction stops at Vermont tram stop. I know its public transport but that's the only way. Tell them also that it's safe to return to Cluidinine. See you soon.'

The tooth communication ceased. Rotan quickly gathered the exchange students together and explained what his daughter had told him. Puzzled looks were a-plenty. Was that real? He advised that they must hurry as their changing form may not be understood and they were at risk of harm. The exchange students had begun to lose their shapes and form into a cylindrical shape. Rotan couldn't wait for Principal Jones for a new set of clothes each. If he was approached and asked about the ill-fitting school uniforms, he'd reply that an incorrect size measure was made and ignore any other forthcoming comments.

'We have to go to the Vermont tram stop where you originally arrived and take the tram home. Quickly, before any of the school community sees you.'

'I was enjoying my time here,' said Casesix. 'It's sad to leave.'

A tear escaped and slid straight down her torso onto the ground to dance with a few dust particles. Her body and those of the others were now sossarges with not a bump on the way down. The "magnificent six" briskly walked the journey to the tram stop, apprehensive about their future. Each had enjoyed human shape and company even though they were sent on a sinister errand. Now they would have to face what Cluidinine had in store for them. Hopefully, Caseone to Casesix would enlighten the darkness of home and change the dreadful black of the environment to anything but that. Hope is a four-lettered word and hung in their minds that the future could only get better. They weren't home yet.

Rotan fussed over them as a shepherd does his flock. He had to ensure their safety. They made it to the tram stop and huddled together like a six-pack at a barbeque. A few random stares headed their way, but no unsavoury comments. It was a week-day when there was a shortage of commuters.

Eyes flitted anxiously as the wait began.

18 HOME AGAIN

he so-called safe space in which the students were waiting, was no longer safe. Miss Alpine had invited herself to join them on whatever journey it was that they thought they were taking. Her appearance was a prevention visit with consequences. It might not end well for all. Miss Alpine slowly recovered from her shock stabbing and returned to the upright danger she represented.

'You snivelling little bastards,' she verbally confronted them with as her first vocal offering of recovery. It's not quite the breakfast language one would want to be treated to each day. 'I'll slice you all into fruit salad chunks and toss you into space,' she continued.

It was noted that her language skills were well toilet-trained as she sought to recall more offensive words. Before she could spray their ears with further colour-changing dialogue and threats, Davidia stepped forward. Her leadership skills, as part of her school education which hadn't been embellished with her time at Senora College, would stand her in good stead.

'That was rather rude. You should treat everyone with respect,' she said. 'My mum always used that old cliché, If you have nothing nice to say, say nothing at all and if you do, say it behind their back.'

'In my world you do as you are told. There is no discussion.'

'I'm not from your world. In my world things are done differently.'

'What's the last request for all of you? None of you will leave Senora College.'

Miss Alpine's face began to glow a bright, deathly yellow, similar in colour to a regurgitated meal. No one wanted to share the love. She criss-crossed her elongated hands in front as a threatening device. Her eyes lacked compassion. Aren't all educationalists loaded with compassion for their students? She wavered, watching the group squirm uncomfortably. *It won't be long now,* she thought. What tasty finish was she preparing?

Halp and Foll surprisingly confronted Miss Alpine. It was unknown for any student or sossarge to confront authority, especially two as vulnerable as Halp and Foll. What had caused this insanity moment of bravado? Without realising it, there it was. They had no blinking konnockers and, somehow, theirs had been switched off so they were no longer under permanent threat of termination. They couldn't believe it. Davidia certainly didn't. The other four students weren't up with everything and Miss Alpine gasped in agony. She thought that simply isn't possible. Her head shook angrily. It was full of upset migraines.

'Miss Alpine, you should free all students from your strict rules and allow more freedom of expression. Nothing on this planet is happy. It's such a miserable existence living in constant fear and anxiety.'

Halp had said her piece cautiously and wondered if she'd ever complete another sentence.

Miss Alpine tuned into the control room. The news was devastating. The reverse buttons had been activated. Senora College was under siege from freedom.

'You mean all the konnockers have been deactivated?'

'Yes,' said a staffer.

'I'll deal with that later.'

It was a situation that she couldn't tolerate. She turned toward the group. This wasn't going to be nice or end as happy families. Suddenly, an annoying droning sound broke the silence.

Davidia recognised the sound as that of one of the most annoying and germ-laden pests from home. She wanted to swat it. She thought that they never did achieve anything useful. Halp and Foll stiffened with fear. The sound frightened them. Miss Alpine stood rigid trying to source its location, what for, she wasn't sure.

It became silent again. That sound had stalled somewhere. Slirander had arrived just in time to prevent a catastrophe to her friends and fellow students. She had landed in Davidia's hair. It was so easy to be lost amongst it. She carefully crawled along her hairline down to an ear and was desperate not to tickle it, in case an attempt at flattening occurred. She whispered into Davidia's ear. Shock registered.

'Don't react,' said Slirander. 'It's me. I've returned in time to avoid your removal.'

'I had it all under control. What are you? Tell me, that sound really wasn't you was it?'

'I'm afraid so. Listen carefully.'

Slirander explained the result of the control room fiasco and how all students were freed from konnockerisation and shouldn't any longer have fear of Miss Alpine. Apparently, she was the final Cluid left. A succession plan of new blood was needed. Were Halp and Foll to be the prime candidates?

'We have to escape from here and we need to do it now. There is little time left. Without Miss Alpine, we're stuffed.'

'What about that armpit fart we saw activated? She needs to do that voluntarily otherwise we're doomed,' said Davidia. 'There is no other way. We need her to do it, now.'

A tear began to form in Davidia's eyes as she recalled the many fun times she had with her family and thought that they may be over.

'It's risky, but I'm the only one able to instigate that action,' said Slirander, 'but it's at grave personal risk. If I don't make it, say nice things about me in the future.'

'Don't be stupid. Get the cow,' said Davidia, using a cross word of her own.

Slirander didn't explain how she was to achieve her aim, only that she was going to do so.

'This isn't goodbye, Davidia. Don't look for me afterwards. Just get on that damn tram when it appears. Wish me luck. Oh, I almost forgot. Halp and Foll aren't coming with you. They have a greater need here. Bzzzzzzz.'

'What do you mean they have to stay here? They're our friends.'

There was no answer.

That dreadful droning sound recommenced.

A war of wills was about to erupt. On the one side was a tiny mosquito trying to achieve good and on the other hand was the evil-willed Miss Alpine, attempting termination.

*

The scene was set. Halp, Foll, Davidia and the students could only stand in a group, herded together for the slaughter yard. Miss Alpine was the executioner dribbling with delight at the hapless lot, soon to be victims of her evil; however, there was one constant interruption that needed silencing before she could proceed with those plans. That droning sound irritated her something chronic, almost to the stage of hysteria. Her body was a tsunami of active water molecules constantly clashing with each other for more room within her body. She was like an enlarged water balloon ready to burst. Her face had turned a bright yellow as if the sun shone from there and not from that other popularised humourous exit.

The droning stopped. Eyes darted everywhere seeking the

purveyor of unpopular noises. Slirander, once again from a safety perspective, had landed in Davidia's hair. She thought that they'd discuss shampoos once they had returned home. She noted that Miss Alpine was wearing a full-length sleeve coverage which loosely draped over her arms. There was no other access other than under that sleeve covering and how to exit would be even more dangerous. It was the right armpit she needed to attack. She observed how Miss Alpine swayed in her agitated state, timed it mentally and fathomed that she could sneak along her arm undetected at certain intervals. It wasn't foolproof. It was courting suicide. The sleeve covering would ebb and flow in a wave-like motion and at each uplift of material, she would advance by either flying or walking quickly in the space provided. If she failed to move carefully, the downward thrust of the material may entrap her. A quick swipe and it would be curtains. No more anything. It was time to go. She didn't have a sound off-button.

In a tactical masterpiece, she flew around Miss Alpine's head to disturb her balance and enrage her dramatically so that she wouldn't be that closely observant of her future sleeve movements. Miss Alpine waited for the onslaught as she heard the sound. She flayed hopelessly at Slirander because her hands were twice their normal size and gave her less control. It was an advantage that Slirander expertly exploited. The sleeves, at that level of whirling and arm waving allowed large spaces for unhindered travel. Slirander seized the opportunity and flew headlong into a dark abyss, albeit a sleeve covering. To a mosquito, that space was a giant cavern. Her sound was muffled as she zigged and zagged avoiding waves of surplus material which fluttered like helpless sails on a yacht in distress: thwap, thwip and thwop.

Suddenly, at elbow location, Miss Alpine bent her arm, which meant she was trapped. The space had disappeared. The material hugged her arm. It was a tight spot. There was only one alternative. As much as it was revolting to her, she stuck her proboscis into Miss Alpine's arm and regretfully sucked, as is a mosquito's lot. Slirander convulsed with revulsion. This wasn't going too well. She withdrew her proboscis and gave it a cleaning blow. Miss Alpine felt the itch perpetrated on her and straightened her arm as she scratched the red welt. That movement released Slirander to continue along her arm, over Miss Alpine's modest "guns", and head toward an aromatic nightmare, the armpit. She didn't know when the last cleansing action had occurred or what fate lingered there.

It was a struggle to remain undetected. A large hand kept grabbing the sleeve as if to squash her and each time she felt claustrophobic. Her tiny, delicate frame was being battered and she didn't know if her fragility could stand the buffeting. After dodging a few more hand grabs, material flutters and nerves, Slirander had made it to that dreaded armpit. She didn't know whether to be exhilarated or not because she possibly knew that she couldn't return with the others if she was trapped.

There was no point delaying her task. It was the moment of truth. She had to instigate that armpit fart to summon the tram and its attachments. There was no light available. It was a dark cavern. She had to guess where the centre of the tattoo was and drill for all she was worth. Having already had a disgusting jab, prod and suck near Miss Alpine's elbow, Slirander felt that it couldn't be any worse. She had to walk around in the dark, sensing its centre. Naturally, it tickled somewhat and Miss Alpine scratched at the irritant. Slirander kept moving and suddenly slid down an embankment which didn't have any attachments. At least she shaved regularly. Slirander felt that she had reached the bullseye and gave an almighty proboscis probe, a real mosquito would brag about, even though it would lead to their demise.

Did Slirander perform her death jab?

Davidia and the others watched Miss Alpine contort her body, snatch at her arm and wriggle like an infected insect. They had no idea if Slirander was alive; however, there was hope seeing Miss Alpine continuously try to itch constantly at a new spot. They had to believe that she was still alive. Any alternative wasn't worth thinking about. They all had to be brave but none of them felt like it. They were miserable and apprehensive. Where was their friend?

Without warning, a remarkable transformation came over Miss Alpine. Everyone was stunned. Remember that the control room fiasco of konnocker reversing had a devastating impact on all those who were konnockered? Well, guess who also had a konnocker that no one was aware of, Miss Alpine. Her body began to elongate like a sossarge and in doing so, her clothes began to slip from the human frame she occupied. This freed up her armpit to the light and hence Slirander could be seen with a stuck proboscis. Miss Alpine felt the infringement and in a fit of rage, tried to squash Slirander by placing a thin, bony, double-sized hand under her armpit. In a coordinated attack, her arm came crashing down as a pincer movement to destroy the pest. An enormous burst of angry wind emanated from there and scared everyone shitless. Nothing had ever been heard like that before. It was an anger burst of hurricane proportions and, yes, it did sound exactly like the butt of jokes people make about wind from the back passage. An armpit fart had erupted. Miss Alpine stood satisfied that the itch perpetrator had been decimated. She stood like a winner, but was actually a loser.

The atmosphere erupted in turmoil. A tram with rails and a station appeared from nowhere. The sign above the tram gave the destination as Vermont. This was the only opportunity of escape. Lose this window in time and it's gone forever.

'Get on board,' yelled Davidia. 'Now!'

The exchange students stumbled forward. Halp and Foll refused to board. They had more important matters to attend to on Cluidinine. They believed their planet needed them. There were only five humans to board. Where was Slirander? Davida was distraught. Where was her friend? The tram could not delay its departure. The doors shut and the tram left with a cargo of only five. Tears began to well up in Davidia's eyes. Had her friend sacrificed herself for them? She checked the tram and, sadly, there was no Slirander. The trip to Vermont was a sad and lonely journey. What would she tell Slirander's dad? It was almost unbearable. She paid no attention to the countryside. Instead, she nursed her inner sadness.

The tram pulled into the Vermont tram stop. All five exited the tram quickly in case they got trapped into a return trip. Rotan was there with his group of six. He encouraged them to board. In moments, the tram had disappeared with a returning cargo. Rotan wondered if he'd ever see them again.

*

Miss Alpine was yellow with rage. She was determined to stamp her authority on Cluidinine again when she attained her previous form. She thought, *Dismiss me, will they? It is at their peril.* With her transformation back into her real-life form as a sossarge, she needed to replenish her body by using her sleep pod as the conduit. It would return her to her former stature and leadership. She disappeared from sight.

Halp and Foll stood there dumbstruck.

'Did you see that? Miss Alpine is a sossarge underneath, just like us. Maybe, she's our parent?' said a wistful Halp, who still hankered a desire for family.

'I don't think so. All the life forms on this planet are our family,' replied Foll, accepting that there was no individuality as to their origin but to embrace every life form as part of the same huge family.

That way, acceptance of whom or what they are would be shared by all. A real team of life forms; however, there was still the issue of control of the planet. That was still unresolved.

In the sleeping pod quarters, Miss Alpine had made it to her individual pod. It looked inviting, restful and the fillip she needed for recovery.

'Those venomous rats will pay for the inconvenience and loss of my powers. All further escorts of any guest will be terminated after their service. That means none of those treacherous life form sossarges could betray me again. I may have come from the same bloodstock, but my powers are far superior. I will rule again with much tighter control. This is one sossarge that can't be eaten.'

Miss Alpine removed the balance of her clothing until she stood tall as a singular shape. She gently lowered her body into her pod. The soothing, rushing, flush of fresh water to replenish her skin and in turn strengthen her, poured out of the collection of pipes seeming happy to spray her. Unfortunately, it was only an imaginary thought. As she lay there plotting, the water gradually turned yellow and began to shrink her torso and not the reverse. The rewiring that Halp and Foll had installed with the negative electronic solution had kicked in. It was too late for Miss Alpine. By the time she had realised what was happening, she had shrunk too much to have any physical strength left to escape from her pod.

'Those bloody parasites. I'll destroy their homeland. No one crosses me. Do you hear me, no one?'

She writhed in agony still spitting cross words loaded with

Cluidinine expletives – that's a whole new dictionary – as she gradually disappeared as a waste product down the plughole, leaving behind a smear trail of fat. Maybe she was a real sausage?

Halp and Foll had triggered their GTD devices and had followed Miss Alpine. They watched her demise from beneath her pod. They both felt sadness at the loss of a member, but quickly recovered relieved that the bitch didn't exist to taunt and enslave the population. It was time for new leadership. They returned to the control room to witness first-hand chaos and weren't disappointed. No life form present had ever had authority to an independent action. That shambles needed rectification. New leaders were required. Were they up to the job if asked? Naturally, they would be.

Whoosh! A tram stopped in the centre of the control room and out popped Caseone to Casesix, all in their natural life form shape. They were greeted as long-lost friends. Hugs were bestowed instead of a session of internment and rectification analysis. They were lost for words. This wasn't their planet, surely?

Halp and Foll stepped forward.

'Welcome home. Cluidinine had undergone some major changes since you had departed and we'd like to discuss the future of the planet with you,' said Halp, who sounded like she had the beginnings of a new leader. Maybe her deputy stood nearby?

There was not one cross word said.

*

'Where's Slirander?' asked an anxious dad when he had counted the return exchange students, only to realise his daughter was missing. His anxiety level at the loss of a precious individual and his only daughter, were highly evident.

Davidia was upset and had no answer to the question, because she didn't know. How could she face school without her friend? The tram stop was feeling miserable, yet it was such a beautiful, sunny day. A few other commuters present, to catch the correct tram into the city, sat and stared at the small group that had appeared from the opposite direction. It was much to their amazement. It must be part of a movie set, thought one commuter. Perhaps it was a sci-fi flash that they had observed. Whatever it was thought to be, no one commented, but would a news report appear in the local paper later that week under extraordinary events? Rotan was at a loss. Davidia sat down and started thumbing the ground in doodle shapes. Her mind was blank. A dark space grew within it, much like what most of Cluidinine represented.

'I wish Slirander was here,' she said, quietly.

'I wish she was here too,' said Rotan.

He had no idea how he would broach the topic with Rolet about their daughter's disappearance.

'She saved our lives,' continued Davidia.

'How did she do that? The last contact I had was that spell I read out to her.'

Davidia briefly explained the events that had occurred. Rotan nodded. Suddenly, an offensive droning noise started up. It was in Davidia's hair, a space not uncommon for the habitation of small insects when regular washing was absent. Davidia and Rotan recognised, not that germ-laden pest, but a different joyful sound. It couldn't be, could it? Slirander was at the end of the timeframe for the spell and had been resting in Davidia's hair after the altercation with Miss Alpine. It was thought that she had been splattered; however, all her resources were exhausted and she had just made it to safety when the tram had departed. She was too tired to warn Davidia that she was safe.

'Slirander, is that you?' asked Rotan, talking to the growing headpiece on Davidia's scalp.

'It's me. What a ride! Don't ask me to do that again,' she replied.

Davidia jumped up in excitement.

'You're safe? I thought you had expired like all unwanted pests. I'm so glad you're safe. I better not hug you, otherwise I would do Miss Alpine's bidding. How did you escape?'

'It was simple, really. When Miss Alpine pulled her arm downwards to squash me, it created a huge draft of wind and I was expelled from her armpit on that large sound that you would have heard. I windsurfed out and made it to your hair nest.'

'When do you become you again?'

'There's still some time to go. Hi, dad.'

Rotan was so overcome with emotion that all he could respond with was a wet, teary smile. The trio headed off toward home. School could wait a day or two before they attended again. The other exchange students had already departed.

'I wonder how Halp and Foll will manage. I liked them,' said Davidia.

Rolet greeted them at the front door looking like a huge sponge hung under each eyelid.

Her water sockets had certainly been emptied. She hugged Rotan and Davidia, but no Slirander. The shock look lasted a moment whilst Rotan explained the reality of the situation.

'I need the bathroom,' said Davidia, as she walked indoors and up to Slirander's ensuite.

A moment passed and when she returned to the bedroom there was Slirander sitting there picture-perfect as her friend. She had returned unharmed. The two girls hugged each other and bounded downstairs to let Slirander's parents know all was well.

There was no place like home.

19 BACK TO SCHOOL

A few days later, Slirander and Davidia attended school, having recovered from their exchange student ordeal. Nothing had changed during their absence, or so it seemed at first glance. Miss Green greeted them warmly.

'Good morning, girls. I trust you enjoyed your new educational experience at that other college. Senora, wasn't it?'

She used plain, normal diction without every third word being the "like" word which they had found irritating.

'Yes, Miss Green. It was an experience. We didn't learn as much as we had hoped,' said Davidia, quite amazed at how Miss Green now spoke in direct, simple and sensible sentences.

'Was there any major improvement that you could suggest that would improve our educational standards?'

The girls looked at each other and neither of them registered a hopeful face.

'We think that what is taught here is fine. Discipline was rigid there, but other than that it's an education we could all do without.'

'The other exchange students were all confused about the whole experience.'

'It's probably an age thing. They are older than us,' said Davidia, confident that she and Slirander were ahead of the game. Youth had its own confidence.

Principal Jones walked by and greeted the girls warmly as well.

'Good morning, girls. Settling in after your short-term exchange visit? Do you want to go on another exchange visit?'

'Not at the moment, sir' said Slirander, having experienced

what could have produced permanent nightmares. 'School here is normal and we are okay with that.'

'Remember, year-end exams are not far away. Good luck with them.'

Principal Jones brushed past Miss Green who turned another colour on contact. Both girls noticed the shift in body behaviour. They smiled.

A couple of fellow students ambled past with one overheard to say, 'They must have taken a sickie the past week for private tuition. Those two don't seem to have much excitement in their lives.'

There was no need to explain previous events to those less than well-informed. It was a judgement call.

'We must attend class.'

Principal Jones was relieved that his students had returned unharmed and no damage was done to them or the school's reputation.

Both families of the girls and others were also pleased to have their loved ones home as well.

They wondered how Halp and Foll were managing their world.

Life returned to normal as the educational programs at Vlad College were still considered some of the best in the State.

Just ask the students.